SWEETNESS

PINE RIDGE
BOOK ONE

ASHLEY A QUINN

TCA PUBLISHING LLC

ISBN is 9798985344110
Library of Congress Control Number: 2022901061

PROLOGUE

Bones aching, Silas Mitchell dragged himself into his bedroom to take a shower and crash. He was getting too old to wrangle cattle like he was in his thirties. Crossing to the dresser, he opened his underwear drawer. His shoulders drooped as he stared down in defeat. He was out of clean skivvies.

His gaze wandered to the heap of laundry in the corner. Dammit. Sighing, he tipped his head back, looking up at the ceiling, exasperated.

He slammed the drawer shut and stomped over to the pile, scooping it up.

"Frickin' salesman, stealing my damned housekeeper away," he muttered, descending the stairs. "I don't have time for all this shit." He entered the laundry room and threw his armload of clothes into the washer. Dumping detergent in the dispenser, he slammed the lid and spun the dial, then punched the button to turn it on.

That task done, he stormed down to the kitchen and grabbed the newspaper off the counter and opened it to the classifieds, looking for a number to call to place an ad. He'd do it first thing in the morning. He leafed through it, but all he saw was a web address.

Everything has to be online nowadays. He sighed and pulled out his phone, scrolling through his contacts until he found the number for his foreman, Chet Red Feather. He pressed send.

Chet picked up on the second ring. "Hi, Silas. What's up?"

"Sorry to bother you. I know we just finished up, and you were looking forward to a bit of family time, but I need a hand with something."

"Oh? What's wrong?"

"I need a woman."

There was a pause. The only sound was Chet's baby, Sloan, squalling in the background.

"I'm sorry, what?"

"A woman. Or a man. I'm not picky. I just need a damn housekeeper. I'm tired of running out of clean skivvies."

Chet laughed. "That's much better than what was running through my mind. Okay. So why are you calling me?"

"I want to put an ad in the newspaper, but it's all online. I don't know how to do that crap. Asa's not here to do it, so can you or Marci come help me?"

"Actually, I can do it here. Hang on a second." Silas heard Chet move through his house, the sound of the baby crying getting louder, then quieter as he moved.

"You want it in the Billings paper?"

"Yep."

Chet paused as he typed, the click-clack of the keyboard coming over the line. "Okay. I have your information entered. What do you want the ad to say?"

"That I want a housekeeper. Someone to clean, maybe do some light cooking. Room and board included."

There was another pause.

"Okay if I use the ranch credit card? Since this is a ranch expense?"

"Yep."

More clicking filled the silence.

"All right, it's in. Any applicants are supposed to send a resume to the ranch email."

Silas breathed a sigh of relief. With any luck, he'd have someone new out here soon to take over Jeannie's duties. "Thanks, Chet. I appreciate it."

"Not a problem. I'll see you tomorrow."

"Yep. Kiss that baby for me."

"Will do."

Silas hung up. His eyes landed on the dishes in the sink. *Jesus*. It's a wonder there weren't flies swarming the house. Rolling up his sleeves, he turned on the water.

ONE

Daisy O'Malley stared at herself in the mirror, fiddling with the ends of her thick auburn hair. Her high-neck, crushed velvet black dress looked like something she'd have worn at one of her high school choir concerts back in the day. God, she looked so dumpy! It was no wonder she was still single.

She scoffed and rolled her eyes. *Yeah, that's why.* It had nothing to do with her six overbearing brothers, who thought it was their job to hand-pick her husband. Case in point, it was Valentine's Day, and she had a blind date. Someone her brother, Kyle, worked with at his software firm. Ethan Byrnes. Kyle swore he was a nice Irish Catholic who did *not* live with his mother still.

She sighed and stepped away from the mirror, stuffing her feet into a pair of black boots. The doorbell rang as she picked up her black clutch. Her cat, Tallulah, jumped up on the back of the couch and meowed as she passed, wanting scratched. Daisy ran a hand over her soft gray and white fur, then continued to the door.

Slipping the security chain off, she flipped open the deadbolts and grasped the knob. She inhaled a deep breath to shore up her confidence and opened the door.

Her eyes went wide as she took in the man on her doorstep. He looked like a bulldog! Stocky and short—so short!—he smiled at her, deep lines bracketing his brown eyes. His light brown hair was combed straight back to within an inch of its life and shellacked into place. The light from the hallway bounced off of it, making it look wet. A light gray suit strained at the seams over his muscular frame. Dark chest hair peeked over the top of the black t-shirt he wore with the suit.

"Wow, you're even prettier than the picture Kyle showed me." He raked his eyes over her, lingering on her chest.

"Thank you. You're... different too." Before she agreed to this date, she made Kyle show her a picture. The last time she went out with one of the men her brothers picked, she'd spent two hours in the company of a man who devoted way too much time to his spray tan. Ethan looked normal in the headshot Kyle showed her. Now she knew why it was his security badge photo she'd seen and not some candid shot.

"Yeah, my hair's grown since I had that picture taken," he said with a smile.

"Mmm, that must be it."

"Are you ready to go?"

She nodded. "I just need to put my coat on." She stepped back to open the hall closet and take out her long wool pea coat. Putting it on, she walked into the hall and locked her door.

"So, where are we going?" she asked as they made their way to the elevator.

"Kyle said you like Italian food, so I booked us a table at Giancarlo's Bistro. I hope that's okay."

"I've never heard of it, but I'm sure it'll be fine," she said, stepping onto the elevator.

"Oh, it's great. It belongs to a friend of mine from school. It's his family's place."

Which meant he wanted them to see him with her. Whether it was to show off or for their approval, she wasn't sure. Maybe both.

The elevator doors dinged, and they stepped off, walking through the lobby of her building to the street. He hailed a cab, and they were soon winding their way through the streets of Chicago to the restaurant.

The drive was short, and the cab pulled up to a building ten blocks away. Daisy got out and glanced around as she waited for Ethan to join her. The area wasn't the greatest, but it also wasn't the worst, and the restaurant looked welcoming.

Ethan held the door for her, and she stepped inside. The heavenly smell of pasta sauce and garlic bread enveloped her. She really did love Italian food.

"Hi, Ethan. Mama said you were bringing a date here tonight." The young woman at the host stand smiled at them.

"Hi Meghan. This is Daisy. Daisy, meet Meghan Turati."

Daisy smiled and offered her a wave. "It's nice to meet you."

Meghan smiled back and picked up a couple of menus. "You too. Follow me, and I'll get you seated."

They wound through the tables to a spot near the back. Ethan pulled out her chair for her, then took his place across the table. Daisy shrugged out of her coat and took the menu Meghan offered.

"What can I get you guys to drink?" Meghan asked.

"I'll take a glass of that nice cab you guys got in. Daisy will have water."

Daisy's brow slammed down. She already knew this date wouldn't end well. "Actually, I'll take a glass of pinot grigio, please."

Meghan raised a brow, her eyes darting to Ethan before

going back to her. She nodded. "Your server is George. He'll be right over with those."

"Thank you," Daisy said.

Ethan fidgeted in his seat, watching Meghan for a moment as she walked away before turning to her, frowning. "You drink?"

She stared at him for a second, then nodded. "I'm not a drunk, but I like a glass of wine now and then, yes."

"Hmm... Kyle said you didn't."

One corner of her mouth lifted. "Kyle would like to think I don't, because he wants me to stay his baby sister. But I'm twenty-eight and can enjoy an alcoholic beverage just like any other adult."

He pressed his lips into a thin smile and nodded.

This was going so well... She opened her menu and rolled her eyes behind it, wondering what else her brother told him. Ethan was no doubt under the impression she was some goodie-goodie who was content to let her man make all her decisions. Truth be told, she couldn't fault her brothers for thinking that. She let them make most of her decisions. But it was really beginning to wear thin.

Their server walked up with their drinks and asked for their orders. She asked for the lasagna while Ethan went with the chicken parmesan. The young man took their menus and disappeared.

Daisy folded her hands in her lap to keep from fidgeting with the silverware. She hated first dates. They were always so awkward.

"So, Kyle said you're a baker."

She nodded. "I work for the place a couple blocks from my apartment. Sugar and Spice."

He hummed. "Never been there."

"You should try it. It's great."

He smiled. "You'll have to bring me some treats on our next date. I'd love to see what you can do."

She gave him a polite smile. Unless the tempo of this date picked up, there wouldn't be a second one. "Tell me, Ethan, what do you like to do for fun?"

"Fun?"

"Yes, fun."

His brow furrowed as he thought. "I box some."

That explained his stocky build.

"What else?"

"Um, I like video games. I just bought a new console, so I've been playing on it a lot lately."

She swallowed a groan. He was a man-child! "That's nice. Do you like to spend time outdoors?" She loved going to the city parks and walking. When she had time, she drove out of the city to some nature trails in the suburbs.

He shook his head. "Not really. I have terrible allergies, so the only time of year I can be outside without being miserable are the winter months, and it's just too cold."

Daisy loved winter. The cold was exhilarating. She bundled up in her parka and mittens and walked the trails just like she would in the summer.

"What about you?" he asked. "What do you do for fun?"

"I hike."

"Oh."

She picked up her wineglass and took a sip, wondering why she kept agreeing to these dates. Ethan seemed nice, but they had little in common. Just like every other man she dated at her brothers' request.

Taking another sip, she set the glass down and did her best to listen as Ethan started talking about his new video game. She was going to kill Kyle later.

The server brought their food, and Daisy dug in, happy to

have an excuse not to talk. That didn't stop Ethan, though. He stuffed a bite of his entrée in his mouth and chewed away while he continued to regale her with stories of his prowess on his latest gaming obsession. Partially masticated chicken wallowed around in his mouth while he did so. It was nauseating. She did her best to keep her eyes on her own plate as she poked at her lasagna, only looking up enough to make it look like she was listening.

"Something wrong with your food?"

Daisy glanced up from her plate at his question. Her lasagna was delicious, but watching him eat and talk killed her appetite. "Oh, no. It's fine. I'm just not very hungry, I guess."

"You better eat. Mama Turati will be upset if you don't eat."

She shrugged. "I'm not going to force myself to eat if I'm not hungry. I'll make sure she knows it wasn't her cooking."

He frowned. "I guess that would be okay. We'll tell her you're on a diet and filled up on water so you wouldn't eat as much. She'd believe that."

Daisy's eyebrows slammed down. "How about we just tell her I'm not hungry?" Because she most certainly was not on a diet.

His expression turned thoughtful. Daisy's eyes widened. How could he not read the hostility in her voice and on her face?

"I think it's better if we tell her you're on a diet. A woman like you, she wouldn't believe you weren't hungry."

"A woman like me? What does that mean?"

"Well, you know." He gestured to her torso. "You're... voluptuous."

"Voluptuous." She set her fork down carefully and folded her hands in her lap.

"Yes. Very. And don't get me wrong, I'm a fan." His eyes landed on her chest and stayed there. "But you have a few pounds to spare."

Humiliation turned Daisy's cheeks bright red. The chair legs scraped the tile floor as she pushed away from the table and stood. "I'm sorry, but this isn't going to work out." She picked up her coat and put it on.

"Where are you going? We haven't finished eating. And there's cannoli for dessert."

She paused buttoning up her coat to stare down at him, incredulous. "Really? You sure my fat ass can handle it?" Shaking her head, she picked up her purse and walked away.

The sound of his chair moving across the floor and his footsteps hurrying after her made her sigh. She just wanted to go home.

"Wait! You can't leave." He ran around to stand in front of her.

She arched a brow. "Why not? You've insulted me, stared at my breasts through most of our date, and frankly, are a disgusting eater. I've had quite enough."

His face turned red, and veins popped out on his forehead and in his neck. "Your brother won't be happy about this."

She shrugged. "That's his problem. Goodnight." She walked around him and hurried out the door before he could follow her.

Her heels clacked on the sidewalk as she strode down the block toward her apartment. A chill permeated the air, but she didn't feel it. She was too angry. The nerve of that man! So she indulged in a pastry or two at work on occasion. Whoop-dee-doo. He was nothing to write home about when he barely came to her shoulders. She couldn't believe Kyle thought that —that pig!—was an acceptable suitor. Her brothers had set her up with some doozies over the years, but Ethan Byrnes might take the cake. None of the other men ever dared insinuate she was fat.

Still fuming fifteen minutes later, she let herself into her apartment. Tallulah ran up and chirped.

"Yes, I know I'm back sooner than expected. Mr. Byrnes is an asshole."

The cat laid down and rolled onto her back, feet in the air. Daisy smiled and bent down to scratch her between her front feet. "Who needs a man when I have you?" She certainly didn't need that particular man.

Rising, she put her coat away. As she shut the closet door, her cellphone rang. She groaned. It was probably Kyle. No doubt Ethan called him to complain.

She took the phone from her purse and looked at the screen. Kyle's face stared back at her. She contemplated not answering, but knew he would just keep calling, eventually showing up at her apartment if she didn't answer.

Daisy slid her thumb over the screen. "Hello?"

"Why did you leave your date early?"

She sank onto the couch. Tallulah jumped into her lap and she stroked the cat's silky fur. "You tell me. What did Ethan tell you?"

"He said you threw a hissy fit about the food, then left."

She rolled her eyes. "I did not throw a fit about the food. The food was fantastic. I just wasn't able to eat it because he insisted on talking around a mouthful of half-chewed chicken parmesan. When I told him I wasn't hungry, he told me that Mama Turati would be upset that I didn't eat. I said we'd just tell her I didn't have much of an appetite. He said we should tell her I was on a diet and filled up on water first so I wouldn't eat much. I argued what I suggested was fine, but he insisted we use his excuse, then told me it was more believable because I could stand to lose a few pounds."

A short silence met her explanation. "Oh."

"Yeah. What could you have possibly seen in that man that made you think he'd be a suitable match for me? I mean, seriously, Kyle. What the hell?"

"Don't curse at me. He's a hard worker and has always

been nice to me."

"You're a man."

Kyle sighed. "Maybe he's just old-fashioned. You should give him another chance."

"When cakes fly!"

"Come on, Dais. He comes from a good Catholic family. Mom and Dad would love that."

That might be so, but she could guarantee her mother would string the man up by his ankles after hearing Daisy's story tonight.

"Well, regardless of what they'd think, I don't see another date with him in my future. Thanks for trying. I'm going to make myself a snack now and go to bed. Gotta get up for work."

"Daisy—"

"Have a good night. Love you. Bye." She hung up before he could say more, then turned off her ringer.

With a sigh, she laid her head back against the cushions. She was so tired of dealing with her brothers. They drove her crazy with their overprotective, domineering attitudes. She loved them, but being treated like a teenager still at the age of twenty-eight was growing increasingly tiresome. It was time to take back some control of her life.

She looked down at Tallulah, her eyes straying to the crushed velvet dress she wore.

Ugh. That control was going to start with her wardrobe. Tomorrow, she vowed, she would go shopping for some different clothes. Nothing too crazy, but she'd like to get something that didn't look like a funeral dress from the eighteen-hundreds.

"Come on, Lulabell." She stood up, holding the cat. "Let's find a snack and hit the hay. I'm tired."

Tallulah let out a short meow, purring as Daisy carried her toward the kitchen and the ice cream waiting in the freezer.

Two

The bell over the door at the bakery tinkled as it opened. Daisy looked up from pouring a cup of coffee for the customer at the register to see her brother, Kyle, walk in.

What did he want? Sugar and Spice was nowhere near the apartment he shared with his wife and kids. Or his office.

She popped a lid on the coffee and handed it to the woman at the counter with a smile. "There you go, thanks."

The woman stepped away, and Kyle took her place, running an assessing gaze over Daisy. "You came to work dressed like that?"

She looked down at herself. Was there a hole in her shirt or something? What she could see of her new v-neck t-shirt and jeans around the brown apron looked fine.

"What's wrong with what I'm wearing?" she asked, looking up.

He gestured to her chest. "Your cleavage is showing."

She glanced down again. There was the start of a vee visible at the top of her boobs above the neckline of her shirt. Barely. She rolled her eyes. "Seriously, Kyle? There is nothing wrong with my shirt. What are you doing here? I know it's not to critique my clothes."

He drew in a breath, frowning at her. "No. I had an appointment on this side of the city, so I decided to stop by. I came to talk about Ethan. He said he's called you several times in the last couple of days, and you won't take his calls or call him back."

Daisy pushed away from the counter and picked up a rag, wiping it along the counter by the coffeepot. "No. I told you the night of our date, I don't want to see him anymore. He is a chauvinistic pig and we have nothing in common. I'm not going to keep going on dates with him when there's no future in it."

"Oh, come on, Dais. You can't know that from one date. Maybe he just had a bad day."

"Yes, I can. Any man who suggests a woman needs to lose weight on their first date is not someone I want to be with. It's the first step toward him controlling my entire life, from what food I eat, to where I work, to who I hang out with. Plus, he hates the outdoors, Kyle. You know I'd rather be outside than in. And he's about four inches shorter than me. I felt like a giant next to him."

"Well, you shouldn't have worn heels."

She glared at him. "I didn't. And it wouldn't have mattered, anyway. I'm five-foot-ten barefoot. He was barely five-six."

He rolled his eyes. "Whatever. I think you're wrong about him, and he just had an off night. You need to give him another chance, which is why I told him you'd be home tonight and would make him dinner. He's coming over around seven."

Daisy froze. "You what?"

"Told him you'd make him dinner. You know. That meal we all eat in the evening?"

"I know what dinner is. But I'm not cooking for that man."

He frowned. "I already told him you would. I know you go to bed early, but I'm sure if you make it clear you have to get up to be here for work in the morning, he won't stay too late."

"It's not about that. It's about the fact you think you can dictate my life. I'm not a kid anymore and none of you seem to understand that. I'm tired of it. If I don't want to date someone, I'm not going to. And even if I wanted to, I certainly don't want you making plans without consulting me. It's none of your business."

He sighed and pinned her with an annoyed look. "Look, I promise to call you first the next time, but he's already coming over, so just make the best of it. He's a nice guy once you get past his rough edges."

So angry she vibrated, she pointed at the door. "Get out."

He frowned. "Dais—"

"No. I'm done, Kyle. Get out." She walked out from behind the counter and spun him around, pushing him toward the door.

"Daisy!" He planted his feet, trying to stop her, but she just tucked her head and pushed harder.

She reached around him and pulled open the glass door, pointing toward the street. "Goodbye."

"You're being irrational. What would Mom think?"

She stared at him, incredulous. "She'd think you're being a total overbearing, idiotic jerk, then she'd slap you and tell you to get your head out of your ass." She put her free hand on her hip. "I'm so sick of your shit. And not just you. All six of you. You don't treat your wives or your daughters this way, so I'm at a loss as to why you do it to me. I'm done. No more dates with your co-workers or friends, no more shopping advice, or advice on what I should eat or do with my hair. I'm not listening to any of it anymore."

He rolled his eyes, clearly not believing her, which only further fueled her anger. "Yeah, okay. You should make steak for Ethan tonight. Men love steak."

"Aargh!" She grabbed his arm and pulled him through the door. "Call him and tell him not to come. If he does, I won't answer the door." She let the door shut in his face and walked back to the counter. That was the last straw. They'd pulled some outrageous shit since their parents died, but this took the cake. Why couldn't they just let her live her life?

Well, from now on, that was exactly what she was going to do, starting with living where she wanted and not where they deemed acceptable.

Her boss and friend, Sandrine Pembroke, stood behind the register and crooked a brow as she neared.

"You finally told your asshole brothers where to stick it. I'm proud of you." Sandrine gave her a bright smile and wrapped her in a brief hug.

Daisy huffed as she pulled back. "I can't take it anymore, Sandrine. I have to get out of here."

"Sure. Go for one of your hikes, and I'll see you tomorrow."

Daisy bit her lip. "Actually, that's not what I meant. I'm giving you my two-week notice."

Sandrine frowned. "What? You're quitting? Why? You love working here. And I love having you."

"I know, and I do, but if I'm really going to make a change and take charge of my life, I have to leave Chicago."

Sandrine gasped. "Leave Chicago? That seems a bit drastic."

Daisy arched a brow. "Have you met my brothers?" She sighed. "If I stay, they will hound me and hound me until I tire of it and give in. I need to go someplace they can't find me."

"You're not going to tell them where you're going? I don't know if that's such a good idea. What if something happens to you?"

"I'll let my aunt know where I am, and I'll keep my number for now. I just won't answer their calls." Now, more than ever, she was glad she set up her own cellphone plan. That happened several years ago, after Ian used her phone to track her down when she refused to answer him once after he pissed her off. He hadn't been happy about it, but he couldn't stop her. Just like now. He would be furious, but he couldn't keep her from leaving.

Sandrine sighed. "If you're sure about this, I'll help you however I can. Your brothers are nice men, but you're right, they need to learn you're an adult. You don't even need to give me two weeks. If you want to leave today, you go. It might be best if you do."

Daisy bit her lip again as she thought about that. "You think so? I mean, I don't even know where I'd go except out west. I love the mountains."

Sandrine shrugged. "So, go. You have quite a nice nest egg, right?"

She nodded. Her oldest brother, Ian, paid her rent because he wanted her in a safe neighborhood. One she couldn't afford on a baker's salary. So, after she paid her utilities and bought groceries each month, the rest went into her savings.

"Live on that until you can find a job somewhere." She nudged Daisy's shoulder. "The world is an open book for you, girl. Go tell your story."

Hope bloomed in Daisy's chest. *Her* story. Not the one her brothers wanted her to tell. Could she really just up and leave her entire life behind?

The phone in her pocket buzzed. She took it out to see a text from Ian.

You're being unreasonable. Stop acting like a child. It's time for you to settle down. Kyle may have overstepped a bit, but he thinks Ethan is a good guy, and what's done is done. Ethan will see you at seven.

Oh, hell no.

She looked up at Sandrine. "Can I have my paycheck early?" She turned the phone around for her to see the message. "I'm leaving now."

THREE

When the elevator doors opened on her floor, she half-expected one or more of her brothers to be waiting outside her door. But the hall was empty. That didn't mean they weren't *in* her apartment, though. Ian had a key. For emergencies. Although, she'd asked his wife, Shelly, to hide it after he'd hired someone to come in and replace her curtains with blackout drapes because they, in his words, "wouldn't let anyone see her silhouette through them, like her sheers."

Unlocking her door, she poked her head inside, ready to turn around and leave if they were there, but only Tallulah greeted her. Daisy walked inside and closed the door, setting her keys and purse on the table beside it and hanging her coat in the closet.

"All right, Lula. I hope you're ready for a road trip." She gave the cat a quick scratch and headed for her bedroom. She had about six hours until Ethan was supposed to show up. She intended to be in another state by then. Which one, though, was the question. She didn't particularly care, so long as it had mountains.

Daisy took out her phone and opened the map app,

zooming in on the mountain states. She closed her eyes, held her finger over the phone and touched the map. Opening her eyes, she looked at where her finger landed.

Montana. Hmm... Zooming in on the state, she repeated the process to pick a city and landed near Billings.

Excitement raced along her spine. Billings, Montana would be her new home.

Putting the phone away, she walked into her closet and took out her suitcases. She was going to pack only the essentials for now. Once she found a place to live, she would contact her Aunt Nori about letting in a moving company to box up her things and ship them to her.

Laying the suitcases on the bed, she started filling them, cramming jeans, sweaters, t-shirts, undergarments, and pajamas into every corner until they could hold nothing else. She flipped the lid closed and tugged on the zipper, but it wouldn't budge. Throwing her weight on top, she grasped the fob. "Come on, you stupid thing. Zip! The less laundry I have to do before I find an apartment, the better." Leaning heavily on the edge, she got the zipper to close, then repeated the process with the other two smaller suitcases.

"Phew!" She hopped off the bed and looked at Tallulah, who watched her from the top of the headboard. "It's a good thing we're not flying. I'd be paying the excess baggage fee for sure."

Tallulah chirped.

Daisy picked up her toiletry case and walked into the bathroom, tossing in the items she used every day. Once that was done, she hauled all her luggage into the living room, then went back to get Tallulah's carrier. She bagged up the cat's dishes and emptied and washed the litter box, putting it inside a trash bag. She added it and the box of trash bags to her stack of things to take, along with the box of clean litter.

Opening her fridge, she rummaged through it, tossing

some items, while others she put into grocery bags to take across the hall to Mr. Tillman. She filled two trash bags and disposed of them in the trash chute in the hall, then dropped off the other items to her elderly neighbor, who thanked her for thinking of him and wished her a safe trip.

She shrugged into her coat and picked up her keys, then wheeled her two largest suitcases into the elevator, taking it to the parking garage below her building. Her car beeped twice as she unlocked it. She lifted the back hatch and hefted the suitcases into the back of her Subaru, grateful she'd sprung for an SUV instead of a sedan. Her brothers thought she was crazy since she lived in the city, but she liked being able to shove her bike and whatever else she wanted in the back and hit the trails. It was one of the few times she'd put her foot down with them on something they disagreed about.

Closing the hatch, she headed back upstairs for another load, getting everything except her cat. She took the elevator up once more to get Tallulah. In the car, she pulled up her weather app to check the forecast for her drive west, deciding it would probably be best to take the more southern route. She programmed her destination into the map app on her phone and started the car, pulling out of the parking garage.

Daisy headed for the interstate. It was just after three, so she should be able to get out of the city in good time. She would be well into Iowa before anyone noticed she'd left.

Well, except her aunt. Nori had tried on multiple occasions to talk some sense into her brothers, but they wouldn't listen to her. So, she did her best to support Daisy in any way she could. The woman wasn't just Daisy's aunt; she was one of her very best friends.

She hit the button on her steering wheel to make a call.

"Call Nori."

The phone rang through the speakers, and Nori picked up after several rings.

"Hey, girl. What's up?"

"So, I did a thing."

"A thing? What kind of thing?"

"I quit my job, packed up my car, and left."

"What? You left? Chicago?"

"Yes. I finally had enough of their shit. You know that guy I went out with on Valentine's Day?"

"The short one who called you fat and only talked about video games?"

"That's the one. Kyle showed up at the bakery at lunchtime today and asked why I hadn't called the guy back. Then, he proceeded to tell me he invited Ethan over to my house for dinner. Told him I would cook for him."

"Without asking you first?"

"Yup."

"Oh my. What on earth was he thinking?"

"No idea. But he wouldn't call him and tell him not to come. Once he left the bakery, I quit and went home to pack. I'm just now getting on the interstate."

"Oh, honey. Are you sure this is what you want to do? Chicago's your home."

"I have to, Aunt Nori. I'll never get out from under their thumb if I don't."

Nori sighed. "Probably not. Where are you going?"

"Billings, Montana. But don't tell them that. Don't tell their wives, either. I don't want to put them in a place where they have to lie to their husbands."

"Your secret's safe with me, dear. What are you going to do about your apartment?"

"I thought once I found a job and a place to live, I'd have a moving service come box up all my stuff and ship it out west."

"That sounds good. If Ian tries to terminate your lease before then—because he's going to be extremely angry with you—I'll make sure it all gets into storage."

Tears welled in Daisy's eyes. She blinked them away so she could see to drive. "Thank you. I wish it hadn't come to this, but I don't know what else to do. I want to live my own life. I love my brothers, but they're smothering me."

"I know, sweetie. It's okay. This might be the best thing for all of you. They'll be mad for a while, but once you've been gone for a bit, and are thriving, they'll see you really can manage things on your own just fine."

"Yeah. That's what I'm hoping." She sighed. "I should go so I can concentrate on driving. I'll let you know when I stop for the night."

"Okay. Be safe. I love you."

"Love you too. Bye."

"Bye, dear."

Daisy ended the call and sucked in a deep breath. She prayed Nori was right. She didn't want to alienate her brothers forever. She just wanted them to see her as an equal.

FOUR

The soft tickle of whiskers on her cheek brought Daisy awake. She opened her eyes to see Tallulah standing on her pillow, sniffing her. The cat chirped when she noticed her mistress was awake.

"Yeah, yeah. It's breakfast time, I know." Daisy sat up and stretched, climbing out of bed. She walked into the kitchen area of the extended stay hotel room she'd checked into in Billings last night. Tallulah hopped up on the counter and meowed as Daisy opened a can of cat food and dumped it into the cat's bowl.

Stifling a yawn, she left the cat to eat her breakfast and started a pot of coffee. She picked up her tablet while she waited on it to brew and pulled up the classifieds for the Billings newspaper. Her first order of business today was to find a job. She picked up a pen, twirling it between her fingers as she read through the ads.

Most of them were patient aide and nursing positions, which she wasn't qualified for, but there were a couple that looked promising; one for a line cook at a diner and another for a housekeeper at a ranch. She jotted down the number for the diner and the email address for the housekeeping position. It was too early for her to call about the line cook job, but she could send her resume for the other one.

She poured herself a cup of coffee, then sat down at the desk and quickly updated her resume and composed a cover letter explaining the Chicago area code on her phone number and her work history. Blowing out a breath, she hit send. She didn't really expect to hear anything back about this job—she figured they'd take one look at where she was from and delete her email—but it didn't hurt anything to try.

Daisy finished her coffee and grabbed some clothes. She would take a shower, then take a walk around the area and explore a bit.

Feeling freer than she ever had, she hurried through her morning routine. Dressed in jeans and a warm sweater, she took the blow dryer to her long hair, then braided it. Back in the main room, she tugged on thick socks and stuffed her feet into her winter boots. She hoped they were warm enough. It was significantly colder here than in Chicago.

As she picked up her coat, she saw her phone screen light up with an incoming call. She rolled her eyes. It was probably one of her brothers. She'd put the phone on silent last night after the fourth call from Kyle.

She shrugged into her coat and walked over to the bedside table and picked it up, then frowned. It was a local area code. She swiped the screen and answered the call.

"Hello?"

"Hi, is this Daisy O'Malley?" The voice on the other end was deep, but friendly.

"Yes."

"This is Silas Mitchell. I own the Stone Creek Ranch. I'm calling about the resume you just sent."

"Oh. Wow, that was fast."

"I checked my email right after you sent it. Would you be able to meet me for breakfast? I'm in town getting supplies."

"Sure. Where?"

"Chester's Diner? They make great breakfast food."

"Do you have an address? I just got into town last night, so I don't know where anything is."

He rattled off the address, and she wrote it next to what she wrote earlier.

"Okay. I'm on my way. How will I know you?"

"I'll leave my name with Cindi. She'll point you to me."

"Sounds good. See you soon."

She hung up and squealed, doing a little dance. Tallulah sat on the counter staring at her.

"Tallie-bell, I think we're going to be okay." She scratched the cat on her head, then picked up her purse and left the room.

It only took her ten minutes to drive to the diner where Mr. Mitchell wanted to meet. She parked in the lot and hurried inside. Montana was beautiful, but the cold was brutal.

"Hi there," a waitress said as she stepped inside. "Give me a sec, and I'll be right with you."

Daisy nodded and removed her gloves, looking over the diner. It looked how she expected from the name. Old-fashioned, but well-kept. Dark wood and red pleather booths ringed the room. Two lines of tables and chairs occupied the middle of the space. There was still a good crowd for nine-thirty.

"Sorry about that," the woman said, reappearing. "Is it just you?"

"Actually, I'm meeting someone." She glanced at the woman's nametag. This was the Cindi she was supposed to find. "Silas Mitchell."

She smiled, then nodded. "He said he was expecting you.

He's over there in the corner." She pointed toward the back of the restaurant.

Daisy looked past her, but only saw the top of a gray cowboy hat as he stared down at the menu.

"You can go on over. You want coffee?"

"Sure. Thank you." Daisy walked past her and wound her way through the tables to stop next to his booth.

"Mr. Mitchell?"

He looked up, blue eyes staring at her from a weathered yet handsome face. He smiled.

"Ms. O'Malley?"

She nodded and held out a hand. "It's nice to meet you, sir."

He rose and her eyes widened as she took in his stature. It wasn't often a man made her feel short.

"Call me Silas, please. Have a seat."

She slid into the booth across from him.

Cindi appeared with her coffee. "Do you want cream?"

"No, black is fine. Can I get a stack of pancakes and some bacon, please?"

"Sure. Silas, do you know what you want?"

"What she ordered sounds good. Add some scrambled eggs, though?"

"You got it." She took their menus and walked away.

Silas smiled at Daisy. "Thanks for meeting me so quickly. I don't come into Billings too often, so I'm glad I was here when I read your email."

"I'm happy too. Like I said in my email, I just moved here."

"What prompted that, if you don't mind me asking? Most people don't just move across the country without another job lined up."

She sighed and fiddled with the silverware in front of her. "I have six brothers. Our parents died when I was ten, and they've carried the responsibility of raising me a little far. I'm twenty-eight, but they still treat me like I'm that little girl. I needed to get out from under their thumb, so I left."

"Just like that?"

She shrugged. "It's been years in the making. I just finally had enough."

"Why Montana?"

She gave a short laugh. "I closed my eyes and pointed at a map."

His eyes widened.

"But I do love the mountains," she hastened to assure him. "I narrowed it down to the western states before I picked."

"Okay. So, what made you apply for the position as my housekeeper?"

"I like to cook and bake, and I don't mind cleaning. I didn't go to college, and I've worked in the food industry since I was in my teens, so my skills are limited. But I promise you, I'll work hard."

"Do you intend to stay in Montana? I'll be honest, I've had three new housekeepers in as many weeks. If you're going to go back to Chicago soon, well, I'm not sure being my housekeeper is the right job for you."

"I have no intention of going anywhere else anytime soon. I want a fresh start, away from my overbearing family. I have always wanted to live out west, but my brothers always talked me out of it before."

"But not this time?"

She shook her head. "No. I didn't even tell them I was leaving. They still think I'm in Chicago, just not answering their calls."

His eyebrows shot up. "They don't know where you are?"

"No. I told my aunt, but swore her to secrecy. If they know where I am, they'll fly out here and try to get me to come home, and I'm not going back."

Silas narrowed his eyes and leaned in. "Are you in some kind of trouble? Did they hurt you and that's why you left?"

She smiled softly. "No. My brothers love me and would never hurt me. They try to shelter me from everything to the point they've smothered me. That's why I left."

"Oh. Okay. One more question. What kind of music do you like?"

She frowned. What did that have to do with anything? "Music?"

"Yes. What do you listen to?"

"I'm not sure what that has to do with this interview, but I like big band style music and classical. Some pop."

"You don't listen to country at all?"

"No."

"What about TV and movies?"

"What types of stuff do I watch, you mean?"

He nodded.

This was the weirdest job interview she'd ever had. But he seemed nice, and she needed the job. "I honestly don't watch much TV. I worked long hours at the bakery. My days off, I usually spent running errands or hanging out with my nieces and nephews. If I went to the movies, it was usually to see some big blockbuster film." She frowned. "Why are you asking about this?"

He sighed and picked up his phone from the table. "I'm going to show you a picture. I need you to tell me if you recognize the man in the photograph."

What in the hell was going on?

He turned the phone around to show her an image of one of the most handsome men she'd ever seen. Dark hair waved over his forehead above blue eyes the color of sapphires. His bright smile crinkled the corners of his eyes and dimples flashed in his cheeks. He was beautiful, but she'd never seen him before.

She looked up at Silas. "I don't know who that is, no. Who is it?"

"My son, Asa."

Her eyes widened. That gorgeous creature was his son? Wow.

She frowned again. "What does he have to do with the questions you asked me?"

"Asa is a singer. And he's been in some movies. He's had some... issues lately with women."

Oh, geez. Some sleazeball was all she needed. "What kinds of issues?"

"Psycho ex-girlfriend and the crazy groupie type. Women throw themselves at him and don't always take no for an answer."

Okay, so maybe he wasn't a sleaze. That poor man. She didn't understand how people could act that way. Everyone deserved privacy.

"I'm sorry about the strange questions, but after the last housekeeper, I had to know you weren't just trying to find a way to get to him."

Daisy's eyes grew large again. "Someone did that?"

Silas nodded. "She seemed like a nice young woman, but I came home early a couple days ago and found her in his room, going through his things. High school yearbooks, journals he kept, stuff like that. She admitted she took the job to get close to him in the hopes of having a relationship with him. Asa comes home to the ranch to rest and get away from the stress of being famous. I can't have someone like that in my house."

"Oh, that's terrible! She should be ashamed. Your son is very handsome, but I'm not looking for anything other than a job, Mr. Mitchell. Even if I did know who he was before today, I would still treat him like any other person. I might be a little star-struck, but I certainly wouldn't make a play for him."

He cocked his head and stared at her. Those blue eyes that

looked so much like the man in the picture assessed her. "No, I don't think you would. You seem like a very straightforward person, Daisy. And you're either a talented actress or telling the truth about not knowing Asa. Tell you what. How about you come out to the ranch tomorrow and I'll give you a tour? If you like the place and can handle living in the back of beyond, you're hired."

"Seriously?"

"Yep. I like you. I think you're just what we need out there. What do you say?"

Daisy stared at him, slightly in shock. She hadn't expected him to offer her the job on the spot. People in Montana sure did things differently.

"Well, I say, tell me how to get there."

His smile was bright as he did just that.

FIVE

Daisy looked up from mashing potatoes as the back door opened. She saw Silas walk into the mudroom and pause to remove his boots before he opened the screen door and stepped inside.

"Hi," she greeted him.

He smiled at her. "Hi. It smells good in here."

"Thanks. I made meatloaf and mashed potatoes. There's apple pie for dessert."

Silas groaned and rolled up his sleeves to wash his hands at the sink. "Girl, you keep cooking like this, and I'm going to gain twenty pounds."

She giggled. "Yeah, right. You burn too many calories working for that to ever happen." She pointed the potato masher at him. "And if anything, you might lose some. You forget, I saw the crap you were eating before I got here. You were a heart attack waiting to happen with all that salt and fat."

He dried his hands with some paper towels, then tossed them in the trash on his way to hang up his hat by the door. "Yeah, well, cooking for one isn't easy."

"I still don't understand why you didn't eat in the bunkhouse with Cookie and the hands before you hired me."

"Because the last thing all those kids want is for their boss to hang out with them after they've spent all day working."

She finished mashing the potatoes and spooned some onto two plates. "Well, Cookie could have at least sent some food home with you. Those TV dinners you had loading your freezer are not meant to be eaten *every day*." She cut the meatloaf and laid slices on both plates, then heaped on some green beans. She handed him a plate and picked up the other, along with a bowl of gravy, motioning to the table. He took some silverware from the drawer and they sat down.

"So, how was your day?" she asked, spooning gravy onto her potatoes.

"Busy." He took the bowl from her when she offered it. "Asa called too. He's coming home."

Daisy's fork paused on its way to her mouth. Mr. Greek God was coming back? She ate the bite of meatloaf, not sure how she felt about that. The last couple of months had been nice. She and Silas had settled into a routine. She'd become comfortable here. Having Asa home would change all that.

But he wouldn't be here forever, she reminded herself. Eventually, he'd go back to L.A.

"When's he coming?" she asked.

"A week or so. His tour wraps up tonight, then he has some things to do in L.A. He said he's hoping to be back early next week."

She nodded. "Okay. I'll make sure his room is ready. Are there any particular foods he likes that I should stock up on?"

Silas shrugged. "He'll eat whatever you put in front of him. He's not picky."

They'd see about that. She'd done some reading on Asa since she met Silas, curious about both her employer and his only child. From what she read, Asa was a bit of a jerk. He had a splashy breakup with some starlet about a year ago. She accused him of being demanding and emotionally closed off.

Daisy had a hard time believing that man was the same one Silas described, but people were different with their family. And fifteen years in the spotlight could change anyone.

It sounded like she would find out what Asa Mitchell was really like soon enough.

"Ow! Dammit! Where the hell did that come from?" Asa Mitchell limped forward, his toe throbbing after he kicked the giant ceramic planter at the base of the stairs. He didn't remember that being there the last time he was home. Shifting the suitcase in his grasp, he hobbled up the steps and threw open the back door, trying to keep the noise down so he didn't wake up his dad. He probably should have stayed overnight in Idaho Falls, but the thought of another hotel room made him cringe, so he kept driving.

Closing the door softly, he set his bag down and walked to the fridge to get a bottle of water. Twisting the cap off, he sat down at the table in the dark and took a sip, enjoying the quiet of home. There wasn't anything like Montana.

The soft shuffle of feet on the wood floors alerted him to someone's presence a moment before a woman walked into the kitchen. For a split second, he thought it was the house-keeper, Jeannie, until he got a glimpse of her silhouette. Unless Jeannie grew a few inches and got breast implants while he was away on tour, the woman humming to herself as she opened the refrigerator door was not their housekeeper. As he watched, she reached inside the fridge. One side of her oversize shirt slipped down to reveal a creamy shoulder.

Jesus. The groupies were getting bold. "Who the fuck are you, and what are you doing in my house?" he growled.

She shrieked and whirled. Before he could react, she hurled a pint-size container of yogurt at him. It bounced off his cheekbone, its cold, clammy contents splattering all over his chest and lap.

He shot out of his chair with a gasp as the yogurt seeped through his clothes and down his arm. "What the hell?" he roared.

She spun around and picked up the milk carton, flinging it at him. He raised an arm to block it. It ricocheted off his forearm and broke open as it hit the floor.

"Get out!" she screeched.

A cupcake splatted against his chest and another one bounced off his face, sticking for a moment before sliding off his chin, leaving behind a streak of frosting.

"Shit, lady. Stop throwing stuff at me!"

"Fine!" She took two steps to the counter and pulled a knife from the block, brandishing it at him. The metal glinted in the light coming from the clock on the stove.

Whoa. Asa held up his hands. "Let's just calm down, okay?"

She sidled toward the wall and flipped the light switch. He squinted against the light to get his first look at the intruder. She was a knockout. About five-nine or so, she wore a pair of miniscule pajama shorts, revealing long shapely legs. A billowy cotton shirt with a wide neckline dipped low over her shoulder and showed off her deep cleavage. Her dark auburn hair spilled out of a messy bun on top of her head.

"Who are you?"

He frowned, straightening. "Who am I? You're in *my* house."

It was her turn to frown. "Your house?" The knife dipped.

Heavy footfalls kept her from saying anything more. Silas came around the corner into the kitchen.

"Asa!"

"Hi, Dad." He smiled at his old man despite his anger at the woman staring at him open-mouthed.

"What are you doing home already? And what happened in here?" He gestured to the mess all over Asa and the floor.

"I decided to drive through. As for the mess," he pointed at the woman, who finally lowered the knife, "ask her."

Silas looked at her.

She shrugged. "How was I supposed to know who he was? He was sitting in the kitchen in the dark. Scared the shit out of me. I just reacted. And he looks different from his pictures."

"Dad, who is this woman?"

Silas sighed. "This is our new housekeeper, Daisy O'Malley. Daisy, my son, Asa."

"New housekeeper? What happened to Jeannie?"

"She quit. Ran off not long after you left on tour and married some salesman she met in Billings. I hired Daisy a couple months ago."

Asa just stared at him for a second. "Why didn't you tell me?"

Silas shrugged. "It hadn't really come up. We haven't exactly talked much lately."

Asa glanced at the ceiling, exasperated. "Yeah, but—"

"And it isn't like you'd have cared who I hired, anyway." He looked at Daisy. "Go get a couple of towels, dear. I'll help you clean up this mess."

She gave Asa one last long look before she laid the knife on the counter and walked out of the room. As soon as she was gone, Silas walked up to Asa.

"I'd give you a hug, but..." He gestured to the muck covering Asa's clothes and face.

Asa grinned. "Aw, come on, Dad. It'll wash."

Silas laughed and shook a finger at him. "Stay away." He held out a hand, though. "It's good to have you back."

Asa shook his hand, gripping his forearm with the other.

"It's good to be back. But did you really have to hire Nolan Ryan for a housekeeper?"

Silas laughed again. "She's spunky, isn't she? But she's a real sweetheart, fastball notwithstanding."

Asa grabbed the tea towel off the oven and swiped at the frosting on his face and the yogurt coating his arm and chest. "Yeah, well, I'll believe it when I see it."

Silas was quiet as Asa tried to wipe the yogurt off himself. He sighed. He needed a shower.

"She's right, you know."

Asa glanced at his dad with a frown. "About what?"

"You do look different. What's wrong, son?"

Asa sighed again. "Nothing. I'm just really tired. Glad the tour is over." He'd done twenty shows in four weeks all over Europe. That was after he finished a three-month nationwide tour in the U.S. There were days he didn't know what country he was in, let alone what city.

"Well, you should be able to get some rest here. Although, it's calving season, so if you want to help out, I'm sure Chet wouldn't turn you away. How long are you planning on staying, anyway? You didn't say."

Asa straightened. "About that—"

Daisy walked in, holding several towels. She handed him one.

"Sorry about creaming you with the yogurt and cupcakes. We weren't expecting you until around lunch or so tomorrow. You really startled me."

He stared down at her. Freckles dusted her cheeks below her green eyes. She was cute. He frowned as the first stirrings of lust curled in his belly. "Yeah, well, I wasn't expecting you, either."

She narrowed her eyes at his accusatory tone. "I wasn't the one sitting in the dark."

"It's my house."

"It's your dad's house."

He blew a breath out through his nose. Who the hell did she think she was?

Silas stepped forward, placing a hand on each of their shoulders. "Okay. I think we need to get this cleaned up and get some sleep. It's very late." He arched a brow at them.

Asa frowned, but nodded. He was right. Getting into an argument with the housekeeper when he was exhausted probably wasn't a great idea.

Daisy hugged the towels to her chest, but nodded.

"Good. Asa, why don't you go on up and take a shower and go to bed? Daisy and I will clean up this mess."

"Are you sure?"

Silas nodded. "Yep."

He glanced at the young woman standing there quietly. She still watched him with wary eyes.

"All right. I'll see you in the morning." Picking up his suitcase, he walked toward the door.

"Make sure you rinse the yogurt out of your clothes before you put them in the hamper," she called after him.

He paused in the doorway and clamped his lips together, his muscles going rigid as he fought the urge to turn around and give her a piece of his mind. It would serve her right if he ignored her request. It was her fault he was covered in yogurt. Keeping his mouth shut, he gave a curt nod without looking back and kept walking. He was too tired to deal with little miss bossy-britches tonight.

Six

The next morning, Daisy looked up at the sound of footsteps on the stairs. Her spine straightened, and the tension made her shoulders stiffen. It was Asa coming down. Silas had been up and out of the house at dawn.

He rounded the corner and stopped in the entryway to stare at her. She took him in. He really did look much different from the picture Silas showed her and from the couple she saw on the internet when she googled him. He looked like he carried the weight of the world on his broad shoulders. He also had a nice bruise on his cheekbone where she nailed him last night.

"You're not going to throw stuff at me this morning, are you?" His low voice rumbled through the room, making tingles race up the back of her neck. She hadn't listened to any of his music yet, but she could imagine how good he sounded when he sang.

She gave him a rueful smile and shook her head. "No. You're safe." She reached into the cupboard and took out a coffee mug, pouring him a cup, then held it out.

He took it, staring over the rim at her. "Thanks."

"Sure. You want some breakfast? There's bacon leftover in the fridge, and I can scramble you some eggs quick."

"Um, that sounds good." He walked to the table and sat down.

Daisy moved around the kitchen as she made his food. She kept her back to him, but could feel his eyes on her. They tracked her movements like a predator tracked his prey.

She rolled her eyes at herself. Asa was not the big bad wolf, even if he was intimidating with his six-and-a-half-foot height, brooding eyes, and dark beard stubble. She could see why they cast him as a cop in those movies he did. She'd spill her guts, too, if he was the detective interrogating her and he stared her down with those deep blue eyes.

"What's with all the cookies?"

She glanced back at him. "They're for the hands. Cookie asked me to make some sweets for them since they're all spending so much time in the saddle monitoring the herd right now. He said it helps boost morale if they don't have to eat his baking."

Asa chuckled. "I can see that. Cookie can cook, but his baked goods could chip a tooth."

Daisy giggled as she cracked two eggs into a small bowl and whisked them with a fork. "Your dad said the same thing."

"Where is he, anyway?"

"He left around dawn to go out with the hands. Calving season is in full swing, so they've all been working long days." She poured the eggs into the hot skillet, then put several slices of bacon on a plate and stuck it in the microwave. Checking the eggs again, she saw they were done and removed them from the heat, adding them to the plate when the microwave dinged. She took a fork from the drawer and set it and the plate on the table in front of him.

"Thanks."

"You're welcome." She turned back to the counter and her cookie ingredients.

"So, tell me about yourself," Asa said. "What made you want to move out here and be my dad's housekeeper? You're a pretty girl. Surely, you have better—prospects—in town."

She paused and looked over her shoulder at him. "Prospects?"

He crunched a piece of bacon and arched a brow. "Come on. You seriously think I don't know what you're really doing here?"

Daisy spun around and crossed her arms, frowning. Oh, this should be good. "Enlighten me."

Asa sat back in his chair and looked her over. "You aren't the first woman who's tried to use my family to get to me." He polished off the last of his bacon and stood, picking up his empty plate, then walking toward her.

She straightened her spine, dropping her arms as he came closer.

He stopped right in front of her, looming. "I don't know what game you're playing, but I won't stand for anyone messing with my dad. He's a good man who has sacrificed a lot for me. So, why don't I help you pack? I'll tell him you had a change of heart about living out here and just couldn't take it another minute."

Was he for real?

"When cakes fly, you will."

He frowned. "Excuse me?"

"You heard me. God, you are so full of yourself. There's a new, young woman employed at your family's ranch, so she must only be there to get her claws into you. I mean, do you hear yourself?" She planted a finger in his chest to emphasize her point. "I am not here for you. Until I came to work here, I didn't even know you existed. I am here for me. So, you can climb down off your high-horse and rest assured that your father is in no danger of being played. Now, if you'll excuse me, I have another several dozen cookies to bake. You can put your plate in the dishwasher on the way out."

His frown morphed into an incredulous stare. "Who the hell do you think you are? This is my house. You work for me."

"This is your father's house, and I work for him," she retorted.

"He hired you, but you work for both of us. That means I can fire you."

"Yeah? Go ahead and try. I'm sure I'll be rehired real quick. Especially since you'll be leaving in what? A few weeks?"

A slow cat-ate-the-canary smile spread over his face. Daisy's stomach dropped. That was a grin she'd seen on her brothers' faces before when they knew something she didn't. She never liked what they had to say in its aftermath.

"Actually, I'm here to stay."

"What?" Her voice dropped an octave as she stared up at him.

"I'm home to stay. That was my last tour. I've decided to retire."

Asa was staying? She had to live under the same roof as this self-centered know-it-all? Great. Just great.

He leaned in, his face inches from hers. "What was that about being rehired quick?"

Daisy wanted to slap the smirk right off his face. She clenched her fists instead. "It's still up to Silas whether I stay or go. He hired me."

"Yes, but I own the ranch. I bought it from him when I first entered the music business to keep it afloat."

She arched a brow. "So, you're going to pull rank on your own father? That's low."

He glared at her, his nostrils flaring. "I don't like your tone."

"Well, I don't like you, period, so there's that."

Asa straightened to his full height. "Go pack your bags, princess."

She crossed her arms again. "No."

"Lady, what part of 'I'm your boss' don't you understand?"

"The part where you aren't my boss. Your father is. So, until he tells me to leave, I'm not going anywhere except to take all these cookies to the bunkhouse."

He stared down at her for a moment, his mouth working at her defiance. "I could call the cops and have you removed."

She gave him a tight smile. "Go ahead. Your dad would love it, I'm sure. So would the media when they get wind of it."

"Oh, you play dirty."

"Honey, I have six older brothers. I'm just getting warmed up."

He stuck a finger in her face. Daisy fought the urge to bite it.

"We'll see what Dad has to say later." With a last glare, he put his plate in the sink and stormed out of the kitchen into the mudroom. A moment later, she heard the back door slam shut as he left.

Daisy sagged against the counter. She didn't know what got into her. She rarely stood up to people like that. It wasn't uncommon for her to butt heads with her brothers, but that —that was a far cry from the arguments they had. He made her furious with his high-handedness. More than her brothers ever had up until Kyle pulled his stunt with Ethan Byrnes.

She blew out a breath and spun around. She hoped she was right and Silas would back her up. Finding another job—

another place to live—wasn't something she wanted to do. She liked it here.

Asa marched across the yard, headed for the barn, seething. That woman had some nerve telling him no. It was his house, dammit. He would not stand for an insubordinate employee, no matter how cute she was.

Reaching the barn, he yanked open the door and stepped inside. He was going to saddle Storm and go find his dad. That woman needed to go. The ranch was his sanctuary. He didn't need some bossy, pretentious, know-it-all around, trying to run his life.

Making quick work of saddling his gray gelding, Asa took off through the pasture. He wasn't sure where Silas was, but figured just getting out of the house would do him some good right now. He needed to clear his head.

Storm carried him over the ranch's gently rolling land. The property covered most of the valley between the mountains in this part of the county, with some higher elevations to the west. After he saved the place from foreclosure, he'd added to it, leaving it in his dad's and his best friend, Chet's, capable hands. But he was ready to be part of things here again instead of a silent owner. Montana was in his blood. So was ranching. He was done being the superstar.

A man on horseback up ahead caught Asa's attention. He kicked Storm into a canter and rode closer. It was Chet.

The other man's face broke into a broad smile as he recognized Asa.

"Hey, man. Silas said you were back."

Asa grinned at his oldest friend, pulling up next to him. He held a hand out. Chet took it, giving it a hearty shake. "Got in late last night."

"Yeah, I heard you startled Daisy."

Asa's smile disappeared, and he rolled his eyes. "Why did Dad hire her? I never thought he'd be swayed by a pretty face."

Chet frowned. "What do you mean? Daisy's great at her job. That house has never been cleaner. She's even got your dad eating better. The first thing she did was throw away all his TV dinners."

"So, basically, she took over." He snorted. "Why do women think they can run a man's life?"

"Whoa. Something tells me this is about more than Daisy."

"No. It's about her. She's just here to get to me. I won't stand for someone using my family. I'm on my way to find Dad to talk to him about hiring someone else."

"Did she tell you she's here to get into your good graces?"

"No. She denied it, of course."

"I'm sure she did, because it's not true. Jesus, Asa, do you hear yourself? Not everything is about you."

"Well, regardless, she needs to go. You should have heard how insubordinate she was. An employee who doesn't respect her employer shouldn't be kept around."

"I've never known her to be anything but polite, so if she was disrespectful to you, I'm sure you started it. You probably need to go apologize."

"Are you for real?"

"Yes. Let me guess. You accused her of taking the housekeeper's job here to get to you. To which she replied she didn't. Then you probably told her you didn't believe her and that she needed to look for a new job."

Asa gave a curt nod. "She told me I couldn't fire her because I wasn't her boss. I own the ranch, so it doesn't matter who hired her."

"So, you're undermining your dad's authority?"

Asa gave him a dark scowl. Why didn't anyone see things his way? That woman was trouble.

"Look, I know you've had some trouble with women in the past, but Daisy's not like that. The last thing she wants is another man in her life. She left six of them behind. Trust me when I say she's just here to work."

"Six men? Did she work as an escort or something?"

Chet broke into laughter, leaning forward over the saddle horn as he guffawed. When he sat back up, he wiped tears from his cheeks.

"Not an escort, I take it?"

"No. Not even close. She has six older brothers who try to run her life. She left to get away from them." Chet sobered and gave him a hard look. "You need to get your head out of your ass. Give the woman a chance. And you can start by riding back to the house and apologizing."

Asa waffled. So he might have overreacted a tad. He still didn't like the woman.

"Where's Dad?" he asked, changing the subject.

Chet sighed. "West pasture, checking for calves."

Asa swung Storm around. "Thanks."

"Make sure you eat crow later!" Chet called after him.

Asa raised a hand in acknowledgement and kicked his horse into a faster gait. He'd be damned if he would apologize to that woman.

Storm carried him over the ranch land on an easy lope. His long strides ate up the ground and soon the west pasture came into view. Asa had little trouble picking Silas out of the herd ahead of him. Several men on horseback rode through the cattle, but only one sat a head above all the others.

Asa steered Storm through the herd toward his dad. Silas swung around to avoid a cow and saw him coming.

"What are you doing out here?" Silas rode up to him, smiling. "I thought you'd sleep until well after lunch."

"I tried." Asa shrugged. "I couldn't stay asleep, though. Besides, I wanted to talk to you."

"Oh? About what?"

"Well, for one thing, I'm home to stay. All my movie and recording contracts have been fulfilled, and I didn't sign any more. I'm done."

Silas's eyes widened. "Are you sure that's what you want?"

"Hell, yes. I'm tired, Dad. And I'm ready to just be Asa the rancher again."

"Well, then," Silas held out a hand, his smile widening, "welcome home, son."

"Thanks." Asa shook his hand, returning his smile. He let go and looked out over the herd, trying to think of a way to bring up Daisy. "So, um, I talked to the new housekeeper again this morning."

"Yeah? Daisy's great. We really lucked out with her."

Asa scoffed. "I don't know about that. I think we should let her go and look for someone else."

Silas tipped his hat back and stared at him for several moments. "Boy, have you lost your damn mind? She's the third woman I hired after Jeannie left and the only one worth a crap. The first one didn't like living so far out of town, and I caught the second one in your bedroom going through your dresser. Daisy didn't even know who you were."

"Yeah, right."

"She didn't. I quizzed her about you before I hired her. There was no subterfuge in her expression. Trust me, after what happened with the second woman, I looked. She's just looking to get away from her family."

"Still, she was insubordinate and downright hostile with me this morning."

Silas arched an eyebrow. "What did you say?"

"To her hostility? I—"

"Not to that." Silas waved a hand, cutting him off. "To

put her on the defensive. Let me guess. You accused her of taking the job to get to you."

Asa's mouth flattened, and he said nothing.

"Uh-huh. That's what I thought." He leaned over and slapped Asa's thigh. "Stop thinking about her like some floozy out to get in your pants. She's not. You do that, and things will be fine."

He sighed. "Dad—"

"No, Asa." Silas waved a hand again. "We're not firing her. She's good at her job, and she's become a friend. I'm sorry. You're just going to have to deal with it." He turned his horse. "I need to get back to work." Before Asa could say anything else, Silas rode away.

Cursing, Asa ground his teeth, biting back a shout of frustration. He spun Storm around to head home. He didn't care what his dad said. He'd find a way to get that woman to leave. His sanity and the peace and quiet he craved depended on it.

His horse covered the ground between the pasture and the barn in record time. Asa led Storm into the corral, tying him to the fence while he unsaddled him and brushed him down. Once he had his horse taken care of, he headed for the house.

As he approached, he could hear music blaring through open windows. Shaking his head, he let himself into the mudroom. Inside, the music was louder. It was some pop song about a girl on fire. He gritted his teeth and toed off his boots before stomping through the kitchen in his stocking feet in search of an off button. He already had a headache from his conversations with Chet and his dad. This racket wasn't helping.

He rounded the living room doorway and stopped in his tracks. Daisy had a duster in her hand, swishing it over the mantle as she sang. Her hips swayed and shimmied with the beat, raising his blood pressure for a different reason. Transfixed, he leaned against the wall and watched. She had a decent voice. Husky, but sweet.

She spun, eyes closed, using the duster as a microphone. When she opened her eyes and spotted him, she shrieked and jumped. Stumbling over the edge of the rug, she lost her balance and toppled forward, landing on her hands and knees.

"Very graceful." His lips twitched, but he held in the grin. "Are you okay?"

She flipped her hair back and glared up at him. "I'm fine." She stood up and straightened her clothes, still glaring at him. "What do you want?"

His eyes moved past her to the stereo on the bookcase. "To turn that down." He sauntered past her and punched the power button. The silence was as deafening as the music. Now, he could hear the angry vibes coming off of her in waves.

She marched over and turned the stereo back on, but spun the dial to turn it down. "Happy? Now scram, so I can finish cleaning."

Asa bit his tongue. Oh, how he wanted to send this woman packing. But his dad refused to fire her, so he had to make nice.

"That's much better, thank you. I have a headache."

She frowned, some of the anger leaving her eyes. "There's a bottle of ibuprofen in the kitchen. Can I get you some?"

He sighed and shook his head. "I'll be fine. I think I just need some caffeine." Which wasn't a lie. He drank several cups of espresso every day. So far, he'd only had the cup of regular coffee at breakfast.

She put down her duster. "I'll make some coffee."

He pushed off the wall. "I'll do it. You finish what you were doing."

"Are you sure?"

"Yeah. Thanks, though." A bit of his ire disappeared at her offer.

She picked up her duster and turned away, finding the rhythm of the music again. Asa caught himself staring at her ass for a moment before he spun on his heel, disgusted with himself.

Ogling the help... What the fuck is wrong with me?

SEVEN

C ar tires crunched on the gravel, drawing Daisy's attention from tending the garden behind the house. Silas had chewed up the ground for her a couple of weeks ago. It was warm enough now she was willing to risk planting.

She glanced back, but didn't see the car. It didn't sound like one of the ranch trucks. With a sigh, she got to her feet to go see who it was. Silas got an occasional visitor from town, but he usually told her when someone was going to stop by.

Daisy rounded the corner of the house and stopped. A tall, blonde woman in heels, a tight short skirt, and a top that barely covered her perfect chest climbed out of a cherry red jeep. Even from this distance, she could tell the woman's nails and lipstick matched the color of her car. This lady was not here for Silas.

"Hi. Can I help you?" Daisy strode toward the woman.

The woman turned at the sound of her voice. She pulled her sunglasses down the bridge of her nose to reveal cornflower blue eyes and gave Daisy an assessing look. Shoving them back up with a sigh, she cocked a hip and rested a hand on it. "I'm here to see Asa. Tell him it's Marla. He'll want to see me."

Daisy smothered a grin. Oh, this should be good. She highly doubted Asa wanted anything to do with this creature. He'd been home a week now and avoided interaction with everyone except his father, Chet, and Chet's wife, Marci. He hadn't even gone to town. She had a feeling that was why this woman was here. If Mohammed won't come to the mountain…

Putting a lid on her mirth, she took her phone from her pocket. "He's out in the field, but I can call and tell him you're here." She dialed Chet's number and put the phone to her ear.

"Yeah, Dais, what's up?" Chet asked when he answered.

"Is Asa still with you?"

"Yes. Why?"

"He has a visitor. Marla."

Chet groaned. "Fuck. That woman is a menace."

She agreed on first impression, but kept her opinion to herself.

His voice went softer as he turned away from the phone to tell Asa what was going on.

There was some static on the line, then Asa's angry voice rumbled in her ear.

"Tell her to get lost. I'm not interested any more now than I was the other times."

Daisy smiled at Marla, who watched her closely, then turned her back and lowered her voice. "How about you come tell her that your own self, because I'm not a bouncer."

He growled. "Daisy, get rid of her. Chet and I are on our way back. I'm hot, tired, and in desperate need of a beer. I don't want to deal with Marla and get octopus arms. She better not be there when we get back."

There was a click as he hung up. She pulled the phone away and stared at it. Who the hell did he think he was, ordering her around like that? Marla was not her problem to deal with.

She shoved her phone into her pocket and turned around. Marla stood there, looking at Daisy over her glasses again.

"Well?"

"He's on his way. Can I offer you some lemonade or tea while you wait?"

As the ranch buildings came into view, Asa noticed the bright red jeep parked next to the house. Anger made his jaw clench. He told Daisy to get rid of Marla.

Chet saw the car and laughed.

"It's not funny."

"Sure it is. You basically ordered Daisy to make Marla leave. I'm not surprised she did the opposite. Don't you know you catch more flies with honey?"

"She's an employee. She's supposed to follow orders."

Chet's face sobered. "You mean like me?"

"Fuck. No, you're different, you know that."

Chet shrugged. "But I still work for you. Am I supposed to just roll over and follow orders when you bark them out?" He scoffed. "I don't know what's up with you, but you need to get your shit straight."

They were about a hundred yards from the house now. Chet pulled his horse to a halt.

"Go deal with them. I'll take Storm to the barn and dress him down."

Feeling properly chastised, Asa dismounted and handed Storm's reins to Chet. His friend took them and started toward the barn without a word. Asa took off his hat and ran a hand through his hair, staring at the house for a moment before he trekked across the grass. He tromped up the back porch steps into the mudroom and toed off his boots, then hung up his hat. Entering the kitchen, he went to the sink and washed his hands. The clack of heels on the hard floor of the hallway warned him Marla's entrance was imminent. He shut the water off just as she scampered into the kitchen.

"Asa!" She threw herself at him, pressing her scantily clad body to his dusty one, and planted a kiss on his lips.

He grabbed her arms with his wet hands and pushed her back. "Hello, Marla." He saw Daisy lean against the wall. She crossed her arms and bit back a smile. He was going to throttle her just as soon as he got rid of his other problem.

Marla pouted for a moment, then pulled her hands free and smacked at his chest lightly. "Why haven't you come to see me? I had to hear from Susie at the Clip-N-Curl you were back."

"Marla, I have no reason to come see you. We aren't dating. Haven't for a long time. I've told you that many times."

A pretty pucker marred her perfect eyebrows. "Don't be silly. I know you just didn't want to do the long-distance thing. But I have it on good authority you're back permanently." She threw her arms around his neck and pressed against him again. "We can be together now," she purred near his ear.

When she licked it, he yanked her away and gave her a hard stare. "Stop. We're not ever going to date again. I think you should go."

Marla balled up her fists, holding them at her sides. She looked over her shoulder at Daisy. "It's this tramp, isn't it? She got her hooks into you with those big boobs." She lifted her nose in the air. "They're all just fat, you know."

Daisy straightened, her expression turning dark. "Excuse me?"

Asa put both hands on Marla's shoulders and steered her out of the kitchen toward the front door. He stopped long enough to get her purse and keys from where she left them in the living room, then ushered her through the door onto the porch. "Thanks for stopping by. I'll see you around."

"Asa—"

He didn't wait for her to say more. He stepped back inside and closed the door, locking it. When he turned around, Daisy stood in the hallway, watching with an amused smile.

"Your girlfriend suits you. Stuck up and prissy."

He stalked toward her, only stopping once he was in her space. "I told you to get rid of her."

She tipped her head and met his gaze. "Exactly. Next time, try asking." She spun around and walked away, leaving him staring after her.

Damn woman... Asa followed her into the living room, where she collected Marla's tea glass and her own.

"Maybe I could have been nicer about it, but would it have killed you to send her packing?"

She sauntered past him. "No. But I'm not about to let you treat me like some second-class citizen just because I'm your housekeeper. I'm still a human being, Asa." She'd had enough of being treated like she was less than an equal with her brothers. She was done being a doormat.

He gritted his teeth, trailing her into the kitchen. She deposited the glasses in the sink. "I don't know what you're used to in your employees, but I'll tell you right now, that shit won't fly with me. I have six brothers. You don't scare me." She marched into the mudroom. "I'm going to finish planting. There are cold cuts in the fridge if you're hungry, as well as a pitcher of tea." Before he could respond, she was out the door.

Cursing, he stomped to the fridge and yanked open the door, making the condiment bottles rattle. He spotted the tea and poured himself a glass. He knew he'd been a little tyrannical, but she brought it out in him. Something about her irritated him.

Sighing, he guzzled the glass, then went back to the mudroom and put his boots back on to go help Chet in the barn. That was a fence he needed to mend. How, he didn't know. He kept putting his foot in his mouth thanks to Daisy, and it was affecting his relationships with those he cared about. But until he could convince his dad to fire her, he needed to get it together.

EIGHT

The bell over the door of Sarafina's diner tinkled as Daisy stepped inside. She was starving. Her plan had been to run her errands and eat lunch at home, but they'd taken longer than she planned. With a half-hour drive back to the ranch, she knew she'd never make it without her stomach growling its way out through her abdomen.

"Hey, girl."

Daisy smiled at Sara Katsaros, the diner's owner and her new friend. "Hi."

"Have a seat and I'll be right over to take your order."

"Can you bring me a chocolate milkshake when you come?"

"Sure can." Sara's messy bun of black curls bobbed as she nodded.

"Thanks." Daisy walked over to a small table near the window and sat down. She plucked a menu from the holder and read it over, settling on a chicken, bacon, and avocado panini as Sara walked up with her milkshake.

"There you go." She set the shake on the table and held out a wrapped straw.

"Thanks." Daisy took the straw and ripped the paper off, dunking it into the thick drink.

"So, what brings you into town today?"

Daisy swallowed her mouthful of shake, then swirled the straw as she talked. "I had some errands to run. I'm working on that vegetable garden I told you about and needed to get some stuff. The hardware store was super busy, though, so it took me longer to get what I needed. Plus, I had about twenty people come up to ask me about Asa." She rolled her eyes. "You'd think he was the pope or something." She shook her head and took another drink.

Sara giggled. "Well, he is the biggest thing to ever happen around here. Everyone loves to say they know him, but few actually do. Hence the questions. How is he doing? I heard he's been a bit surly."

Daisy scoffed. "That's an understatement. I don't know what he's normally like, but he's been a bear. Growling at me, growling about me. He needs to get over himself."

Sara laughed. "I think you rub him the wrong way."

"Oh, I know I do. The feeling is mutual."

"It's not for the reason you think, though."

"What do you mean?"

"I've known Asa a long time. You're just his type of woman, but he's had some issues with the fairer sex lately, so he's probably sworn them off for a while. Being confronted with you is not helping him."

It was Daisy's turn to laugh. "That's rich. I'm Asa Mitchell's type? Have you seen the women he dates? They're all like size zeros. I'm about ten sizes too big."

Sara waved a hand at her. "That's because he was surrounded by them. I think his manager, Martin, had a lot to do with who he dated too. Asa was very young when he left. We'd just graduated. Martin got his hooks in him and convinced him he needed to put up a certain façade if he wanted to be taken seriously and make it in the music world. That type of woman was a part of that. I think it's finally getting to him."

Daisy frowned as she processed Sara's words. She did not want to think of Asa as a victim. The man was an asshat. But if what she said was true, Daisy had made some seriously wrong assumptions about him, and she didn't like that. She'd been judged poorly more than once—by strangers and her brothers —and it wasn't a nice feeling.

Sara straightened and flipped open her order pad. "But that's just my two cents. Do you know what you want to eat?"

Mood dampened, Daisy gave her order, then slouched in her seat, her milkshake in her hand as Sara retreated. The straw hung out of one corner of her mouth as she took a deep draw, thinking. Had she misjudged Asa? Maybe she should cut him some slack. He couldn't be all bad. He was Silas's son, after all, and that man was a gem. She sighed and sucked down another mouthful of the chocolatey drink. Men. It didn't matter where she lived; they always created problems for her.

Lost in thought, she didn't realize how long she sat there contemplating her famous housemate until Sara walked up with her food.

"One chicken, bacon, and avocado panini with chips." Sara set the plate on the table. "Can I get you anything else?"

Daisy shook her head. "I'm good, thanks."

"Holler if you need me."

"I will." Daisy picked up her sandwich as Sara walked away, taking a large bite, so hungry she could eat a whole chicken by herself. In no time flat, she polished off her meal. Picking up her water, she took a sip to wash everything down and glanced at her watch. *Yikes!* It was later than she thought. She needed to get back to the ranch. Her garden wouldn't plant itself.

Slurping up the last of her shake, she slid out of the booth.

As she walked up to the counter to pay her bill, she noticed the woman who'd been out at the ranch the other day—Marla—checking out. Daisy stepped up behind her, waiting her turn. Marla turned and saw her, stopping for a second to offer her a glare before sauntering out, a to-go cup in her hand.

"Good to see you, too," Daisy muttered, rolling her eyes as she walked up to the counter to pay her bill. Sara grinned at her as she took the check and her credit card.

"What'd you do to Marla?"

"She thinks I'm after Asa."

Sara giggled as she punched buttons on the register. "That woman's had a thing for him since we were kids. He never should have given her the time of day in high school. It only encouraged her."

"She can have him." She giggled as she remembered Asa's face when Marla laid a big, fat kiss on him. "Although I don't think he wants her."

Sara laughed. "No. He doesn't."

Daisy took her credit card and stowed it in her wallet. "Well, she's still his problem to deal with. I gotta go. I'll see you later."

Sara waggled her fingers. "See ya."

Daisy returned her wave and left. As she pushed through the door and headed for her car, she saw Marla standing next to it and let out a little groan. She didn't want to talk to the woman, but it looked like she wouldn't have a choice.

"Hi, Marla."

The woman's blonde head jerked up and Daisy saw the keys in her hand. Inches from the long, deep scratches now in her paint job.

"Hey!" She took several quick steps in Marla's direction.

Eyes wide, Marla straightened and backed up.

"Why did you key my car, you crazy bitch?" Daisy ran a finger over the lines marring the paint.

"Stay away from Asa!"

Daisy opened her mouth to tell Marla where to shove it, but never got the words out. She raised her eyes just in time to see Marla's to-go cup coming at her. The paper cup bounced off her chest, the plastic lid flying off, allowing the cold, gloppy vanilla shake to splatter all over her clothes.

"Oh!" Daisy gasped as the freezing liquid slid down the neckline of her shirt and between her breasts. She plucked the material away from her torso, looking up to see Marla running across the street and jumping in her car. "What the fuck?" she muttered. Marla backed out of her parking space, almost hitting an oncoming car, and sped off with a short squeal of her tires.

"Daisy? Are you okay?" Sara came out of the diner. She held out several bar towels.

"I'm fine. Just wet." She took a towel and swiped at the mess. "And sticky. Thanks for the towels."

"Oh, sure. I saw the whole thing. I can't believe she did that."

Daisy could. That woman was certifiable.

"Do you want me to call the police?"

Sighing, Daisy stopped dabbing at herself and looked up. "I suppose. I don't think the scratches she put in the paint are going to just buff out."

Sara peered around her and made a face. "No. I'll go call."

Before she could step inside, a cruiser rolled down the street. Sara saw it and stepped to the curb, waving her arms. The officer pulled over and parked behind the cars, turning his lights on before getting out.

"Hi, Sara. Is there a problem?"

Her dark curls bobbed as she nodded. "Marla Wilkins just keyed my friend's car and threw a milkshake at her." She pointed at Daisy.

Daisy waved a hand, still clutching the bar towel.

The officer frowned and moved away from his car, shutting the door and walking over to them. "What happened?"

"I came out of the diner to leave, and she was standing next to my car. I thought she wanted to talk out here where it's private, but she was keying my car. I said, 'Hey!' and asked her what she was doing. She didn't answer. Instead, she told me to stay away from Asa, then chucked her shake at me."

The officer's lips pursed. "Asa Mitchell?"

She nodded.

"Why would she want to talk to you in private? You two have a disagreement?"

Daisy shrugged. "Not exactly. I'm the Mitchell's housekeeper. She came out to the ranch the other day to see Asa, and he threw her out. She seems to think I'm the reason he doesn't want anything to do with her. I'm not, though. I barely know the man."

"And you didn't have words in the diner?"

"No, sir. I said hello to her. She glared at me and left."

"I can confirm that," Sara said, raising a hand and holding up one finger. "I was at the counter checking Marla out. Daisy came up behind her to check out as well."

The man nodded. "Okay. Let me grab the paperwork." He turned and jogged back to his car, returning a moment later with some papers. "I need you both to write a statement. I'll turn it over to the prosecutor's office for charges to be filed. They'll issue a warrant for her arrest, then."

Daisy took the paper and pen he offered, frowning. "I thought you'd just give her a citation, or something."

"No, ma'am. She committed two misdemeanors. Destruction of property and battery. They aren't ticketable." He quirked a brow at her. "Do you still want to file charges?"

Daisy looked at her car, then heaved a sigh. *Dammit.* "For the vandalism, at least. It won't be cheap to get the paint fixed." Turning around, she laid the paper on the hood of her car and started writing, grumbling under her breath about men and their drama. She should just make Asa pay for the damages. He was the reason his crazy ex keyed her car in the first place.

Pen flying over the page, she wrote out what she just told the officer, then signed her statement, handing it and the pen back to the man. Sara did the same.

"I'll get these turned in. Hopefully, we'll get her picked up today or tomorrow. The court will contact you with more information once that happens, Ms. O'Malley. You have a nice day now." He backed up a step, then glanced at Sara, tipping his hat. "Sara."

"Thank you," Daisy said. He retreated to his cruiser and drove away. "Well, that was fun." She took another swipe at her sticky clothes as she watched him drive down the street. Realizing she wasn't making any headway with the towel, she handed it back to Sara. "Thanks for the towels. I should be going."

"Okay. If you need anything, let me know. I hope Marla leaves you alone now."

"Me too. Thanks again." She hit the button on her remote to unlock her car and climbed inside, waving at Sara as she backed onto the street and headed for the ranch.

Halfway home, her teeth started to chatter. It was warm out, but just cool enough that the breeze coming in the window left her chilled. If she rolled the windows up, the sun beating down made the interior stifling and the vents just made the cold, wet material of her shirt flap against her skin. She gave up trying to find a happy medium and just sped up, pushing her car over the speed limit and praying she didn't get pulled over.

Turning onto the ranch drive, she drove up the gravel lane faster than wise and came to a halt at the back of the house in a cloud of dust. Still shivering, she got out of the car, leaving her purchases, and hurried up the back steps to the mudroom.

"It's about damn time you got back. Dad asked me to help you work on your garden and I've been waiting almost an hour now."

Daisy skidded to a halt in the doorway as an angry Asa rounded the corner and stopped to glare at her. His expression altered, though, as he took in her appearance. "What happened? What's all over your shirt?"

"Marla's milkshake." She stormed past him to go to her room.

"Marla's—?" His boots scraped the floor as he turned and followed her down the hall. "Why are you wearing her shake?"

"She keyed my car, and I caught her in the act. It was her getaway tactic."

"What? Why did she key your car?"

"You," she tossed over her shoulder.

He grabbed her arm and spun her around to face him. Daisy blew her hair out of her face and stared up at him, annoyed.

"What do I have to do with any of this?"

She pulled her arm from his grip. "According to her, I'm what's standing in the way of her getting to you. She wouldn't even listen to me so I could explain she's out of her damn mind." She narrowed her eyes. "You need to get control of your girlfriend."

"She's not my girlfriend. Hasn't been since I was eighteen."

"Whatever. I don't care. Just talk to her. She's already facing criminal charges for what she did. Let's not have to make them worse because she does something else."

"Wait. You called the cops?"

She frowned up at him like he was dense. "Of course I did.

She keyed my car. Do you know how much it's going to cost to have it repainted?"

He groaned and pinched his nose. "That's just great. Just fucking fantastic. More press. Exactly what I need. God, can't you think of someone besides yourself before you do things?"

Whoa. Daisy planted her hands on her hips and squared her feet to face him. "Excuse me? Who's being the selfish one around here? I'm just trying to live my life and was doing fine until you showed up. Now, I've got some crazy blonde bitch throwing drinks at me while she takes out her sexual frustration on my car. *Maybe,*" she poked him in the chest, "if you had *talked to her* like a civilized person last week, she wouldn't see me as the competition. Because I'm most certainly not."

"That's for damn sure," he muttered, looking down his nose at her. "Like I'd ever want to date you."

Daisy's old insecurities about her body reared their ugly heads, but she put a determined lid on them. Being away from her brothers had already helped her see her body in a different light. Especially with Marci and Sara's help. They'd been begging her to let them take her shopping for better clothes. Something that flattered her fuller figure instead of hiding it. Like the cold, wet shirt she still had on.

"You know what? Screw you." Unable to stand the feel of the clammy fabric any longer, she whipped her shirt over her head. A smile tugged up the corners of her mouth as she spun around. She'd seen the involuntary flare of desire on his face as he got an eyeful of her ample chest covered only in her satiny blue bra before she turned away.

Maybe Sara was right. Maybe she was his type. That thought made her bold, and she added a little extra sway to her hips as she continued down the hall.

NINE

The sound of Daisy singing floated out the kitchen window as Asa stretched chicken wire over a post surrounding the vegetable garden. Her sultry voice rang clear on the light breeze. After their fiery exchange in the hallway, he'd done his best to avoid her. Not because he didn't want a repeat, but because he did. When she'd whipped off that t-shirt to reveal those beautiful breasts, he'd been struck dumb. Anything he'd planned to say went sailing out of his mind at the sight of all that creamy flesh encased in bright blue satin. It had been a week and he still couldn't get it out of his head. Coming home wasn't the retreat he hoped it would be.

Dust rose in the distance as a car turned off the highway onto the drive. Asa picked up his water and took a drink, staring at the trees while he waited for the car to emerge. He didn't know who it could be, but it was either one of Daisy's friends, or someone come to hound him. Several of his "old friends" had dropped by in the last few weeks since he'd been home, wanting to get reacquainted.

He swiped at the sweat dripping down the side of his face and shook his head. It would be a wonder if he ever made a genuine friend ever again. He hated his fame. The only good it had ever done him was to save the Stone Creek. He wouldn't have a home to come back to if it weren't for his music career.

A sleek silver SUV broke through the tree line, and Asa groaned. There was only one person he knew who would drive a car like that out here. Sighing, he took off his gloves, shoving them into his back pocket as he walked toward the front of the house to greet his guest.

The car came to a halt, its purring engine cutting out as the driver turned it off. Asa stood in the shade of the large oak next to the drive with his hands on his hips, waiting.

"Asa!" Martin Frost's dark head popped above the door as he got out.

Expression thunderous, Asa stared at his manager. "What are you doing here, Marty?" He should have known Marty would show up eventually. Asa had been avoiding his calls and texts since he left Los Angeles, but he had zero desire to go back, which was likely what Marty was here to convince him to do. When he said he was done, he'd meant it, though. He wasn't going back.

Marty held out his arms and walked around the front of the car. "Is that anyway to greet a friend?"

"Sorry. How was your trip? I hope it was good and that it'll be the same going back to L.A."

"Come on, Asa. Don't be like that." He dropped his arms, propping his hands on his hips.

Asa sighed, some of the starch leaving him. Daisy's words about dealing with people instead of shoving them away rang in his mind. He hated to admit it, but she was probably right. "Can I offer you a drink?"

Marty grinned. "That'd be great. It's hot here. Hotter than I thought it would be."

Asa shrugged and turned toward the house. "Welcome to

Montana. Come on. Daisy made a fresh batch of sun tea yesterday. I think there's still some left."

Marty followed him up the front steps onto the porch. "Who's Daisy? And who's singing?"

"Daisy. She's our housekeeper." Asa pulled the door open and led his manager inside, the singing growing louder as they approached the kitchen. He couldn't help but stop and stare as they crossed the threshold. Daisy sang along to the music flowing through her earbuds as she rolled and punched down a ball of dough on the counter. Flour dusted every surface around her, including the floor and her clothes.

"Daisy."

She kept dancing and kneading.

"*That's* your housekeeper?" Marty pointed at her, disbelief and male appreciation on his face.

Asa narrowed his eyes at Marty's expression, but nodded before calling Daisy's name again.

When she still didn't hear him, he rolled his eyes and strode forward. His hand landed on her shoulder as he called her name a third time. She shrieked, throwing her hands in the air, the cup of flour she just picked up showering over them.

She whirled around. Eyes wide, she plucked an earbud from one ear. "You scared the shit out of me! Quit doing that!"

Asa blinked. Flour fluttered off the ends of his eyelashes to float in front of his face. "Maybe you should turn your music down a bit. I called your name twice."

Her cheeks turned red. "Oh. Sorry." Her eyes roamed over him, and a small giggle slid past her lips. "You're covered in flour."

He ran a hand over his hair. It flew around him in a fine mist, sticking to the sweat on his face and arms. "So are you. What are you making?"

"Bread."

Marty cleared his throat. Asa glanced back, having forgotten about him for a moment. "Daisy, this is my manager, Martin Frost. Marty, our housekeeper, Daisy O'Malley."

Marty stepped forward, a hand outstretched. "It's nice to meet you. Call me Marty, please."

Daisy smiled and took his hand. "It's nice to meet you too. Sorry about the mess."

He waved a hand. "Don't worry about it. Do you have any already baked? I'd love to try some."

"Not yet, no, but it'll be ready in time for supper."

"He's not staying," Asa cut in.

They both frowned at him, but he pushed ahead. "We came in for some tea. Is there any left?"

She nodded and turned to take two glasses from the cupboard.

Asa took them with a nod. "Thanks."

"There are cookies in the cookie jar if you want some. I baked them this morning." She pointed to the white jar labeled "Cookies" on the counter.

"You don't have to tell me twice." Marty stepped over to the jar and removed the lid, taking out two fresh chocolate chip cookies. He took a bite and moaned. "You can bake as well as sing like an angel? Marry me."

Daisy giggled. Annoyance skated over Asa's nerves, making his movements jerky. He sloshed tea over the side of one glass, adding to the mess on the counter. Swiping at the puddle with some paper towels, he handed a glass to Marty. "Let's go into the study and talk." Anything to get him away from Daisy. The last thing he needed was to have her enamored with his manager. The man ran through women like cheap wine.

Marty pulled one more cookie from the jar and waved it at Daisy as he backed out of the room. "It was lovely to meet you, my dear."

She smiled, blushing prettily, adding to Asa's annoyance. He tugged on Marty's sleeve, pulling him out of the room.

"Slow down, Asa. I was just saying goodbye."

"Leave her alone. She's not like your other women."

"Maybe that's a good thing. I could go for a country girl. I hear they're wild in the sack."

Asa stopped, rounding on the shorter man. It wasn't often Asa used his size to intimidate someone, but he did now. "She's off-limits. End of discussion."

Marty's eyes widened a fraction before a smile spread over his face. He took another bite of cookie. "You like her."

Jaw muscles twitching, Asa spun away and continued down the hall, entering the study. "I don't. But she's a nice girl. And not cut out for the likes of you, so keep your hands to yourself."

Marty polished off his cookie and raised his palms. "Fine, fine. I'll behave."

"Good. Now, say your piece so I can get back to what I was doing." He sat down in the chair behind the desk, ignoring the seating area on the other side of the room. This was not a social call.

Marty frowned, glancing at the couch, but sat down in the wingback chair across from Asa. "Why don't you want to take my calls? It's been three weeks."

"You know why."

"Oh, come on, man. You weren't serious. Who gives up a career like yours in its prime?"

"Me. I'm tired of the life, Marty. I meant it when I said I was done. All my contracts have been fulfilled. Except for a charity gig here and there, I'm retired." His gaze didn't waver as he gave his speech. He wanted to make sure Marty understood this time that he was dead serious about getting out of the business.

Marty pressed his lips together, taking in a deep breath

through his nose. "Asa, you can't quit." He sat forward, leaning his chin on his steepled hands. "You're in your prime. I've had the movie studios clamoring at the door, wanting to know if you'll consider their films. And your label wants to know when to expect your next album."

Asa shook his head. "Never. I mean it. I'm done." He sighed. "I know you don't understand why I would get out at this point in my career, but it's for my own health. The stress —I just can't handle it anymore. Always having to be 'on,' never getting more than a few days off, and even then, being stuck behind closed doors if I don't want to have my picture splashed all over some paper. It's not me. The man they want —that's who you made me into, but it's not me. This," he gestured around him, "is me. I'm just a rancher from Montana. It's all I've ever wanted to be. Music was a means to keep that dream."

Marty stared at him for several moments. Asa could see him processing his words, trying to find a way to turn the argument around and get Asa to do what he wanted. He'd done it many times in the last fifteen years, but in this case, there wasn't anything he could say that would change his mind. He was home. To stay.

"How about I set up one last tour? A farewell to your fans. You owe them that."

He was thankful for his fanbase, but he refused to let himself get sucked back in. Months from now, he might release a final song, but right now, he needed a clean break. For his own sanity. "I think they'll understand why I quit."

Marty scoffed. "Most will, but there'll be a few who might come looking for you."

He'd thought of that, and after Marla's easy access to the property, he'd decided to look into adding a better gate to the driveway. One that needed a code and had cameras. "I'll deal with that if it happens. But I mean it, Marty. I'm done."

Marty blinked several times, staring. "You're sure I can't change your mind?"

"I'm sure."

"Well," Marty stood. "I guess I should go, then."

Asa rose, relief flooding through him that he didn't have to fight any harder to get his independence. "Yes, you should." He moved around the desk. "I'll walk you out." He ushered Marty to the door and down the hallway. Daisy stepped into the kitchen doorway as they passed.

"Leaving already?"

Marty smiled. "Afraid so. Asa's not interested in coming back to L.A., no matter what I have to say."

"Well, I hope it wasn't an entirely wasted trip and that you at least got a bit of a break from work by coming all the way here."

Marty stepped closer and took her hand, bringing it up to place a kiss on the back. "Meeting you made it worth it."

Daisy blushed, and Asa frowned. What was he up to? "Marty."

The other man glanced back and winked. Asa narrowed his eyes. He was definitely up to something.

"You get tired of washing his boxers, give me a call. With your voice and looks, the record labels would love you."

"Marty!" Asa took a step forward, making the other man let go of Daisy's hand. He held them up, giving Asa an imploring look.

"I'm on the lookout for new talent. Seems I have an opening." He winked at Daisy and took her hand again, patting it. "Work on him, would you? Convince him to see the light?"

"Trust me, I'd love to get him out of my hair. But I think that's a decision only Asa can make. *Without* anyone pressuring him." She arched a brow at Marty. The man had the good grace to look chagrined.

"I get the message. Again, it was nice to meet you."

"You too."

Asa cast a surreptitious glance at Daisy as he ushered Marty out the door. Why had she defended him? He knew she'd like nothing more than to be rid of him, so why would she say those things? Dumbfounded, and with no explanation, he filed it away in his brain to mull over later. Right now, it would just give him a headache.

"I'm sorry you came all this way for nothing," Asa said, walking Marty to his car. "I know I've disappointed you, but I hope you understand."

Marty opened the door, holding the frame. "I do. And I hope you understand that I'll be back." He sank into the seat. "You're too talented to waste away out here in the middle of nowhere. I'll give you some time, but I'll be back." He tugged the door closed and offered Asa a wave before starting the engine and driving away.

Asa blew out a breath. Well, that was one hurdle he didn't have to worry about for a while, at least. He just hoped Marty did what he said he would and gave him some space for the foreseeable future. Asa had his doubts. Marty had capitulated much too easily.

Shaking off his thoughts, he tugged his gloves from his pocket and headed back to the garden to finish the fence. If he didn't get it done today, he'd have a more immediate problem to deal with—Daisy.

TEN

Purse in hand, Daisy stepped off the back porch headed for her car just as Asa pulled past in one of the ranch trucks. He came to a stop next to her, the pickup's big diesel engine purring like a big cat.

He rolled down the window and rested an arm on the sill. "Where are you off to?"

"I need to get groceries. *Someone* ate the last of my yogurt." She glared up at him. "And the hands requested cupcakes. It's Benny's birthday. I need a few things to make them."

"I'm headed to town myself. Hop in."

Ride a half an hour there and back with him in the confines of a vehicle? She didn't think so. "Oh, that's okay. I'll take my car."

"Why? It's a waste of fuel. I only need a few things at the feed store, so it's not like one of us is going to be gone longer than the other. Get in the truck."

She bit her lip. Dammit, he was right. "Fine." She walked around to the passenger side and heaved herself into the seat, glad the pickup came equipped with running boards. After closing herself inside, she buckled her seatbelt, and he steered the truck down the drive.

"So, what do you need to get at the feed store?"

"Milk replacer and a couple more bottles. We've had more than the average number of calves abandoned by their mothers this year. There were two born last night that neither mother wanted. We're hand-feeding all of them until they're ready to be weaned."

"That's terrible. Why so many?"

He shrugged, turning onto the highway. "Probably the drought. It takes a lot of calories to produce milk, not to mention feed a cow through pregnancy. One of the mamas who abandoned her calf yesterday almost didn't make it through the birth. It's not uncommon for them to not want the calf after that."

"That's sad. If I can help at all, let me know?"

"We've got a rotation going, but if we get shorthanded, I'll keep you in mind."

Daisy nodded and made a mental note to stop in the barn when they got back to see the setup they had for bottle-feeding the calves. Maybe she could convince one of the boys to show her how.

Her phone rang, interrupting her thoughts. She rooted through her purse to find it, cursing when she saw the number. It was her brother, Ian. No doubt wanting to harangue her for not returning his gazillion messages. Or any of those left by their other brothers. She still hadn't talked to any of them.

She clicked the button to silence it and shoved it back in her purse.

"You're not going to answer it?"

She glanced at Asa, then looked back out the windshield, folding her hands over her bag. "No."

He frowned. "Why not? Solicitor?"

If only. "My brother. I don't want to talk to him."

"How come? Does this have something to do with why you left Chicago? Dad said you had family troubles."

"Yes. I don't have anything to say to him, and there's nothing he could say to me that would convince me to come back."

"Maybe he's calling to apologize. Did you ever think of that?"

She scoffed. "Yeah, right. The great Dr. Ian O'Malley is never wrong. And even if he was, he'd never admit it. He just moves on. No, he's calling to tell me I'm being silly, and that I need to come home and do what they say." She folded her arms over her chest, clenching her teeth as she seethed. Talking about her brothers always sent her blood pressure skyrocketing.

Asa was silent for a moment. "Why did you leave? What did he do? I mean, it must have been something wild for you to move across the country."

She stared out the window, watching the scenery roll past as she answered. "It was a combination of things, really. Our parents died when I was young, so he and my other brothers raised me. They kept me sheltered and basically ran my life for me until I left. I was content to let them when I was young, but as I got older, I wanted to make my own decisions, and we butted heads over it. Especially about the men I dated. That was the last straw, actually. My brother, Kyle, set me up on a blind date with some guy he works with. For Valentine's Day. It was a disaster."

"Oh, ouch."

"Yeah. It sucked. Kyle wouldn't let me break things off, though. After the awful Valentine's date, I refused to take the guy's calls. Kyle took it upon himself to invite Ethan over to my apartment for dinner. Without asking me first. When he showed up at my job and told me what he did, I threw him out of the bakery, quit my job, packed up my stuff, and left."

"Without a destination in mind?"

"I closed my eyes and picked a place. It led me here."

Asa chuckled. "Lucky us. So, how come they haven't shown up here to drag you back? From what you said, that sounds like something they'd do."

"They would if they knew where I was."

"Wait. They don't know where you are? Do they even know you're safe?" He tensed as he spoke, shifting in his seat.

"Relax. I told my aunt where I was. But she's been sworn to secrecy. All she's told them is that I'm all right and happy where I am."

He sagged back into the seat. "Good. I'm glad someone from your old life knows where you are." He shook his head. "I can't imagine not knowing where my dad is. I'd be frantic if he just disappeared."

"I'm pissed at them, but I'm not heartless. They were good to me when they weren't trying to dictate my life." She glanced at him, curious about what he said. Or, more accurately, what he didn't say.

"Do you have any other family besides Silas?"

Asa clenched and unclenched his hand on the steering wheel, his jaw working as he formulated an answer. "My mom's alive as far as I know, but I don't know where she is. She ran off when I was three."

Daisy's eyes widened. "You haven't seen her in thirty years?"

"She showed up at one of my concerts once, not long after I really hit the big time. *That* was awkward. It was at a meet and greet after a show, and I had all these other fans around when she comes up and tells me who she is." He shook his head. "I couldn't deny it, either, because even though she ran away, Dad kept some photographs of her for me. I knew what she looked like."

"What did you do? What did she want?"

"To be part of Asa Mitchell's life and ride my coattails. Though that wasn't what she told me then. I'm just sorry it took me almost a year to figure out she wasn't there for me. Once I did, though, I told her to just leave me alone. I wasn't interested in a mother who wanted to use me for my fame. She bought a hundred-thousand-dollar car without my knowledge just by using my name and her relationship to me."

Daisy gasped. "And a dealership let her?"

He nodded. "Her picture and our relationship were all over the tabloids, so they didn't question it. They gave her the papers to take home to have me sign, and she forged my signature. Once I found out, I cut her off and made sure everyone knew it. She left not long after. I heard from her once more about a year later. She got arrested for theft and called me for bail money. I didn't give it to her."

Daisy's eyes widened. "Oh my goodness. I'm so sorry."

Asa shrugged. "It was a long time ago." He sighed. "So, short answer, no, I don't have any other family besides my dad."

"That's not entirely true. You have Chet. And Cookie."

One corner of Asa's mouth lifted. "Yeah. Chet and I grew up together, and Cookie's like a fun uncle. He showed up one day when I was just a kid, looking for a job. Said he couldn't ride and didn't know shit about cattle, but he could cook."

"Why didn't he get a job at a restaurant, then?"

"PTSD. He was in Iraq. Crowds made him anxious, and for a long time, they gave him flashbacks. He needed the peace the ranch provided. Dad hired him on the spot after hearing his story. He's been a fixture ever since and is much, much more than just the ranch cook."

"I've noticed. He's like a mother hen." The older man

hounded the younger hands to clean up after themselves, but also offered them a place to go when they needed to talk. He did a lot to keep up morale on the ranch.

"He is, and him being here is the only reason I agreed to leave and try to make it in the music industry. I knew he'd take care of Dad."

"I think it's mutual." Silas provided as much support for Cookie as he got in return.

"It is. They've kept each other company over the years."

"Why didn't either of them marry?"

"Cookie did, but his wife didn't like ranch life. He tried living in town with her for a while, but was miserable. She was too, and they split up. I'm not sure why Dad didn't. He never even really dated much. At least not while I was still living at home. I don't know about since then." His expression closed. "I haven't been the best son the last fifteen years."

The clench to his jaw told Daisy he was done talking. She turned her attention to the road in front of them, not wanting to push him. That was the best talk they'd had in the three weeks he'd been home. She didn't want to ruin the tentative truce they seemed to have reached.

The last few miles into Silver Gap sped by, and they were soon pulling into the grocery store parking lot. Asa steered the truck up to the entrance and stopped.

"I'll be down the street at the feed store. Text me when you're done?"

"Can't."

He frowned. "Why not? You have your phone."

"But I don't have your number."

"You could have just said that." He rolled his eyes and held out a hand. "Give me your phone."

Daisy took it out of her purse and unlocked it, then handed it to him. He added himself to her contacts and handed it back.

"Now will you text me when you're done?"

"Yep. Or I'll just start walking that way if you aren't back yet. I don't need much." She opened her door and slid down to the ground, praying she didn't break an ankle. Men and their trucks. She understood why the powerful vehicle was necessary on the ranch, but did it have to be so damn far off the ground? Her feet hit the pavement, and she closed the door before walking into the store to get what she needed.

Asa pulled out of the grocery store parking lot and back onto the street, rumbling down the road to the feed store where he parked beside the building. Grabbing a ball cap from behind his seat, he tugged it over his hair. It wasn't much of a disguise, but it would hopefully hide his face from the casual observer. He hated being mobbed, which was why he'd avoided town since he returned. But he couldn't hide forever.

Opening his door, he stepped out, making his way inside the store. The owner, Bill Kaczmarek, looked up as Asa entered.

"Asa! I heard you were back. It's good to see you, boy." The older man stepped around the counter and held out a hand, offering Asa a genuine smile.

Asa took it, finding himself smiling back. Bill and his family were old friends. Asa went to school with his middle son, Wade. "Hi, Bill. How've you been?"

"Can't complain. Yourself?"

"Better now that I'm home."

"Silas said you were back for good. That true?"

"Yep. I retired from the music business. It was time." More than time. He'd stayed a good five years longer than he really wanted to.

"Good. I know your dad's missed having you around."

"I've missed him too."

Bill patted his shoulder. "So, what brings you in today?"

"I need some bottle-feeding supplies for calves."

"That's a popular item. This drought is playing havoc on livestock all over the county. I think I still have some left, though. Let's go look." He led Asa down an aisle toward the back of the store. "Here's what I've got." He gestured to the display. The bell above the door jingled, drawing Bill's attention. "Let me know if you need anything else."

"I will, thanks."

Bill nodded and walked off to greet his new customer. Asa turned his attention to the bottles on the shelf, picking up several. He took them up front, setting them on the counter before wandering back out into the store. He still needed milk replacer, and Chet mentioned they were low on a couple supplements they fed the horses. He might as well pick those up while he was here and save someone else a trip into town later. Arms full, he walked up front a few minutes later.

"Asa Mitchell, is that you?"

Asa bit back a groan. Bill's other customer was Janice Barlow. She was a notorious gossip. It would be all over town that he was at the feed store about thirty seconds after she left.

"Hello, Mrs. Barlow."

She batted her eyes at him and smoothed down her hair. "It's not Mrs. anymore. Neal and I got divorced last year."

Great.

"I'm sorry to hear that."

She waved a hand at him and took the receipt Bill held out to her. "Don't be. He was a jerk."

He couldn't argue with her there. Neal Barlow was an asshole of the shittiest caliber. Asa didn't know why she married him in the first place.

"Well, then, congratulations."

She grinned and picked up her items. "Thanks." Walking closer, she looked him up and down.

Asa adjusted his grip on the items in his arms, hoping she'd get the hint and not touch him.

"You should call me sometime. I'd love to welcome you back to town."

"Um, thanks." He cleared his throat. "I'll probably be busy for a while, though. Getting back into the groove of ranching and all that." He tipped his head toward the stuff he held.

She smiled at him for several moments before nodding, that gleam in her eyes that said she wanted to eat him alive still shining bright. "Well, if you get some free time, let me know." With a wink, she turned and sauntered out.

Asa dumped his load on the counter, shaking his head. "That's why I've avoided town."

Bill grinned. "What? You don't like women fawning all over you?"

"Trust me, it grows tiresome quickly."

"You need a girlfriend," Bill said, ringing up his purchases. "Someone to act as a buffer."

Asa scoffed. "Any woman I'd ask would expect an actual relationship. No, women only complicate things, and that's the last thing I want or need right now."

Bill arched a brow, but said nothing. He finished ringing Asa up and read him his total. Asa swiped his card, then scooped the bottles and milk replacer into his arms and looped the sack with the feed supplements over his fingers.

"You need help?" Bill asked.

"Nah. I'm good." He gave the older man a farewell smile. "Thanks. Tell Wade I said hello."

"I will. Have a good day."

Asa nodded and walked out of the store, using his hip to push open the door. He rounded the building and stopped at his truck. Realizing he couldn't get to his keys with his arms full, he stooped to put the stuff on the ground so he could fish them out of his pocket.

"Hi, stranger."

Shit. He hung his head at the sound of a woman's voice behind him. *I was so close*! Rising, he turned to see another blast from his past standing at the corner of the building, smiling at him.

"Vanessa. Hi." Vanessa Hodgins was another classmate. They'd never dated, but that hadn't stopped her from trying.

She strode closer, putting extra sway into her step. Asa clenched his teeth. It was going to be a long time before he came back to town.

"Why haven't you come to the Rusty Nail to say hi to everyone? It's all over town you're back for good, but no one's seen you. What's been keeping you so busy you're ignoring all your friends?"

He fought not to roll his eyes. None of the people he would see at that bar would ever be considered his friend. Not unless Chet and Marci went with him or Wade showed up.

"Been busy. Look, I hate to be rude, but I need to go." He gestured to the stuff on the ground. "We've had a run on calves that need bottle fed."

"Oh, those poor creatures! It's too bad they grow up into those ugly beasts. I wish they could stay cute."

"Yes, well, we don't breed them because they're cute. The American populace likes its beef."

She giggled. "Very true. I do enjoy a good hamburger." She ran a nail down his chest, plucking at one of his buttons. "I bet you grill a great burger. You should cook for me sometime."

"He's busy."

Asa turned his head to look past his truck at Daisy, who walked toward him.

Vanessa frowned. "Who are you?"

"I'm—"

"My girlfriend." The words popped out of his mouth before he could stop them. His eyes widened a fraction before he sent Daisy an imploring look.

"Your girlfriend? I didn't know you were dating anyone."

"It's new," Daisy said, looking up at Asa as she walked up beside him. "Are you ready to go? These cupcakes won't make themselves." The look she gave him said she'd like to throw them at him again.

"Yeah." He dug in his pocket for the keys and pushed the button to unlock the truck.

Daisy opened the back door and set her bags inside, then picked up his things and began loading them. Asa bent over and picked up the bag of supplements, handing it to her. She closed the door and walked around the front of the truck.

Asa opened the driver's door. "It was nice to see you, Vanessa."

Lips pressed together and brows drawn down, she nodded. "Yeah."

He hopped inside and closed the door, starting the engine. With a wave, he pulled away. Leaning his head against the headrest, he sighed. "Thank you."

"I only did it so we didn't make a huge scene. Though I'm not sure this is any better. She's probably already on the phone to spread the news."

He grimaced. "Yeah. Sorry. I didn't think. Bill—the feed store owner—planted the idea that I needed a girlfriend to keep the women away in my head. Then I came out to her. When you walked up, it just popped out."

"I get it. After Marla, trust me, I do. Which is why I didn't contradict you. But now that we've set that ball in motion, what are we going to do about it?"

Asa propped an elbow on the windowsill and rested his

head on his fingers. "Do you mind pretending to be my girl-friend? Just in public. We don't have to go anywhere together. Just don't tell anyone otherwise when they ask you about it. I just want to keep the women away." Fatigue colored his voice.

Daisy sighed. "I guess I can do that." She was quiet for a moment. "I'm sorry things are like this for you. If it's any consolation, I think all the women throwing themselves at you are disgusting hussies."

He barked out a laugh. "Thank you."

She giggled. "You're welcome."

"Seriously, though, thank you. I appreciate you going along with things back there. I know I've been a bit of an ass, so it wouldn't have surprised me if you left me out to dry."

"A bit of an ass?" A smile kicked up one corner of her mouth.

"That's all I'm admitting to, yes."

She giggled again. "It's better than nothing, I suppose. But I get why you've been a dick. To a degree, anyway. The noto-riety—I can't imagine it's easy to deal with."

"It's not. And it's why I left the business. I never wanted to do this long-term. My hope was to make enough to pay off the ranch mortgage, then come home. I never dreamed I'd end up a superstar."

"Why didn't you quit after your first album?"

"Because I was young and dumb. I liked the attention, and I was greedy. I wanted to add to the ranch, upgrade our equip-ment, increase our stock. By the time I did all that and got to a point I was done with the music industry, I was in too deep to quickly extricate myself. I had contract obligations, which included a second and third movie. I was trapped in a life I didn't want anymore. With no way out, I made some mistakes in my personal life, and now I have a reputation that doesn't want to stay in L.A."

"With women, you mean?"

"Yeah. Only part of the stories in the tabloids are true." He sighed. "It doesn't stop women from thinking I'm always out looking for a good time, though." He glanced at her. "Maybe if they think I'm involved with someone, they'll back off. I just hope it doesn't draw too much media attention."

Daisy frowned. "What kind of attention?"

"Gossip columns, mostly. A paparazzo or two might show up, but they won't get much. We don't go to town really, especially together, and the locals will stonewall them."

"You sure about that? Marla and that woman at the feed store would both love to see me suffer. They might help them just to spite me."

He frowned. "I hope that doesn't happen, but if it does, we'll just have to deal with it."

She turned in her seat. "Asa, you don't understand. If my name gets connected to yours and ends up in some gossip rag, my brothers could find me. They will descend on the Stone Creek so fast we'll never see them coming."

"Look, I get that you don't want to talk to them, but—"

"It's not just that." She blew out a breath. "En masse, they're a force to be reckoned with. It won't just be me they come down on. It'll be you too. And your dad. I don't want to drag you into my problems, and that's exactly what will happen if they show up here."

"What are they going to do to us? You're here of your own free will."

"Yes, but they will make us miserable until I agree to go back to Chicago."

He stared out the windshield with a thoughtful look on his face. "You know I've been a proponent of you leaving since I got home, but I don't want you to go because you feel bullied into it." He glanced at her. "Not even by me. Dad and I will stand by you if they show up and try to make you go home."

She stared at him with wide eyes, then reached out and poked him on the cheek.

He swatted at her hand. "What? Why are you poking me?"

"Who are you and what did you do with Asa Mitchell?"

"Very funny." He rolled his eyes.

She smiled. "I'm not sure what prompted you to do a one-eighty, but I appreciate it."

He shrugged. "You still annoy the shit out of me, but I'm about seventy percent certain now that you didn't take the housekeeping job to get close to me."

Her eyebrows slammed down, and she crossed her arms. "There he is." She shook her head.

He sighed. "Can we just call a truce? You scratch my back, I'll scratch yours." He held out his right hand. "Deal?"

Daisy stared at him, then looked at his hand. She huffed. "Fine. Deal."

When she slid her strong, slender hand into his, an electric zing sailed up his arm. He let go and put his hand back on the steering wheel, flexing his fingers around the leather as the tingle continued. *What the hell was that all about?*

ELEVEN

"Oh, Daisy. This one's gorgeous."

Daisy glanced over to see the dress Sara held up. She'd finally given in to peer pressure and let her and Marci take her shopping. The deep green sundress Sara held was beautiful. But she wasn't sure it would look good on her. "I'm not sure. Those straps are tiny."

"So?"

"So, my bra straps will show."

"Get one with thin straps, or wear a strapless one."

Daisy arched a brow. "You make it sound so easy. Do you know how hard it is to find a bra in my size that's supportive and doesn't have thick straps? And I'd rather not wear a strapless one. They never stay put. I end up tugging at it all the time to keep it in place." Her double D's did not like to stay contained. There was a reason she opted for the grandma-style bras or a sports bra. She was just glad she could get the grandma ones in pretty colors now, even if they did cost her a fortune.

Sara frowned. "I still think you should at least try it on. If it looks as amazing as I think it will, the strapless bra might be worth it."

She eyed the dress. It *was* pretty. "Fine. I'll try it on."

"Yay!" Sara looped the dress over her arm with the others.

Daisy eyed the pile. There was more there than she'd agreed to. She opened her mouth to say something, but Marci bustled forward with an armload of her own and grabbed Daisy's arm.

"Come on. Time to try stuff on." She snagged a corner of Daisy's t-shirt and pulled her toward the dressing rooms.

"I can walk, you know."

Marci grinned. "I know. I just can't wait to see you in some of this stuff. You have such a stunning figure. The t-shirts and jeans you wear don't do it justice. We're going to fix that."

She glanced down at herself. She liked her clothes. They were comfortable. And she'd picked the shirt out in defiance of her brothers. It had a v-neck, which they hated. But Marci was right. It was a little sloppy.

Sara opened the louvered door and hung up her armload of clothes. Daisy's eyes went wide as piece after piece filled the hook. Marci stepped in and hung up hers. Not everything fit, and she had to lay some of it on the bench.

Daisy swallowed hard. She was going to be here forever.

"We'll be right outside," Marci said.

"Yep. We want to see everything."

"Everything?"

Sara nodded. "Everything."

Daisy sighed and nodded. She shut the door and looked at the pile of clothes. Where the hell did she start?

The green dress beckoned. "Oh, what the hell," she whispered. She drew her shirt over her head, then kicked off her sandals and unfastened her jeans. She stepped out of them, then grabbed the dress off the hanger and slid it over her head.

"Whoa." She stared at herself in the mirror. The bodice dipped low, exposing her cleavage, but not indecently so. A band of fabric with embroidered flowers accentuated her waist before the skirt flared out, ending just below her knees.

Daisy swished the skirt, loving the feel of the flowy material. The only thing ruining it was the thick band of her bra underneath the spaghetti straps. She pulled the chunky straps down and tucked them into the bodice to get the full effect of the dress. Excitement zinged through her veins. She'd never seen herself like this.

Nervous about what Marci and Sara would say, she opened the door and stepped out.

They both gasped. Marci covered her mouth, and they both stared.

"Girl, that dress is fire."

A slow smile formed on Daisy's face. "You think so? I mean, I like it, but I've never worn anything like this before."

"Yes. You need to buy that dress. I don't care if you have to duct tape your boobs in place, you need that dress."

Daisy and Marci laughed.

"She's right. You need that."

"But where will I wear it?" She looked down at herself, running her hands over the fabric. "I mean, it's lovely, but I can't exactly cook and clean in it and it's too low cut for church."

Marci cast her a sly smile. "Maybe you should make Asa take you out. Since he's your boyfriend and all."

Daisy groaned. "You heard about that? Man, I was hoping that wouldn't make the rounds. We only told Silas so he wouldn't be blindsided by it in town one day."

Marci giggled. "You told Vanessa Hodgins. She's one of the biggest gossips in the county. I knew by nightfall."

"Why didn't you say something? It's been two weeks!"

"Because we understood why you two did it," Sara said.

"Asa needs a buffer right now, and you're too much of a softy to say no when you know someone's hurting."

Daisy frowned, disconcerted that Sara had her pegged after only knowing her a few months. Was she really that easy to read? "Well, regardless, it's all a sham, so there will be no dinner date for Asa and me."

Sara shrugged. "I say buy it, anyway. Even if it sits in your closet for a while, one day you'll have an opportunity to wear it. And you will knock the socks off of everyone who sees you in it."

She glanced at herself once more, biting her lower lip. It really was a beautiful dress, and it fit so well. "Okay, fine." With a huff, she whirled around to go back into the dressing room.

"Woohoo, now try on something else," Marci said.

Confidence boosted, Daisy shut the door and stripped out of the dress. For the next thirty minutes, she paraded in and out wearing a multitude of outfits. Some were great, and some not so great, but in the end, she found some amazing clothes to update her wardrobe. And it was just as comfortable as her big t-shirts and saggy jeans.

"Now you need shoes," Sara said, hauling her toward a shoe store down the street.

Daisy groaned. "Can we eat first? I'm starving. And I need a drink after trying on all those clothes." She could honestly use a rather stiff drink, but would settle for a glass of iced tea.

"We sure can," Marci said. She steered them into a pub across the street.

Inside, a young man showed them to a table in the back. Daisy sank into the booth, piling her packages on the seat beside her. Marci and Sara slid in across from her.

"I'm glad we decided to come to Billings to do this. They have some nice shops downtown. It's nice to get away from the baby for a bit too."

"Who has him? I saw Chet on the ranch this morning."

"My mom. She practically shoved me out the door, ready to spoil him for the day." She rolled her eyes. "More like spoil herself. I doubt she'll put him down unless she has to pee."

Daisy smiled at the picture Marci painted. She wished her mom was around still. She would have been a great grand-mother to all Daisy's nieces and nephews.

Their server stopped at their table to take their order. Daisy asked for a glass of tea, as did Marci and Sara. They ordered a few appetizers to share, preferring not to weigh themselves down with a heavy lunch.

"Okay," Sara said when the server left. "What put that frown on your face?"

"What? What do you mean?"

"We were talking and laughing, then your whole expression changed. Why?"

Daisy sighed. "What Marci said about her mom made me think about mine and how great of a grandma she would have been. Life just sucks sometimes."

Marci reached over and covered Daisy's hand. "I'm sorry. I didn't mean to make you sad."

"You didn't. More like... contemplative and wistful."

"What were your parents like?"

"They were great. My dad was a doctor, like my oldest brother. But when he was home, he made time for us. He'd listen to us talk about our day. I loved it when he would come up to my room and play tea party with me or just sit with me while I colored or drew pictures. He'd play sports in the back-yard with my brothers. Baseball and flag football were their favorites."

"What about your mom?"

Daisy smiled. "She was a regular June Cleaver. I learned to bake from her. I was only ten when she died, but she taught me a lot in those ten years. And not just about baking. She taught me how to be a lady. My brothers made sure I never forgot."

"Is that why you let them control so much of your life for so long?"

The server walked up again and passed out their drinks before she could answer. Daisy thanked the young woman and put a straw in her cup, taking a drink before continuing. "Partly. At first, I was too young to care. My parents were dead, and I was suddenly living with my twenty-five-year-old brother and his wife. He had no idea what to do with me. He tried to do what he thought Mom and Dad would want, but once I hit puberty, he freaked a bit, especially once it became obvious I was, um, curvier than most girls my age."

"His wife didn't try to curb his actions?" Sara asked.

Daisy shrugged. "She did some, but she came from a rather conservative family herself. She always dressed very modestly and let Ian run the house. She still does. He values her opinion, but she rarely disagrees with him. I think she likes having him make the decisions around the house. And, at the time I went to live with them, they'd just had their first child. Their second soon followed. She didn't have a lot of time for a kid who could mostly take care of herself."

Marci wrinkled her nose. "That had to be tough. Not having a mom at that age. I couldn't imagine going through all those changes without my mom around. I was a wreck; emotions all over the place."

"Actually, Shelly was good about helping me sort through my feelings. At least with school and kids my own age. I never really talked to her too much about Ian. She never contradicted him when he told me to do something I didn't like, and I didn't want to create waves."

"Your brother sounds like a real peach."

Daisy fiddled with her straw. "He's not a bad guy, and he

loves me. But I think I came into his life at a time when he had a lot on his plate—new baby, med school, just lost his parents—and he didn't know how to be a parent to a young girl. Not yet. He's not as strict with his daughters as he was with me. They still dress fairly modestly, but not as modest as I did. And his oldest daughter just started dating, and she's sixteen. He's a bit of a pill about the boys she dates—making sure he knows them well first before she goes anywhere with them and keeping her to a strict ten p.m. curfew when all her friends get to stay out until midnight—but she gets to pick her own boyfriends."

"You don't get to pick your own boyfriends?" Sara asked.

Daisy giggled. "I do. But they don't like it because they haven't vetted them first. That's why they keep trying to set me up on all these disastrous blind dates. They're all men they know personally and they tick the right boxes. Gainfully employed, good family, no criminal record, that sort of thing. When I pick the guy, they don't know any of that and it drives them nuts. I also think some of the issues we have now are just holdovers from when I was young. They all still see me as that little girl."

"I think I understand better why you left," Marci said. "This break will be good for all of you."

"Yeah. I needed to live my own life on my terms. I'm just hoping we can mend the rift someday. I love my family. I just want to spread my wings."

"If they love you as much as you say they do, I think they'll come around."

Daisy hoped so. As much as she enjoyed being on her own, she missed her family, especially her nieces and nephews and her sisters-in-law.

Their food arrived, and they continued to talk as they ate. Belly full and her spirits buoyed, Daisy followed her new friends back out to the street and let Sara drag her into a shoe store where they talked her into two pairs of flats and a pair of killer heels she wasn't sure she'd ever wear outside the house, but had to have. Her savings took quite the hit today, but she didn't care. It felt good to spend some money on herself for once instead of just putting it in the bank for a rainy day. This was her rainy day.

Back at the ranch, she stumbled through the back door with her packages, startling Tallulah. The cat jumped back and stared at her from the doorway.

"Oh, sorry, Lula." She walked past the cat to head down the hallway to her room, setting her bags down on the bed. Tallulah followed her in and hopped up beside them, chirping at Daisy.

"I didn't get anything for you, silly." She scratched the cat's head, then dug into her bags to put all her new clothes away. She took out the green dress and held it up against her body, turning to look at herself in the full-length mirror, letting out a shriek as she caught sight of Asa standing in the doorway.

"Good lord." She pressed a hand to her chest. "Knock, would you?"

He grinned. "Sorry."

"No, you're not."

He chuckled. "Looks like you spent some money today." His eyes roamed over the dress she still held against her body. "That's a nice color on you."

Daisy blushed and laid the dress on the bed. "Thanks. So, did you need something or did you just want to scare the daylights out of me?"

"As fun as it was, I did actually have a question. I'm going out of town tomorrow for a few days to look at some live-stock. I need you to make me some food to take along so I don't have to stop except for gas and to use the restroom."

She arched a brow. Was he incapable of making his own sandwiches? "Uh, okay. I guess I can do that. But out of curiosity, why can't you make yourself some sandwiches?"

"Because I don't want sandwiches."

What the hell else would a person take on a road trip? "What do you want, then?"

"Something more substantial. Meatloaf, fried chicken. Stuff that's still good when it's cold."

"Sandwiches would still be good cold. They're meant to be eaten that way."

He rolled his eyes. Daisy crossed her arms and glared at him.

"A sandwich won't get me very far. Plus, I can only eat so much lunch meat in a week before I can't take it anymore. I ate a sandwich today because you were gone. That's about my quota."

Was he for real? She knew he grew up on bologna and ham sandwiches. Silas still ate them when she didn't have something else for him for lunch. Hell, sometimes he asked for them. But apparently, that wasn't frou-frou enough for The Great Asa Mitchell.

"Fine. I'll come up with something."

"Great. So, when's dinner? I'm starving."

She grinned. "It's in the fridge. Or in the cupboard. Depends on if you want more lunch meat or peanut butter this time. Silas gave me the whole day off."

Asa frowned. "What?" He groaned. "Come on. I worked all day. You can't whip up something quick?"

Her eyes narrowed. She *had* been going to tell him there was leftover casserole in the fridge from yesterday he could reheat, but she wasn't telling him shit now. He could figure it out on his own.

She walked forward, putting a hand in the middle of his chest to push him out of the room as she grabbed the edge of the door. "I think you'll be okay." She stepped back and flung it closed, twisting the lock. Jackass.

TWELVE

"Finally." A blue "Rest Area Ahead" sign whizzed by as Asa drove down the highway. He'd needed to pee for over an hour. He passed a slow-moving truck and flipped on his blinker to move into the righthand lane to exit the interstate. Cruising down the ramp, he pulled into a parking space and cut the engine. From the passenger seat, he picked up his ball cap and settled it on his head, then climbed out of the truck. With his eyes down, he hurried into the building, praying no one recognized him.

The rest area was busy; summer travel season in full swing. He rounded the corner to the men's room and stepped up to the urinal to relieve his full bladder, then washed his hands and went back to his truck.

Stomach growling, he opened the back door to get into the cooler Daisy packed for him. His mouth watered at the thought of her fried chicken or meatloaf. The woman might annoy him, but she was one hell of a cook. And a baker. He hoped there were chocolate chip cookies too.

Asa flipped open the lid, then frowned as he got a look at the food inside. There wasn't a chicken leg or slab of meatloaf to be found. What there was, though, was a hodgepodge of things. He quickly inventoried the cooler's contents. Two bananas, a container of raspberries, a bag of pre-chopped lettuce, a carton of grape tomatoes, a bottle of ranch dressing, four hard-boiled eggs, a block of cheddar cheese, and two cans of tuna all sitting on top of several ice packs. He grimaced as he picked up the tuna. He hated canned tuna. She knew that, too.

Temper rising, he reached for the reusable grocery sack on the floorboard he'd found sitting atop the cooler this morning. Inside, he found paper plates, napkins, and plastic forks, along with a can opener for the tuna and an envelope. He took that out and tore it open, fuming.

I didn't have time to make fried chicken or meatloaf since yesterday was my day off. I hope you understand. But there's no lunch meat, as requested. Enjoy!

~D

P.S. Next time, say please. And maybe thank you.

Unbidden, one corner of Asa's mouth lifted as he read her note. The woman had sass, he'd give her that. And she had done as he asked and skipped the lunch meat. He looked inside the cooler again. But did she have to give him tuna? Peanut butter would have been preferable.

"Yuck." He passed on the tuna and picked up the eggs. She had a point. He could have been nicer about it when he asked. But he hadn't been able to stop imagining her in that green dress she held. It looked like it would show just enough skin and hug her curvy frame in all the right places. His gruffness came from his effort to keep his libido in check as that image ran through his mind. She drove him crazy, but she was a knockout and didn't even know it.

Asa gathered a few other items from the chest, then got back in the driver's seat and turned the air on while he ate. He peeled a banana, then brought his phone up and opened his texting app, scrolling through his contacts until he found Daisy's number. He fired off a quick text to her.

You could have at least packed some cookies.

A few seconds later, he got a stern-faced emoji in response. *Be thankful you didn't get a jar of beets. Say thank you next time and maybe you'll get more than just the basics,* she replied.

Grinning, he ate another bite of banana and texted her back. *Don't laugh too hard, sweetness. Payback's a bitch.*

Three dots appeared on his screen as she typed out her reply.

Bring it.

He laughed. Messing with her was fun. He could picture her. She was probably in the kitchen, making lunch for herself and his dad. Those pouty lips pursed as she stared down at her phone, her fingers flying over the keyboard as she scolded him for his attitude yesterday.

The first stirrings of lust curled low in his belly. Asa frowned and turned off the screen, doing his best to shut down his reaction. He didn't want to be attracted to her. Women were nothing but trouble. Getting involved with his housekeeper would be a grade A mistake. Plus, she drove him nuts most days.

But the makeup sex would be fantastic.

He groaned and closed his eyes for a moment. That was enough of those sorts of thoughts. Asa picked up his trash and got out of the truck to dump it all in the garbage can nearby.

Two women walking up stared at him, and he realized he left his hat in the truck. Recognition dawned on one woman's face. He didn't wait to see what she did next. He spun on his heel and hurried back to his truck, climbing inside and starting the engine. As he backed out, he noticed the women standing on the sidewalk, watching him. He offered them a smile and a small wave, then pulled away, glad to have escaped before he got mobbed. Because it wouldn't just be those two. Other people would notice, then he'd have a throng. It never failed.

Asa sighed and leaned his head back. He was grateful for his fans. The success he'd seen wouldn't be possible without them. But fame was no longer what he wanted. He wanted to melt away into obscurity. It would take time, but one day, he would be able to go somewhere without attracting a bunch of attention. Until then, he would skip restaurants and other crowded places and run whenever he thought he'd been recognized.

The hum of the road helped calm his nerves, and soon he was singing along to the radio, drumming his thumbs on the wheel as he drove. He stopped once more a few hours later to stretch his legs and eat more of Daisy's lunch buffet, then was back on the road. He pulled into Knox's ranch a couple hours later, parking next to the house. As he got out and shut the door, Knox's dog, Jai, an Irish Wolfhound, came running around the side of the house straight at him.

Asa's face broke into a wide grin. He held his arms wide. "Hey, bud." The dog barreled into him, his massive paws landing on Asa's chest. He stumbled under Jai's weight, planting his feet so he didn't topple over. Jai licked his face, whining in excitement.

He laughed and tipped his head forward to touch his forehead to the dog's nose. Part of the reason he loved this dog and Knox's other one, Maeve, was because it wasn't often an animal could look him in the eye. Horses and wolfhounds were about it.

A bark alerted him to Maeve's presence. He turned to see her loping toward him. Knox followed.

"Hey, Asa. How was your drive?" The tall blonde man held out a hand as he reached him.

"Good. Quick. Something wrong with her?" He shook Knox's hand, then pointed at the dog now standing next to him. She wagged her tail, but didn't stand up to greet him like she usually did.

"No, she's fine. Just hugely pregnant."

"Really?" He tipped his head to look at her abdomen, which, now that he looked closer, was distended.

"Yep. I'm about to have seven dogs." Knox propped his hands on his hips and ran his tongue over his teeth as he shook his head. "I don't know what I was thinking by breeding them."

Asa eyed Maeve thoughtfully. "You were thinking that I would love a dog and knew I would want a wolfhound." He gave Jai a gentle nudge to get down, then crouched next to Maeve and rubbed her ears. "What do you say, Mae? You think I could have one of your pups?" Her tongue lolled out, and she licked his face.

Knox laughed. "I think that was a yes. But seriously, you want one?"

"Yeah." He stood. "I'm home for good. No more touring or movie shoots. It would be nice to have a dog again." He grinned. "It'll have the added benefit of creating more work for my housekeeper. She'll love all the dog hair and potty training accidents."

He chuckled. "You still feuding with that woman?"

Asa shrugged and ran a hand through his dark hair. "Sort of. We still irritate each other, but we're learning to live together. Dad won't let me fire her."

"Yeah, because you don't have a good reason."

"Yes, I do. She never listens. I ask her to do something and she ignores me, or does it in some way that annoys the shit out of me."

Knox grinned. "I think I like this woman already. Have you tried asking nicely?"

Asa snorted. "You sound like her. And I always intend to be nice, but then something happens and the words that come out of my mouth aren't so polite."

"Something happens? From the time you start to ask to the time you finish?"

He nodded. "If you met her, you'd understand. The woman's got some major sass." And a body that short-circuited his brain.

Knox shook his head. "I call bullshit. There's more there than you're saying." He held up a hand. "But I won't pry. You get enough of that from other sources."

Asa let out a breath. This was why he continued to get his horses from Knox. He could get great cutters in Montana, but down here, he got a friend, too.

He smiled. "Appreciate it. So, you want to show me these animals I drove all the way down here to look at?"

"Sure." Knox smiled and ambled toward the barn, calling the dogs. Asa fell into step beside him.

"So, how have things been around here? I know they were a little crazy when I was here for Tara's wedding." Late last year, he'd performed at a wedding for some of their friends. When Knox asked if he would, and he heard Tara's story, he'd made Martin rearrange his schedule so he could be there. It was an honor to do something special for someone who'd been through so much and found happiness again.

"They're good. Calmer, finally. No more child traffickers or murderers lurking around. We're back to the standard domestic disputes and some drugs. Oh! And Tara had her babies."

"I saw pictures. Brady texted them to me. They're cute."

"They are. And spoiled rotten between all their aunts and uncles, not to mention Lee and Jenny. I've never seen two people more excited to have grandchildren."

Asa smiled. "Well, when you have five kids and they're all in their thirties except one and you don't have grandchildren, I can see being excited once you do."

Knox chuckled. "True. I'm sure your dad will be excited once you start a family."

Asa scoffed. "No. That's not happening. I doubt I'll ever find a woman I could trust enough to marry, let alone have kids with."

"Give it a few years. Once you're out of the spotlight a while, things might change."

"Maybe, but I doubt it." Bitterness at what his fame had done to his life churned in his gut. He hated that his future was limited because he was famous. It had been his choice, he knew, but he wished things were different. Fame was never what he wanted. Just security. He had that in spades now. But the family ranch would probably still end up in a stranger's hands after he died with no heirs to pass it down to.

"Just keep an open mind is all I'm saying."

"This from the man who's older than me and still single?"

Knox shrugged. "I know. But I'm a loner. Always have been. Not many women get that I like my space and that I'm not a talker."

"Excuses, excuses." Asa chuckled.

Knox rolled his eyes, a smile tugging at his mouth. "Come on. Let's look at some horses." He opened the side door on the barn and let them inside.

Asa took a deep breath of the sweet but pungent smell of

hay and horse as his eyes adjusted to the dimmer interior. "How many are you looking to sell?"

"I have four ready and a couple that are close. You can look at them all." He led Asa through the barn to a pasture out back. "That dappled gray is ready, so is that dun." He pointed to two horses grazing to the right. "I have two sorrels as well. That paint and the buckskin way at the back of the herd will be ready in a couple months."

Asa asked about their temperament, running an assessing gaze over the herd. Knox brought each one of the available horses into the barn for him to look over. He really liked the dappled gray. The paint was great as well. But they only needed one. His ranch hand Jasper's horse, Danny, was getting too old to be worked so hard. It was time for him to be a lazy senior horse and enjoy his golden years. He thought Jasper would like the gray horse, but the paint was beautiful and very sweet. Asa was tempted to get both, but he didn't know what they would do with an extra horse.

"Man, I wish I needed two. He's just beautiful." He stroked the paint's neck. "But I know Jasper will like the gray better. He's better suited to cutting and herding and is just headstrong enough for him. I think the paint is more of a trail horse."

Knox nodded in agreement. "Yeah. He's a nice, smooth ride, but the gray is definitely more assertive." He eyed Asa, a speculative gleam in his eyes. "What about your housekeeper? She need a horse?"

"Daisy?" He hadn't even thought about whether she wanted to ride. "I don't know if she knows how to ride." He waved a hand. "It doesn't matter, anyway. I'm not buying her a horse. When she leaves, I'll be stuck with an animal I don't need."

"I wouldn't be so sure she'll leave."

"She's a city girl, Knox. From Chicago. One day, she'll get tired of the boonies and go home."

Knox held up his hands. "I'm just playing a bit of devil's advocate. As much as you want to believe she'll go home on her own, she might just surprise you. That's all I'm saying."

"You haven't even met her."

"No, but I've heard Silas talk about her. He thinks she hung the moon."

Asa frowned. He didn't need the reminder. "I'm aware. Can we talk about something else? Anything else?"

Knox flattened his mouth into a thin line, but nodded. "What do you want to talk about?"

"Horses." He stepped forward to further assess the gray gelding. "Can I take him for a ride?"

"Sure. Lead him into the barn, and we'll get him saddled up."

Asa unhooked the horse from the corral fence and led him into the barn, perturbed. Maybe a nice ride would get Daisy out of his head. Something needed to. She didn't belong there.

Thirteen

A warm breeze blew through the kitchen, lifting the tendrils of Daisy's hair that fell out of her ponytail. She was wrist-deep in soapsuds, washing all the baking pans that hadn't fit in the dishwasher. The hands were out of cookies at the bunkhouse, so she made another batch this afternoon. Plus, Asa would be home soon. She tried to tell herself that wasn't why she made his favorite, but she felt a little bad about the food she sent with him. Especially the canned tuna. He hated it.

But, dammit, he punched all the wrong buttons with the way he asked. It was too much like the way her brothers acted. Years of pent-up frustration boiled over as she stood in the kitchen, staring at the pantry to figure out what to put in the cooler besides cold-cut sandwiches. So, he got tuna. And a bunch of other stuff she didn't have to cook. Well, other than the eggs, but those were easy.

It gave her hope, though, that she hadn't received a blistering phone call once he discovered what she packed. The texts were actually funny. Despite her best effort, she was starting to like him. Just the teeniest bit. He was still an arrogant asshole.

A shout from outside, followed by several more and the bellow of a cow, drew her attention. She rinsed her hands and dried them, then stuffed her feet into her barn boots and hurried out the back door. Her eyes widened as she saw Jasper and Chet trying to free their orneriest bull, Terminator, from some barbed wire. He had a piece wrapped around his horns. Some of the prongs dug into his face, close to his eyes. She could see the blood dripping off of him from where she stood.

Daisy didn't think. She sprinted toward the pasture and slipped through the fence, hurrying to the bull's side.

"Daisy!"

She ignored Chet and moved into Terminator's eyeline. "Easy there, big fella."

He bellowed again and tossed his head, pulling against the rope around his neck. Jasper held on as the bull dragged him sideways, his boots sliding through the dirt.

She held out a hand to the bull, letting him get her scent. "It's okay, sweet pea. Chet and Jasper just want to help you get that gnarly stuff off your head." The bull bellowed again, but didn't move. She edged closer. "If you hold still, it'll all be gone in just a couple snips." Her eyes flicked to Jasper. "Jazz, give me the rope."

"Are you nuts? You'll never be able to hold him if he bolts. He drags me as it is."

"Just trust me, please?" What neither man knew was that she and this bull were friends. He'd charged the fence one day not long after she arrived on the ranch. Instead of freaking out and running, she stood her ground. The bull stopped and watched her, then ambled off. The next day, he did the same thing, but she came prepared with treats and fed him several pieces of apple. It became a routine of theirs whenever he was in the pasture near the barn. She would bring treats with her when she went out to collect eggs from the chicken coop in the mornings. She wished she had some now. It would go a long way to keeping him calm.

Jasper huffed a sigh, but handed her the rope. Daisy wound it around her hand, laying the other one on the bull's muzzle. He gave a soft moo.

"I'm sorry. I don't have any treats. But I'll get you some as soon as they're finished."

"Treats?" Chet said. "You've been giving Terminator treats?"

"Yep. He's my buddy. Right, sweet pea?" She rubbed his nose. The bull leaned into her touch.

"If that isn't the damnedest thing I ever saw..." Jasper shook his head.

"You can try to cut him free now. Just go slow."

In the distance, she heard a car door slam. As Chet made the first cut, a string of curses uttered in a deep male voice carried through the air.

"What the fuck? Daisy, get out of there! Chet! What the hell is she doing?"

The commotion Asa created as he ran toward the pasture and hopped the fence startled Terminator, and he took several running steps backward, tossing his head and towing Daisy with him. She dug her heels into the dirt and leaned back, trying to stay on her feet.

"Asa, stop!" Chet waved him off.

Daisy ignored them all, her focus on staying on her feet. "I know the bad man scared you, sweet pea, but he's going to stay back there." Terminator pulled against the rope she held. Daisy tugged back. "Let us fix you up and you can go find your lady friends again, you big oaf." He mooed, then snorted, shaking his head.

"Asa, go get an apple from the barn," Chet said.

"What?"

"Just do it."

Daisy heard him take off through the pasture. Terminator let out a loud bellow and dipped his head.

"Don't you even think about it, you butthead. I will never bring you another treat again if you charge me."

"Daisy, give me the rope. You need to get out of here," Jasper said.

"No. We just have to get him calm." Asa needed to hurry with that apple. They'd been so close before he showed up.

Terminator snorted and shook his head again, backing up several steps as he bellowed. The first whisper that this was a bad idea floated through her mind. Feeding a bull some apples from outside the fence was one thing, but climbing inside and holding him by a rope with barbed wire wrapped around his head was quite another. She needed to do something fast, because he was losing patience with all of them. So, she did the one thing that always soothed her when she was restless. She started singing. Words to the lullaby her mother used to sing to her filled the air.

The bull stopped. He mooed and snorted, but stayed still. Daisy continued to sing even as she saw Asa running along the fence line toward them. As he got closer, he slowed, walking at a fast pace until he was out of her sightline. She could hear his feet thud against the ground as he got closer. Prickles of awareness lifted the hairs on the back of her neck as he stepped up behind her. He held out the apple.

Daisy glanced away from Terminator, letting her song trail away. "Slice it up." She kept her voice at the same soft pitch as her singing.

While he did as she asked, she started the lullaby over, and inched toward the bull. She took a piece of the apple and held it out to him. "Look, sweet pea. Apple." The bull blew a puff of hot air through his nostrils and took a step forward. She fed him the apple. He chewed it up, then bumped her hand for more.

"I'll be damned." Asa handed her another piece.

She grinned. "Chet, cut the wire off." She gave Terminator another slice as the foreman made the first cut. Daisy stretched out the interval between slices to give Chet and Jasper time to get him free of the wire. As they did that, Asa called the vet. The bull had several deep cuts on his face.

Chet cut the last piece of wire. Daisy used the remaining slice of apple to lead him into a smaller pen on the side of the barn, so they didn't have to chase him down for the vet.

Once he was secured and munching away on some fresh hay, Daisy headed into the barn to wash up. Her hands burned. She looked down to see red marks and a smear of blood on her palms from the rope. It had rubbed her flesh raw in some places. Asa found her at the sink, cleaning the dirt out of her wounds.

"What the hell do you think you were doing out there? Why didn't you let Chet and Jasper handle him? He could have killed you! And look at your hands. At least they were smart enough to wear gloves."

Red tinged her cheeks as her anger surged. She glanced up, ready to give him a piece of her mind. The look in his eyes stopped her. He wasn't so much angry as he was scared, and she didn't think he knew it. But it was there, lurking in the depths of his blue eyes.

She took a breath. "I'm sorry if I scared you. I ran in—without gloves—when I saw what was going on. Terminator and I are on good terms. I feed him treats all the time. I figured if anyone could get him to calm down long enough to let Chet cut the wire off, it was me."

"I don't care if he follows you around like a whipped puppy. He does it because you have treats. If you don't have those, there's no telling what he might do. Bulls are incredibly unpredictable, and at the end of the day, he's still a testosterone-fueled, one-ton battering ram with spikes. He's not some giant dog you can keep as a pet."

She frowned. "I know that, Asa. I'm sorry, okay? I saw the blood dripping off his face and just reacted. Sue me."

"I should fire you. I'd like to, but Dad still won't let me. Though for this, he might."

Daisy doubted it, but she had a feeling she'd get a stern talking to from Silas later. He knew she snuck treats to the bull, but Asa was right. Terminator wasn't to be trusted, even if he did shadow her most mornings.

"I'll be more careful in the future. But I can't guarantee I won't jump in to help again."

Asa sighed. "Just think about what you're doing first next time? You could have done the same thing from the other side of the fence."

Her mouth pulled. "If we could get him there. He didn't exactly want to cooperate."

He growled. "We could argue like this all day, but I have a horse to unload and your hands need tending." He took her by the arm. "Come on. I'll patch you up."

"What?" Her feet barely touched the floor as he led her out of the barn. "Asa, where are we going?"

"Inside. There's better first aid stuff in my bathroom. What's out here is meant for the field. Wraps and heavy-duty band-aids. I have gauze and tape inside."

"They're really not that bad. Band-aids would work just fine."

He glanced back at her. "They'll fall off the second you try to do anything. And the gauze will offer some padding."

Daisy stared at the back of his head, not willing to admit aloud that he was right. Instead, she let him lead her inside and upstairs to his bedroom. She tensed as they stepped over the threshold. She'd been in here before to clean, but never with him. He filled the space, dominating the room with his tall, muscular frame. She tried to stop the little shiver that ran through her as he hauled her past the bed to the en suite bathroom. She could envision him tangled in the unkempt sheets, one thick leg hanging out, his chest bare, and the sheet just covering what his pants hinted at every day.

"Are you okay? You look a little flushed." Asa eyed her with concern as he pushed her down onto the edge of the bathtub.

Daisy resisted the urge to fan herself. She knew she was beet red. She could feel it. She shoved thoughts of Asa covered by only a bedsheet from her mind and cleared her throat. "I'm fine. Just warm. It's hot today."

He frowned. "Sure." He shook his head and turned to dig in the cabinet in the corner for the first aid kit. He kneeled in front of her and opened it, removing several items, then setting the box on the floor. "Let me see your hands."

She flipped them palm side up and let them rest on her thighs. He lifted one to examine it. All the tingles she'd managed to get rid of came back at the feel of his big hand cradling hers. She clamped her teeth together and stared at a point over his shoulder. He opened the tube of antibiotic ointment and squirted some on her hand.

"I can do this, you know. Go unload your horse."

He arched a brow, but didn't look up from his task. "You can hold a gauze pad on your hand *and* wrap it with your other hand. Which is injured as well? And then do the other one with that one bandaged?"

Daisy fought to keep her neutral expression. He would have to realize that. Her plan was to find Silas or Cookie and have one of them help her. She wasn't telling Asa that, though. He'd just ask why he couldn't do it. She didn't want to tell him it was because he turned her insides to jelly.

So, she sat there and let him doctor her hands and tried to

take shallow breaths so she didn't inhale the scent of his soap wafting off his skin as he worked on her hand. When he leaned in to get a better look, she held her breath.

"There. That should do it." He sat up, then frowned at her. "Are you sure you're okay? Your face is red again."

She sucked in a breath. "I'm fine." She stood up, forcing him back. He rose to stand in front of her. Daisy's breath caught again. He was so big! The bathroom shrank to the size of a closet with him standing in it. She swallowed hard. "I should get back downstairs. I have cookies to box up for the hands yet."

"You made cookies?"

"Chocolate chip, yes."

He groaned. "Did you save some for here?" Before she could answer, he held up a hand. "And before you say anything, I'm sorry I was such an ass about the food thing. You're right. I should have said please. And thank you." He paused. "Thank you."

Daisy blushed. "I appreciate that. And I'm sorry about the tuna. I know you don't like it. I should have given you a jar of peanut butter."

He chuckled. "There was enough other food in there to make up for it. I lived on eggs and cheese. And produce."

She smiled. "At least you didn't starve."

"No, I didn't. But I had a big steak once I got to Knox's."

That made Daisy laugh.

"So, am I forgiven?"

She eyed him, tapping a finger against her chin. "Yeah. We're good. I'm sure we won't be later, but for now, you can have a cookie."

Asa whirled and headed for the door. "I'm going now before you change your mind."

Giggling, she followed him out.

Fourteen

The sun beat down on Asa's neck as he unloaded fencing supplies from the bed of his truck to fix the section of fence where Terminator found his barbed wire hat. Beads of sweat dotted his brow, and he swiped them away. Man, it was hot. He picked up the wire cutters and tossed them on the ground, then hopped down. Jasper found this downed section riding fence the other day, and Asa told him he would take care of it. He regretted that now. He'd forgotten how hot Montana summers could be.

He picked up the wire cutters and walked over to the broken section to clip off the rest of the wire. He would just stretch new wires all the way across. Careful not to stab himself on the barbs, he picked up the first broken wire, frowning when he got a look at the end. It didn't look like it broke. It looked like it was cut.

Great. Asa sighed. A rustler was just what he needed. He made a mental note to tell the guys to count cattle as he took his phone out to take some pictures of the wire. It rang just as he snapped the last image. His manager's name flashed across the screen, and he cursed. Asa did not want to talk to Marty.

He was no doubt calling to talk him into coming back to Los Angeles.

Asa pressed the button to silence the ringer, then shoved the device in his pocket and picked up his wire cutters. The phone rang again as he made the first cut. He silenced it again and went back to his task. When it rang a third time, he yanked off his gloves, throwing them to the ground, then answered the phone.

"What, Marty? I'm busy."

"You need to get online. The tabloids are having a field day with your new girlfriend."

"My what?" He frowned. "I'm not dating anyone."

"You sure about that? Because the rags say you and your housekeeper are hot and heavy. Their source is someone local."

Asa groaned. "Where the hell did they—shit. Vanessa." Dammit. He knew telling her he and Daisy were together would come back to bite him. He just didn't imagine it would be like this. Daisy was going to kill him. This was exactly what he didn't want to happen. He'd just wanted to keep the local women off his back.

"Who?"

"A woman here. She thinks Daisy and I are dating. We knew she spread it around town, but I was hoping that was as far as it would go."

"How did she get that idea?"

"It doesn't matter. What matters is she called the tabloids. Probably because she was pissed at me. Or she thought she could run Daisy off by bringing those vultures into it. Have the papers called you for comment yet?"

"Yeah. I haven't returned any of their calls, though. I wanted to talk to you first. What do you want me to tell them?"

"That it's categorically false." He didn't want a relationship—real or fake. Letting the lie spread around town was a mistake. Why couldn't the press just leave him alone?

Marty sighed. "Are you sure? They're not going to let this go. Not when they've got a hometown source that puts the two of you together."

He groaned. "I know. But I'd rather have it on record that it's not true. Maybe if I keep denying it and they don't get any juicy pictures, it'll send them back into the woodwork."

"Okay, you're the boss. I'll call 'em back."

"Thanks, Marty. And thanks for the head's up."

"Not a problem. Talk to you soon."

"Yep. Bye." He hung up and let out a string of curses. This was just what he needed. Why couldn't they leave him in peace?

Asa hurried through replacing the cut wire, then tossed everything in the back of his truck and hightailed it back to the house and barns. He wanted to get a look at the pictures and see just how damning they were. He couldn't imagine they were anything too scandalous. He hadn't touched Daisy in any romantic way.

The truck rocked to a halt near the horse barn in a cloud of dust. He shut off the engine and took out his phone, getting online now that he had internet access. Fingers flying, he typed his name into the search bar, followed by the word girlfriend. The first result had the headline, "Asa Mitchell Finds Love with Housekeeper." He groaned and clicked on it, hating that he was feeding the algorithm. But he needed to know what they said and what pictures they took.

An image of Daisy in short shorts and a tank top as she looked up at him with a spatula pointed at his face while he grinned down at her was the first thing he saw when the webpage appeared.

"Goddamn, son of a bitch!" He remembered that day. It was a few days after the incident in town with Vanessa. He'd come in from spending all day in the heat, sunburned and hotter than Hades, and she had the air off. Said she was airing out the house because she mopped all the floors and everything smelled like fake forest. Knowing that ordering her to turn it back on wouldn't work, he commented on her lack of clothes, hoping she'd feel self-conscious about showing so much skin around him. He told her he liked the shorts, but that she'd be even cooler in just that blue satin bra she showed him.

His mouth quirked. She'd been like a little kitten, claws out, when she pointed that spatula at him and told him it would happen when cakes flew. He reminded her they already had, to which she growled at him and went back to fixing dinner. His tactic worked, though. Once she finished making supper, the air came back on.

Asa's smile died as he realized whoever took the picture would have done so through the window above the sink. It bothered him to no end that a stranger had been so close to the house and none of them knew. It also explained the cut wire. They'd have noticed a car coming up the drive, but if someone snuck in overland, they wouldn't know it.

He scrolled down the page, seeing several other pictures of Daisy doing different tasks around the ranch. Everything from cooking to gardening. It was the last series of pictures and their caption that sent his blood pressure through the roof, though. They were from the day Terminator wrapped his head in barbed wire. The first couple shots were of her with the bull while he looked on, concerned. In the last one, he had his hand around her bicep as he led her into the house to bandage her hands. He'd been walking fast, and the shutter closed at just the right time to make it look like they were jogging inside. The caption read, "Asa and his mystery woman hurry inside for a passionate tryst after their harrowing encounter with the bull."

"Jesus." They would say anything to sell papers. Apparently, they were still running with the idea he was a ladies' man.

He sighed and got out of the truck. He hoped he could avoid putting cameras up on the ranch, but apparently, they were a necessity if he was to continue living here. Asa couldn't risk the safety of everyone else because the press didn't want to leave him alone.

His long legs ate up the ground between his truck and the house. Every step felt like he had lead weights attached to his feet. Daisy was going to go ballistic. He remembered what she said about her brothers. If they saw these pictures, they would be here in a heartbeat. Six angry men, hellbent on protecting their little sister, was not something any of them needed. He could see the firestorm that would erupt in the tabloids if they appeared.

Reaching the back door, he paused with a hand on the handle. He ran his other hand over his face. He could hear Daisy singing as she worked inside. Oh, this conversation was going to suck.

Hips swaying to the music, Daisy belted out the song blasting in her earbuds as she folded towels. The door to her left opened, and Asa stepped inside. She smiled and waved, but continued singing.

He stopped, hands on his hips and a serious look on his face. Trepidation skittered down her spine. She didn't like that expression. Taking out her earbuds, she paused the music app on her phone. "What? Why are you looking at me like that?"

He blew out a breath and looked past her at the wall for a moment. "Can we go sit?"

That bad feeling got worse. "Why?"

He motioned to the kitchen. "Just go sit. Please?"

Daisy huffed and stomped inside, pulling out a barstool. "Okay, I'm sitting. What's going on?"

"Well," he started. He sat down next to her and turned on his phone screen, scratching his temple. "Um, you know how you were concerned it would get out to the press that we told Vanessa we were dating even though we're not?"

Dread settled low in her belly. "Oh, you've got to be kidding. How bad?"

"It's bad." He set the phone on the counter and swung it around so she could see it.

She pulled it closer and scrolled through the article, her eyes growing wider the further she went. "Oh my God!" she breathed. "This is terrible!" If her brothers saw these pictures, they would be on the next plane to Billings. She put her elbows on the island and covered her face as tears threatened. They had *finally* stopped calling her multiple times a day, and according to Nori, they were starting to accept that she was fine on her own. All that progress, wiped out with a few pictures.

"I know it looks bad."

She dropped her hands to glare at him. "You think?"

"But I already told Marty to deny it."

She frowned and let out a snort. "Will it do any good?"

He shrugged. "Probably not. You're a young, beautiful woman living in my house, and I have a reputation as a player. They'll never believe nothing's going on. At least, not right away. We just need to avoid being photographed together."

"That's hard to do when we live in the same house and they're not above taking pictures through the windows."

"I know. And I know you like to have the windows and curtains open, but we need to keep them shut. It doesn't matter that our relationship is purely business. Sex sells. Platonic relationships are boring. They'll make up whatever they want to sell papers."

Her frown deepened. "I really hate that you're famous."

"Me too, sweetness."

Daisy sighed. "So, how do we go about getting our lives back?"

"We let my manager, Marty, handle the tabloids. He's going to deny the relationship, then ask for privacy. I'll make sure he lets the papers know if we see any more pictures of us on the ranch in their magazines, we'll sue them for trespassing. I'm also going to have some cameras installed around the buildings so we can monitor things. It should limit the paparazzi to town."

"So, I'm stuck here?"

"No, you can still go out. They'll probably snap a few pictures of you when you're there at first, but if we don't go together and they can't get anything of the two of us, they should leave eventually. It'll be too costly for them to stick around long."

"Okay. That solves your problem. What about my brothers? Someone is going to see this and tell them about it. There will be six pissed off Irish Catholic men lined up at the door within the week."

He sighed. "Yeah. I've got nothing except we present a united front. I'll do whatever you want. Whatever you think will convince them you're fine. I'm so sorry you got dragged into my life. Your only option to avoiding any of this now is to leave."

She narrowed her eyes at him. "You'd just love that, wouldn't you? How do I know you didn't invite paparazzo here and tell him to take those pictures to scare me off?"

"What? Hell, no. I would never invite the press into my life like that. I'd just as soon they left me the hell alone for the rest of forever. Look, Daisy, you and I may not have seen eye-to-eye at first, but even I can admit you improved things around here. You still drive me crazy most days." He pointed at the phone and the picture of her with the bull visible on the screen. "Terminator is case in point. But my dad smiles all the time, the house is clean, and there are always cookies. Would life be simpler without you? Yes. But would it be better? I'm not so sure."

Flabbergasted, Daisy could only stare at him. He liked having her around? She knew they'd been getting along better, but when had he decided he wanted her to stay? That was news to her.

Her phone rang from her pocket. "Fuck. That's probably Ian." Annoyed at the situation, she yanked it from her shorts to look at the screen, expecting to see her brother's face. But it wasn't Ian. It was her aunt.

"It's my Aunt Nori." Frowning, she answered and put the phone to her ear. "Hello?"

"Daisy Jane O'Malley, what the hell are you doing out there? Ian showed up bright and early this morning to show me pictures of you cavorting with Asa Mitchell. And that bull! What *were* you thinking?"

Daisy cringed. It had been a long time since Nori scolded her. "It's not what it seems. Well, the bull thing is, but not the rest of it." She sighed. "I just found out about all this myself. Nothing is going on between me and Asa. Some photographer snuck onto the ranch and took those pictures. The tabloid published them out of context."

"The article says they have a verified source that you're dating."

"That's because we told a woman in town we were. She and several other women around here have been hounding Asa, and he just wanted them to leave him alone. It was just meant to get them to back off, not for us to end up in a tabloid."

"Well, regardless, your brother is furious. After he left

here, he was going to go talk to the others. I think they're making plans to come out there now that they know where you are."

Daisy groaned. She glanced at Asa, then took the phone away from her ear and put it on speaker. "Nori, Asa's here with me. We were just talking about what we were going to do if they showed up. I really don't want them to come out here. Not just for my sake, but because it'll draw more press. Those pictures with the bull are only a few days old, so the photographers are probably still in the area. Having my family descend on the ranch will only add fuel to the fire. Can't you talk them out of coming?"

Nori sighed. "That depends. What am I supposed to tell them? If they think he's using you, nothing will stop them from getting on a plane."

"I'm not using her, ma'am."

"Yes, you are," Nori retorted. "That's exactly what you're doing. But I understand why. And I don't think you meant to put Daisy in this position."

"No, ma'am. It was just meant to get me a little space. I figured Vanessa would tell people around town, but not that she'd call some national tabloid and sell them the story."

"Well, she did, and what's done is done, so let's figure out what we're going to do. Daisy, I can probably keep your brothers in Chicago if I come out there and check on you."

"I'm not a toddler, Aunt Nori."

"Don't give me sass, girl. You know what I mean. Ian's going to want eyes on you. Better me than him. Besides, I miss hanging out with you. I love that you've spread your wings, but I miss having you around."

Tears welled in Daisy's eyes. "I miss you too."

"Good. That's settled. I'll be there tomorrow. Now, what do I tell Ian?"

"Just tell him we're handling things, and it was all a misunderstanding. And don't let him call any of the papers and ream them a new one. That's the last thing we need." She sighed. What a mess.

"I'll try, but you know how stubborn he can be."

"I know. Just do your best." She sighed again. "I'm sorry, Aunt Nori."

"This isn't your fault. And it's not yours, either, Asa. You both are victims of circumstance and greed. All right. I guess I'm off to calm your brothers. I'll text you later with my flight information."

"Sounds good. Thank you." She was so glad she had an ally in her fight to keep her brothers in check. "I really appreciate you doing this."

"Of course, my dear. I'm happy to help. I just want what's best for you."

"I know, and I love you for it."

"I love you too. I'll talk to you later."

"Okay." They said goodbye, and Daisy hung up. She groaned and folded her arms on the counter, dropping her head onto them. "This is a disaster."

His hand landed on her back. "It'll be okay. Take it from someone who's had years of experience with this sort of thing. We just have to weather the storm until they move on to someone else."

She sat up. "You left the business because of the storm."

"Of constantly weathering different storms. One day, once I've finally faded into obscurity, they'll leave me alone. But I'm not there yet, unfortunately."

Daisy blew her bangs out of her face. "Okay. Well, if Nori's coming tomorrow, that means I need to get the guest room ready. And we need to tell Silas what's going on."

Asa grimaced. "Yeah. I'll handle that."

She nodded and stood. "I'm not arguing with that. Good luck."

He waved a hand. "He's used to this stuff by now. Although, it's been awhile since it landed on his doorstep."

"Well, hopefully, your manager can keep it to a minimum." She patted the counter. "Thanks for telling me about all this before I found out in town—or by my brothers showing up."

He offered her a soft smile. "I'm sorry I had to at all."

She held his gaze for a moment, then nodded again. "I'm going to go get the spare room ready. I'll see you later." She backed away and turned, blinking furiously as she walked away. Her heart ached as the realization her whole life could be ruined by a few innocent pictures taken by a greedy man.

FIFTEEN

People flowed around Daisy as she stood next to the baggage carousel at the Billings airport, waiting on her aunt. She was both excited and nervous to see her. Excited because she'd missed the older woman, but nervous because she wanted Nori to be proud of the life she'd built for herself over the last few months.

The crowd parted, and she saw Nori's salt and pepper head striding through the atrium, pulling a carry-on behind her. Daisy squealed and ran forward.

Nori caught her in a tight hug. "Oh, it's so good to see you, girl."

Daisy pulled back to take her in. "You too." She wrapped her in another hug, then let go and took her arm, leading her toward baggage claim. "I'm so glad you're here."

"Me too. Honestly, I'm a little happy about the predicament you're in. It gave me an excuse to come out here and see what you've been up to."

Daisy smiled. "You didn't need an excuse. I'm happy to have you visit anytime."

"I know, but I didn't want to impose on your boss. Bosses?"

"Boss. Asa likes to think he's the boss since technically, he owns the property, but Silas is in charge."

Nori laughed. "I bet that goes over well."

"Swimmingly." Daisy chuckled as they stopped next to the carousel. "Do you see your bag?"

Nori stepped forward and pulled a lavender suitcase off the belt. "Let's hit the road. I want to see this ranch. And your bull."

"Oh, God." Daisy pressed her hands to her cheeks. "I'm never living that down, am I?"

"Nope. That riled your brothers up almost as much as your relationship with Asa. But not as much as those clothes you had on. Speaking of, I like this." She motioned to the dress Daisy wore. It wasn't the green one, but it was a pretty navy blue with large flowers in shades of orange, pink, and yellow. The bodice dipped in front, showing a hint of cleavage. The skirt swirled around her legs, stopping mid-calf. Strappy white wedge heels completed her look.

"Thanks. I made some friends here, and they took me shopping."

"They have good taste."

"I agree. Come on. Let's get out of here." She took Nori's suitcase, pulling up the handle to roll it behind her. They exited the front doors and crossed the street to short-term parking.

"Where did you park?"

Daisy pointed to the right. "Over there." She dug her keys from her purse and led the way through two rows of cars to her Subaru. Unlocking the doors, she opened the back and put Nori's suitcase inside. Her aunt stowed her carry-on next to it, then shut the hatch.

"Phew! It's hot," Nori said, getting into the car.

"Yeah. Who knew Montana was a sweatbox in the summer?" Daisy started the car and turned the air-conditioning on full blast.

"The ranch house is air-conditioned, right?" Nori pulled her blouse away from her chest, trying to cool off.

"Yes. That was one of the first changes Silas made when Asa hit it big. That and repainting, I guess. And a new barn. It's a nice place now."

"Sounds like it. So, tell me more about those two. You mentioned they're father and son, and I will admit, I did some research on Asa. He sounds different from the way you described him. Not so—down-to-earth?"

Daisy giggled. "He's a stuck up prick some days, but he's also very grounded. The tabloids make him out to be some playboy, but he's not really. He is rather used to having assistants do things for him, but he's getting better about ordering me to do stuff."

Nori arched a brow. "He orders you around?"

"He tries. Or he used to. After he ordered me to pack him food for a business trip to Colorado and I sent him a bunch of random things, he's gotten better about asking. We've come to a truce. Sort of."

"Sort of?"

"Yeah. We're civil with each other, but there are still moments where we argue. Like this morning. I knew I had to be here to pick you up and that I wouldn't be back until close to dinnertime, so I told him and Silas they were on their own for dinner. Silas was happy to eat a sandwich, but Asa has a thing about lunch meat."

"How do you have a thing about lunch meat?"

She shrugged. "He just doesn't care for sandwiches that much unless they're hot. I tried to tell him there was leftover lasagna in the fridge, but he talked over me, saying he would have to go into town to get a decent meal. I just glared at him and walked out."

"Was his dad there?"

Daisy nodded. "He just smirked and ate more bacon. He knew there was lasagna because he watched me put it away last night."

Nori laughed. "Do you think he'll tell Asa?"

"Probably not. We usually let him figure out he's being an ass on his own."

"Smart man."

For the rest of the drive, Daisy told her aunt about the ranch and its inhabitants, including the hands who lived in the bunkhouse. Nori asked about the friends she made, so she told her about Sara and Marci. By the time they reached the ranch, Nori was ready to throw a party so she could meet everyone. Daisy wasn't opposed, but she wasn't sure Asa would like it, even if it was all people he knew.

Daisy made the turn onto the ranch drive, kicking dust up behind them as she drove toward the main house.

"Oh, Daisy, this is darling!" Nori leaned forward to look through the windshield at the two-story white farmhouse.

"It really is," Daisy agreed. With its wraparound porch, light blue shutters, and wooden front door, it gave her a cozy feeling every time she looked at it. It felt like home. "The inside is even better."

Nori smiled. "I can't wait to see it."

Daisy parked the car in her space in the four-car garage adjacent to the house, and they climbed out. After retrieving Nori's luggage, they walked down the short walkway between the two buildings and up the steps to the back door. The screen banged closed behind them.

"Oh, it feels nice in here."

Daisy giggled. "I told you there was air-conditioning."

"It's an old house. I imagined window units that turn some rooms frigid and leave others just on the edge of cool."

"Nope. Central air. Come on. I'll show you to your room." Daisy stepped into the kitchen, towing Nori's suitcase behind her.

Silas stepped into the room from the hallway.

"Silas, hi." She smiled at the man. "I didn't think you'd be home yet."

He smiled and came closer. "I figured I should be here to greet your guest." He held out a hand. "Hello. I'm Silas Mitchell. Welcome to the Stone Creek."

Daisy's eyes widened as she watched her aunt blush. Nori tucked her hair behind her ear and took Silas's hand.

"It's nice to meet you. I'm Noreen Brannon. Nori."

"Nori. That's a pretty name."

"Thank you." Nori tittered.

Daisy coughed to cover her surprise. What the hell was going on? Were they flirting?

"Excuse me. I have a bit of a tickle in my throat."

"Do you need some water?" Silas asked.

She waved a hand. "No. I'll be fine. I was just about to take Nori to her room."

"Oh. I'll show her. You get a drink."

"That's okay. I'll be all right."

Silas reached for the suitcase handle. "I insist. I can show Miss Nori to her room just fine. Get some water." He took the suitcase away from her. "Come on, Nori. It's this way."

Daisy stood to the side to let her aunt pass. Nori barely spared her a glance as she followed Silas from the room.

Once they left, she stared at the empty space for a moment before shaking her head and moving to the cabinets next to the sink. She needed the drink just to clear the shock now running through her. She'd never seen her aunt act that way around a man before. Not even around her uncle when he was alive.

She filled a glass with water from the fridge and took a sip just as the back door opened. She looked over the rim to see Asa walk in.

"Hey. Sorry I'm late. I was in the barn and lost track of time."

"You didn't need to be here. Silas didn't, either."

"It's our house, and it's only polite to greet guests, even if they're technically here to see you." He frowned and glanced around. "Where is she?"

"Your dad took her upstairs to show her to her room."

"What? Why didn't you do that?"

"He wouldn't let me."

Surprise crossed Asa's face. "Why not?"

She shrugged. "Might have something to do with the fact they were attracted to each other."

Asa scoffed. "No. Dad doesn't date."

"That you know of."

He frowned. "Still, she's just visiting."

Daisy lifted one shoulder. "I don't know what to tell you. She took one look at him and forgot I was here. Surprised the shit out of me. I coughed to cover my shock and Silas insisted he would take her upstairs so I could get a drink, even though I told him I was fine."

Asa glanced at the hallway. They could hear Silas and Nori walking around upstairs, the murmur of Silas's deep voice coming through the floor. "Have you hydrated?"

She giggled and set her glass on the counter. "Yes."

"Come on." He took off for the door.

Daisy lengthened her stride to keep up, running up the stairs as he took them two at a time. "Geez, Asa. They're not going anywhere."

He didn't slow, though, and she scurried after him as he reached the landing. They stopped in the doorway to Nori's room.

"Hello." Asa stepped inside, Daisy right behind him. Silas and Nori stood near the window, her aunt holding Tallulah as they looked outside. He walked forward, hand outstretched. "I'm Asa. It's nice to meet you."

Nori turned, her brow furrowed as she assessed him. "So, you're the man causing my niece so much grief."

Asa balled his hand into a fist and let it drop. "Yes, ma'am. I am sorry about that."

Her face broke into a grin. "I'm just teasing. I know none of this is your fault." She put the cat on the bed, then held out her hand. "It's nice to meet you."

He chuckled and took her hand. "I'm glad. How was your trip?"

"Uneventful."

"Nori and I were just talking about what to do for dinner," Silas said. "Neither of us thinks Daisy should have to cook, and no one wants to eat anything you or I make, so I propose we all go into town to Sarafina's."

"Dad, I don't know if that's such a great idea. We're trying not to let the press see us together." He motioned to Daisy.

"There's nothing wrong with all of us going to a family dinner, and I refuse to be bullied into hiding."

Daisy grimaced, echoing the expression on Asa's face. She knew Silas was right, but it didn't change the fact she disliked having her picture and life plastered across some gossip magazine.

She shared a glance with Asa and shrugged. "Sara's is safe, at least. She won't put up with anyone taking pictures of you, or the crap from any of your women."

He growled. "They're not my women, sweetness."

She grinned. "Marla was."

"Fifteen years ago."

Nori laughed. "Oh, I like you. Come on. I'm starving."

"Same here," Silas said. "It's been a busy day." He held out an arm to Nori. "Shall we?"

She beamed up at him. "We shall."

The older couple flounced out of the room, leaving Daisy and Asa to follow. Asa motioned her to precede him. She sighed and followed her aunt downstairs. This day had turned weird.

Asa tried to make himself smaller as they walked into Sarafina's in the hopes it would disguise his presence from the other patrons. He stayed behind his father, letting his bulk shield him as well. He glanced around the restaurant, looking for potential trouble, pausing as he saw Sara. She stared at him with wide eyes from behind the counter bar.

He offered her a small smile and straightened to his full height. He wasn't fooling anyone. All his posture did was make his neck hurt.

"Well, hello." Sara walked up, draping the towel in her hands over her shoulder. She grinned. "You decide to come out of your lair and finally visit me?"

"I haven't been that bad." Asa stuffed his hands in his pockets and frowned. He'd stopped in here a couple times since he'd been back to pick up a to-go order. And he'd seen her at the ranch when she came out to visit Daisy and Marci.

She rolled her eyes. "Whatever." She turned her attention to Nori. "You must be Aunt Nori. I'm Sarafina Katsaros."

Nori smiled. "Are you the Sara who took my niece clothes shopping?"

"Yep, that's me. Doesn't she look fabulous?"

"She does. It's nice to see her out of those drab clothes she wore to make her brothers happy."

Sara grinned and gestured for them to follow her. "After

she got over her aversion to color, she did pretty well on her own."

"I do not have an aversion to color."

Sara rolled her eyes. "Honey, everything you owned was gray, brown, black, or white."

"Not true. I had some blue shirts."

"I stand corrected." Sara chuckled and held up her hands, then pointed to the booth she stood next to. "Is this okay? It's as about as secluded as I have right now." She glanced at Asa.

"It's fine. Thank you, Sara." Asa sat down, sliding over so Daisy could sit next to him. His dad and Nori sat down across from them.

"Do you guys know what you want to drink?"

"Iced tea for me," Daisy said.

"I'll have the same," Nori said.

Sara wrote both on her notepad. "Asa?"

"Water."

"I'll have tea as well," Silas said.

"Okay. Three teas and a water coming up." She spun around and headed for the counter.

"This place is cute." Nori picked up her menu as she glanced around at the diner's interior. Light blue walls gave the restaurant a cheerful feeling. Black lanterns hung above every reclaimed wood table and natural wood floors finished off the space.

Asa followed her gaze around the room. He liked Sara's diner. It was a happy place and reminded him of her. She was a cheerful person. And a good friend. Something he hadn't been for a long time. He blew out a breath and opened his menu.

"So, what's good?" Nori asked, perusing her own.

"Everything," Silas said.

Nori giggled. Asa glanced at her, then at his dad. A bright smile lit Silas's face. He frowned.

"I can't eat everything. What's the best?"

"She makes great fried chicken. It rivals Daisy's."

"Silas, stop. Mine isn't better than Sara's. Nothing I make is better than her food."

"I like your meatloaf better. And your cookies," Asa muttered, his eyes back on the menu as he tried to ignore his father making goo-goo eyes at Daisy's aunt. When silence met his words, he glanced up to find them all staring at him. "What?"

Sara reappeared with their drinks, and he turned to look at her. She set their drinks on the table, then took out her order pad. "You guys ready?"

"I am," Asa said. He looked around at the others, who nodded.

"Okay, Daisy, what do you want?"

"The trout basket."

Sara scribbled on her pad. "Asa?"

"A burger with everything and fries."

"M'kay. Nori?"

"Silas says you have wonderful fried chicken, so I'd like to try that."

"Good choice. Do you want mashed potatoes or a baked potato? Or fries?"

"Mashed potatoes, gravy on the side, please."

Sara nodded. "You get another side. I have green beans, corn on the cob, glazed carrots, or broccoli and cheese."

"Oh, that last one sounds great."

"Broccoli it is. Silas?"

"I'll have the same, except I want green beans and extra gravy."

Sara finished writing down his order, then gathered their menus. "All right. I'll have it out in just a bit." She smiled and left.

Asa glanced around the room again, then out the window,

which overlooked the back of the lot. Tension put a hard set to his shoulders and kept him on edge.

Daisy elbowed him softly in the side. "Relax, would you? It's just a family dinner. You keep looking like that, and people will think we kidnapped you and dragged you here against your will. Won't that give the tabloids something to talk about?"

He frowned, then sighed. "Sorry. I just feel a little exposed. I've spent the last few months avoiding public places and the camera around every corner."

"You poor man," Nori said. "I can't imagine not having any privacy. Hopefully, you'll get that soon."

"Thanks. I know I just need to give it time." He shifted, trying to relax, and his thigh touched Daisy's. Awareness shot through him, putting the tension back in his shoulders for an entirely different reason. Daisy glanced up at him through her lashes as he looked down. A pretty blush stained her cheeks, and something passed between them, sending an electric jolt through his system and kicking his heart rate up a notch.

Asa forced himself to look away, taking a sip of his water as he gathered himself. What was that about? He looked across the table, his gaze landing on his dad. Silas grinned at him. Asa narrowed his eyes. The old man was up to something.

Choosing to ignore his father for now, Asa cleared his throat and looked at Nori. "So, Nori, tell us about yourself. What do you do for a living?"

"I retired last year, but until then, I was a real estate agent."

"You're young to be retired," Silas said.

Nori smiled. "I'm glad you think so, but I'm probably older than you."

"Well, I'm sixty. Sixty-one in October."

"I turned sixty-six in February."

"You don't look it."

Nori beamed. "Thank you."

Asa stared at his dad. He'd never seen him flirt. He didn't know the man knew how.

"I wanted to travel. My husband passed away ten years ago, and we always wanted to see the world. We went to a few places—Alaska, the Bahamas—but I want to go to Australia and Rome. Athens, and of course, Ireland." She gave him a cheeky smile.

"Travel sounds wonderful. I'd love to take a nice long vacation. Now that Asa's home for good, maybe I can find time to do that."

"You didn't go see him when he had concerts in exotic locales?"

"A couple times. I went to the UK to see him. And Mexico. But it's hard to get away from a working ranch. It's easier since Chet came on board as foreman five years ago, but I can't just drop everything and take off. It takes planning."

"Well, it will be easier for you now, Dad. You deserve to take all the time off you want. I can take up the slack."

Silas grinned at his son. "Oh, I'm counting on it."

"You know, Silas, I have a trip planned to Ireland in the fall. Maybe you could join me?"

He considered her with a thoughtful look. "I might have to take you up on that. Where all are you planning to go?"

Asa leaned down and put his mouth close to Daisy's ear. "What the hell is happening?" he whispered.

"I don't know," she whispered back, staring at the older couple.

They sat there and watched as Nori and Silas talked, oblivious to the pair across from them. It wasn't until Sara walked up with their food that they noticed their surroundings again.

"Here you go." She set their plates on the table, arching a brow at Asa, who had leaned toward Daisy as he watched his dad flirt.

He straightened, but didn't scoot away from her. To be honest, he liked the feel of her against him. Probably more than he should.

"This all looks so good," Nori said. "Thank you."

Sara smiled. "You're welcome. Let me know if you need anything else."

Asa picked up his burger and took a bite as she left. Daisy speared her fish with her fork. Conversation turned to more general topics while they ate. They didn't linger in the diner, because Nori wanted to walk through the downtown area. It was Friday, so many of the shops were open late.

Silas held the door as they exited Sarafina's. On the sidewalk, he offered Nori his arm, and they strolled ahead of Asa and Daisy.

"I feel like I walked into an alternate universe." Asa stared at the back of his dad's head.

Daisy giggled. "He's sixty, not dead."

Asa scrunched his nose. He did not want to think of his dad that way. "That's not an image I wanted."

"Me either, but it's there." She tilted her head, studying them. "They're cute together, though."

He sent a sharp glance her way. "Are you trying to marry him off to your aunt?"

She gave him a disgusted sigh. "I have no ulterior motive. For anything."

He frowned and looked in the shop windows as they passed. "Everyone has a motive."

"Of course they do. But it's not always nefarious."

"So, what's yours, then?"

"To get away from my brothers and spread my wings. I have no desire to be in a relationship. I need to work on myself first."

He scoffed. "All women want to be in a relationship. You just don't know you do."

She snorted, and he saw her roll her eyes in the reflection of the shop windows. "And you're an expert on what women want?"

He chuckled. "The tabloids would tell you I am."

"And they always tell the truth." She grinned.

"Bogie, ten o'clock," Silas said, dropping back with Nori.

"What?" Asa looked that way.

"I saw a man with a fancy camera in the park. It had a long lens on it."

Asa cursed and took Daisy's hand, hauling her inside the shop. As soon as he stepped inside, he knew he made a mistake. It was Marla Wilkins' consignment store. She spotted him from across the room, and her eyes lit up, a predatory smile ticking up one side of her mouth.

Until she saw Daisy. Her face closed off, and a dark scowl descended. Asa felt Daisy stiffen next to him.

"Oh, Asa, I shouldn't be in here."

"Me neither." He turned around to leave, but Silas and Nori stood in his way. His dad looked past him, frowning as he saw Marla. Nori's attention was on the clothes and furniture around her.

"This is a cute store."

"You'll have to come back. We're leaving." Asa walked forward.

Nori's brow scrunched. "Why?"

Silas took her arm and turned her toward the door. "We'll explain outside."

"Oh. Okay?" Confusion marred her pretty face, but she followed Silas to the door.

"Asa Mitchell! You have a lot of nerve bringing that woman in here."

He closed his eyes for a moment, stifling a groan of frustration, then turned around. "I have nerve? You're the one who keyed her car and threw a milkshake on her."

"Wait, what?" Nori said. "Daisy?"

"It's okay, Aunt Nori. I'll explain later."

Anger flashed in Marla's eyes, and she glared at Daisy. "So I lost my temper. She didn't have to press charges."

"Would you have fixed the damage to my car if I didn't?"

Marla glanced away before answering. "Sure."

Daisy rolled her eyes. "Somehow, I don't think you're very sincere about that."

Marla's eyes narrowed to slits. She pointed to the door. "Get out."

"Gladly." Daisy spun around. "I'll see you in court." She marched toward the exit, Asa on her heels.

His hand shot out to hold the door, so it wouldn't hit him in the face as she barreled outside. "Daisy, slow down."

She whipped around, her hair fanning out around her. Her eyes glittered with fury as she stared up at him. "That woman is the devil. If there weren't witnesses, she'd claw my eyes out. All because she thinks I have what she wants. Those pictures and that story only made it worse."

"Marla's harmless. Yes, she has a temper, but keying your car is about the extent of what she'll do."

"I wouldn't be so sure of that. A woman scorned carries a lot of rage."

"I didn't scorn her."

"She thinks you did, and that's all that matters."

"Can we take this inside?" Silas asked, coming up beside them with Nori. "You're giving our photographer friend quite the show." He nodded toward a man leaning out from behind a tree.

"Jesus, they're not even trying anymore." Asa shoved his hands in his pocket so he didn't do something dumb, like flip the guy off.

"I think maybe we should go back to the ranch," Nori

said. "I can come back to town by myself another day and shop."

"I think you're right," Silas said. "Come on, son. Let's go home."

Asa huffed, doing his best to let some of his anger go. "Yeah." He looked at Nori. "I'm sorry I ruined your first evening here."

She waved a hand. "Nonsense. I had a lovely time. Photographer and crazy shopkeeper notwithstanding."

"Good." He held an arm out to her. "How about a ranch tour instead?"

Nori grinned up at him and hooked a hand through his elbow. "Oh, you are a charmer." She glanced at Silas and winked. "Like father, like son."

Asa looked at his dad, who just smiled, then chuckled. "Come on. There's a bull I'm sure Daisy would like you to meet."

SIXTEEN

Daisy hummed along to the music playing through her earbuds as she sorted through the mail. She'd walked down to the mailboxes and picked it up a few minutes ago, getting some exercise in. She planned to make cookies later for the party tomorrow night, and she wanted to eat a few without feeling guilty. The half mile to the mailbox and back was the perfect way to accomplish that.

She turned over the letter with her name on it, curious about who it was from. It had a Denver postmark, but no return address. Probably more junk mail. She received plenty of that. Picking up the letter opener, she slid it under the flap and sliced it open, then pulled out the single sheet of paper inside, unfolding it. Her eyes widened as she read it. This was not junk mail.

Hands trembling, she laid it on the counter and took a shaky breath, unsure what to do. She read the letter again, hoping the words would change, but they didn't. Someone was angry about the photographs in the tabloids. Enough so to warn her away from Asa.

"Good morning, dear." Nori walked into the kitchen,

dressed in a gauzy, short-sleeved dress. The rust-colored skirt with its small blue and white flowers fluttered around her legs. She stopped in front of the coffeepot and reached for a mug. "Did you have a pleasant walk? I saw you head down the drive when I got up."

"Yeah, it was fine." Daisy stared down at the letter.

Nori set the pot down after pouring herself a cup. "Everything okay? You sound distracted."

"Huh?" She glanced back. "Oh, yes. It's fine." She laid the letter down. "Just some strange mail."

"Strange mail? What kind of strange mail?"

Daisy hesitated. Her fingers fiddled with the edge of the paper before she nudged it toward her aunt. "I got this today. I'm not sure what it means."

With a frown, Nori picked up the letter and scanned it. Her eyes went wide. "Daisy, this doesn't sound good. Someone's very upset with you."

"I know, but really, how bad could it be? I mean, nothing's actually going on between us."

"It doesn't matter. Someone thinks there is. Honey, I think you need to show this to the police. Maybe it's got fingerprints on it and they can track down the sender. At least warn them to back off. You should know where the threat's coming from."

Daisy picked up another letter, the electric bill, and sliced it open. "It's not a threat, though."

"Hmm, really? 'Asa's mine. Back off, bitch,' seems like a threat to me."

She rolled her eyes. "Okay, so it's a little threatening. But they didn't threaten me with any actual harm. Just told me to back off. Can't really back off more than I have."

"No, but you can tell the police. Make a record of it, so if this person does more you can establish a pattern and have a protection order put in place."

Daisy sighed. "Fine. I'll go into town later and show it to the police. Right now, though, I need to finish sorting the mail and start my baking. You do want cake and pie tomorrow, right?"

Nori snorted. "That's a silly question." She pushed away from the counter, pointing a finger at her niece. "I'll hold you to your word. If you don't go to the police, I'll tell Silas."

And she would, too, Daisy knew. She nodded. "I promise. After I get the baking done."

Narrowing her eyes, she held Daisy's gaze a moment longer, then spun toward the refrigerator. "Good girl."

Daisy giggled. "I'm so glad you're here."

Nori leaned out around the fridge door to grin. She ducked back in, then shut the door, holding the cream cheese. "I called Ian last night. Gave him an update."

"Oh, God. How did that go?"

"Fine." She took a bagel from the bread box and put it in the toaster. "I told him I saw with my own eyes that you two are just friends. And that you're doing just fine."

Daisy's mouth flattened. "Did he believe you?"

Nori shrugged. "Maybe. He's staying put, so he didn't not believe me." She took a sip of her coffee. "Besides, you *are* doing fine. It's not like I lied."

"True." She finished splitting the mail into piles, and opened a drawer, taking out a rubber band. She wrapped it around all the mail for the boys in the bunkhouse and set it aside. "I just don't want him to come here. Not until I know I can stand up to him when he tries to tell me I'm not doing things right."

"Oh, honey." Nori frowned, moving closer. "I don't think it's so much that he thinks you're doing things wrong, it's just that, well, he never really came to grips with the fact you grew up."

"Duh." She moved all the mail to the kitchen table to get it out of her way. She'd take it where it needed to go later.

"You leaving was a good thing. It's forced them all to realize you're not a kid anymore. Will he try to hold on to that image when he sees you again? Undoubtedly. But I think once you show him you won't let him run your life for you anymore, he'll back down. At the end of the day, Ian loves you and just wants what's best for you."

Daisy sighed. She pulled her canisters forward and started measuring ingredients into a bowl. "I know. It doesn't mean I'm looking forward to the confrontation, though."

"I know, dear. But I promise to be there for you when that happens. I'll help you get through until he comes around."

"Thanks, Aunt Nori." She smiled at her, so very glad she was here. It was nice to feel connected to someone again.

Laughter rang out over the yard, carried on the warm breeze. Asa rolled his shoulders and tried to relax, knowing he was among friends. Real friends. It was difficult to shake the anxiety, though. The last party he went to ended with a loud, public fight with his ex-girlfriend and his inability to commit.

It wasn't that he didn't want to commit. He just knew she wasn't right for him. Asa only stuck with her because it was mutually beneficial. She got the publicity from being Asa Mitchell's girlfriend, and he kept the women—most of them —off his back. Plus, she wasn't bad in bed. And he liked having someone to talk to. But he didn't love her and knew he never would. If it hadn't happened in the year they were together, it wasn't going to.

Then the entire breakup got plastered on the front page of every tabloid for all the world to see. It was the last straw for him. After that, he couldn't wait for his tour to end so he could step away from the fame. He just wanted to be Asa again.

A burst of feminine laughter drew his attention. He glanced over to see Daisy laughing at something Jasper said. The ranch hand asked her to dance several songs ago. They'd been twirling past him, laughing it up ever since.

"You know, your life might be easier if you did what the papers suggested."

"What?" He turned to see Chet standing beside him, holding out a beer. Asa took it. "Thanks." He took a drink.

"If you and Daisy dated. Life would be easier for you."

"Hardly. The women in town already think we're together, thanks to my encounter with Vanessa Hodgins. And the papers would just double down, trying to get some juicy pictures of us. I just want all the attention to die a swift death."

Chet shrugged. "Maybe, but man, it would be fun when the reporters weren't around."

Asa frowned. "She's not the type you can mess around with, Chet. You know that."

"Hey," he held up his hands. "I didn't mean any disrespect. She's a good woman. She puts up with your ass."

Asa gave him a look.

"I'm just saying. You should make your move before she ends up with someone else. Like Jasper."

"I'm not interested in Daisy."

"Sure. That's why you can't take your eyes off of her."

Asa glared at him and turned his attention back to the dance floor. It wasn't his fault Daisy looked amazing in that green dress. It was sexy and alluring, but still modest. She looked playful and fun, but in an adult way.

Chet grinned.

More feminine laughter floated through the air. What were they talking about that was so damn funny?

"Dude, just go ask her to dance."

"Will you leave me alone if I do?"

Chet's grin widened. "Sure."

He handed his beer back. "Hold this. And don't spike it. I can tell the difference now."

"That was one time." Chet laughed. "And we were seventeen."

Asa pointed two fingers at his eyes, then flipped his hand around to point at Chet. "I'm watching you."

"Yeah, right. You get that woman in your arms and I guarantee you'll only have eyes for her."

He was probably right, but Asa wasn't about to admit it. With a final look, he walked away to break up the laugh party on the dance floor.

Walking up behind Jasper, he tapped him on the shoulder. "May I cut in?" he asked when his ranch hand turned around.

"Oh, sure. Yeah. Sorry. I didn't mean to monopolize her. We were having fun."

"You're fine, Jazz. Go grab yourself a beer."

Jasper nodded, then turned to Daisy, raising her hand. "Until we meet again, my dear." He kissed the back of her hand. He offered her a roguish smile and walked away to her giggle.

"Having fun?" Asa took her hand and pulled her into his body as the music changed to a slower song.

Her free hand landed on his chest, then slid up to his shoulder. "I was, yes. Why'd you have to break it up?"

"Figured he needed a break."

"Only *he* needed a break?"

Asa made a noncommittal sound in the back of his throat and kept moving to the music. He ignored her question and asked one of his own. "Has Nori met everyone?"

Daisy looked around. "I think so. She's spent most of her time with Silas, though."

He'd noticed. The two of them were glued at the hip. They ate supper together, then ate Daisy's delicious desserts while standing side-by-side at the edge of the section of yard designated for dancing while they waited for Chet to hook up the sound system. Once music poured through the speakers on the back of the house, they'd danced most of the evening. It was freaking him out a bit, to be honest.

Asa turned his attention back to the woman in his arms, becoming aware of her lush body pressed against his. Dancing with her suddenly didn't seem like the best idea. Particularly since parts of his anatomy didn't want to listen when he told them to simmer down.

His phone rang, saving him from himself. "Sorry." He let her go to take it from his pocket, frowning when he saw his manager's number on the screen. What did he want now? He slid his thumb over the screen and answered. "Yeah, Marty."

"Who's Marla Wilkins?"

"Marla?" He glanced at Daisy, who openly listened to his end of the call. "She's my high school girlfriend. Why are you asking about her?"

"Because she's claiming *she's* your girlfriend, not Daisy."

"What? How did we get from a 'confirmed source' stating Daisy and I are together to I'm dating Marla?" Jesus, someone needed to stop guessing about his love life. The next thing he knew, they were going to link him to Daisy's aunt. He was sure they had pictures of him walking arm in arm with her as they left town a few nights ago.

"I don't know, but there's a whole interview from her."

Asa sighed. "Why would she do that? Especially when she thinks Daisy and I are really together."

"I don't know, Ace, but she's worked the rags into a frenzy. This one article has details. Juicy ones."

"What? Jesus. Text me the links. I'll read them and call you back."

"And quickly. We need to do some damage control. If you're serious about retiring and wanting the press to leave you alone, we need to cut this off now. She's just fanning the flames."

He pinched the bridge of his nose, letting out a breath. "Yeah. Send me the links." Asa resisted the urge to crush his phone beneath his boot heel as he pulled it away from his ear. "Dammit."

"What? More pictures?"

"Probably, but not necessarily of us." His phone dinged as the text from Marty came through. "Dance time's over. I have to deal with this."

"Deal with what? What's going on? I heard you say Marla's name. What did that crazy woman do now?"

He took her hand and led her away from the other dancers toward the house, where he found a quiet spot on the back porch. "That was Marty. Apparently, Marla told the tabloids they got it wrong. That she and I were dating, not you and me."

"What? Why would she do that? She has to know you'd deny it."

"I don't know. I stopped trying to figure out why she does the things she does a long time ago." He opened the text message Marty sent and clicked on the link. Daisy crowded in next to him to read along.

"Oh, dear lord. 'Playboy Asa Mitchell Breaks Housekeeper's Heart As He Goes Back to High School Flame, Marla Wilkins.'" Daisy read the headline aloud, rolling her eyes.

Asa groaned. "I'm going to kill her. This is a fucking exposé about our relationship." He snorted as he read. "She lied through her teeth, though. I was not her first. Not by a long shot."

They looked through the articles, which mostly said the same thing, though only one carried an interview with her.

Asa turned off his phone screen in disgust and shoved it into his pocket. "She must have tracked down the reporter in town and given him an interview."

"Isn't there anything you can do to stop her?"

"Not really, no. She didn't really slander me. Some of the details aren't right, but the gist of the story is true. Except the current relationship part. She's just pissed at me and striking where she knows it'll hurt me the most. My privacy."

"Everything okay, son?"

They turned to see Silas and Nori approaching.

"We saw you on the phone, then you stalked off."

Asa gave them a quick rundown of what Marla did.

"That's terrible," Nori said.

"It is, but it's who she is. I just wish I realized it before we dated. Then she'd just be some crackpot looking to get her fifteen minutes of fame instead of someone the papers actually want to hear from. I just need to figure out how to shut her down. Money won't do it—not that I'd offer to pay her off anyway."

"What if you give the papers a better story?" Silas said.

Asa frowned. "What do you mean?"

Silas held out a hand. "Before you shoot me down, hear me out."

"Why would I shoot you down?"

"Because I think you should confirm that you're in a relationship."

Asa reared back like he'd been slapped. Metaphorically, he had. Why would his dad suggest such a thing? "You want me to tell the tabloids Marla and I are dating?"

"No, not Marla. Just that you're in a relationship. They're determined that you are." He shrugged. "Why not give them what they want? There will be some speculation, sure. But I think once the newness wears off, they'll back down and leave you alone."

"Not if I don't give them a name. They'll scrutinize every relationship I have with every woman in the area. I don't want to bring that kind of attention to any of them."

"Then tell them it's me," Daisy interjected.

Daisy had no idea what came over her to make her offer to be Asa's pretend girlfriend for the press. She felt sorry for him, and it just popped out.

"You had a cow the first time they linked us together, and now you want to invite them into your life?"

She shrugged. "They're going to speculate anyway. This way, we control the narrative."

A curious frown overtook Asa's face. "So, we give them what they want to kill the wild guesses?"

She nodded. "And it'll discredit Marla's story. Who are they more likely to believe? You or her?"

"But, honey, what about your brothers?" Nori interrupted. "They think it was a misunderstanding that led to the first story."

"We can explain we were trying to keep things quiet because I'm not comfortable with the attention. That's only a partial lie."

"Daisy, I appreciate you trying to help, but I don't want to create more problems for you. I'll just issue a statement that Marla's story is false."

"And you'll end up in a war of words with her, and more paparazzi parading around. Don't worry about me. I can handle my brothers. Especially since Nori's here." She glanced at her aunt. Nori nodded in agreement.

He covered his eyes with a hand, pressing his fingers into the sockets. "Why do I have a feeling they're going to paint me as a playboy with multiple women?"

"Tell them you're engaged," Silas said.

"Engaged!" Nori turned to look at him.

"Dad, that's crazy."

Daisy agreed. A fake relationship was one thing, but a fake engagement?

"No, it's not. Think about it. Not only are you dispelling Marla's story, but you're adding credence to yours. And it takes away the playboy angle and makes her appear like a scorned ex, looking for revenge."

Asa shook his head. "Who are you and what have you done with my dad? He would never suggest so blatantly lying."

Silas shrugged. "I'm tired of seeing you stressed and angry. I know a lot of the reason for that is the constant publicity and the lack of privacy."

"Announcing an engagement won't give me any more privacy. It might make it worse."

"At first, yes. But then they'll get bored with you. There won't be any excitement because you won't be the playboy bachelor anymore." He held Asa's gaze for a moment, then looked at Daisy. "This isn't solely his decision. You need to agree. I know it's asking a lot."

She tipped her head, considering his suggestion. It wasn't hard to understand where he was coming from. Silas loved his son and wanted to help him. And she had a feeling he was right about how everything would play out. But could she subject herself to that type of scrutiny until it did? Especially the type she would get from her brothers?

Daisy glanced at her aunt. Having her here would help with her family. The boys trusted Nori to keep an eye on her, which should keep them in Chicago.

Nori raised an eyebrow, letting Daisy know it was her decision. Taking a deep breath, Daisy looked at Asa. "Let's do it. Tell them we're engaged."

He dropped his hand. "What? No. I can't do that to you.

They're like vultures. They will rip your life apart to squeeze out every sordid detail."

"So? It's not like I have anything to hide. You couldn't pick a more boring person for your pretend fiancée than me."

He scoffed. "You all have lost your minds. This is insane."

Daisy shrugged. "I'm not doing this just for you. This is for Silas too. You're stressed, which makes him stressed. And it's for me as well. I want the paparazzi to go away as much as you do. If faking an engagement makes that happen faster, then I'm all for it. I've found a home here, and I'd like to keep it. The quicker we get rid of your reporter shadows, the better off we'll all be."

Asa stared at her, assessing her. Daisy held his gaze, hoping he'd see the light. Silas was right. An engagement to boring old her seemed like the best way to get Asa out of the spotlight. Finally, his shoulders dropped, and he nodded. "Fine. But we need to make this look legit. You need a ring."

"Take her to Billings tomorrow and get one," Silas said. "Make a spectacle of leaving town together, so that photographer follows you. There won't be any denying your story if he photographs you buying a ring together."

Asa sighed and scraped a hand through his hair. "I swear, I'm just going to buy an island somewhere and never leave." He looked at Daisy. "Fine. If you're game, let's do this. So, Daisy O'Malley. Will you marry me?"

SEVENTEEN

"Are you sure you want to do this?"

Daisy paused to look back at Asa as she turned to get out of the truck. Her stomach churned as the reality of what they were about to do hit her. There was no going back after this. But it was the right thing to do for all of them.

"I'm sure." She pulled on the door handle and stepped down from the truck. Asa came around and took her hand. They both ignored the SUV that was parked half a block away. Just like they ignored it the whole way from home. It had been camped out on the road near the ranch drive and followed them first into Pine Ridge, where they stopped at Sara's to get coffee, then when they left town. She was sure tomorrow's headlines would be huge.

Asa held open the door to the jeweler's and ushered her inside. Behind the counter, an older man in a gray suit looked up, smiling as he saw them.

"Hello. Welcome to Barton's. My name's Johnathan. How can I help you?"

"We're looking for an engagement ring."

His smile broadened. "Wonderful. We have quite the selection." He motioned to a case to his right. "What style are you thinking, young lady?"

Daisy glanced up at Asa, who nodded. She walked toward the case the man gestured to and looked inside. Diamonds of all shapes and sizes winked back at her in the sun coming through the windows lining the front and one side of the store.

"Um, nothing too big. I work with my hands a lot, so maybe something that won't get caught on everything and get in the way?"

He nodded and unlocked the case, pulling out a couple of trays. "A bezel or halo setting might be best, then. This is what we have in those."

She looked at the rings, overwhelmed with the choices.

"Can you tell me a little more about what you like?" The jeweler asked, noticing her hesitation. "Maybe we can narrow it down some more."

"Not large," Daisy said. "I don't like drawing attention to myself."

"You picked the wrong man for that." He smiled and nodded at Asa.

Asa stepped closer and wrapped an arm around Daisy's waist. She did her best not to stiffen. She knew she needed to get used to him touching her when they were in public, but she wasn't there yet. But Asa had obviously been recognized, so they needed to maintain the ruse.

"She loves me, so she's willing to step outside her comfort zone a little. Right, sweetness?"

Daisy turned her head to look at him, forgetting how close he was. His mouth was only inches away. She felt her cheeks heat.

"Right." She tried to smile and prayed it didn't come out like some weird grimace. She cleared her throat and glanced down at the rings.

"Feminine," Asa said, answering the jeweler's question about her style. "She's kinda girly, so something pretty. But not overly flashy."

"I am not girly."

"You are in those new dresses you bought. And what about this hair of yours?" He lifted a section of her wavy auburn locks. "You use all kinds of stuff on it."

"So I like my hair. I'm as happy to put on barn boots and help with chores as I am baking cookies for the ranch hands, you know that."

He shrugged. "I'm just saying. You've got a girly side."

"What about something vintage in look?" The jeweler suggested. "That style is a good blend of no-nonsense and feminine. Like this one here with the floral design, or this filigreed one. Both are feminine, but understated in their elegance."

Daisy looked away from the small tilt to Asa's mouth to check out the rings. Her eye caught on the filigreed one. It looked like branches twining up to hold the stone. Smaller diamonds hid in the branches, catching the light. "That one." She pointed to it.

He took it from the tray and handed it to her. Before she could slip it on her finger to try it on, Asa took it from her and held her left hand in his.

"What?" he asked when she frowned at him. "We should do this right. I asked you without the ring, but I'm still going to be the one to put it on your finger."

"I'm just trying it on."

"Don't care." He slid the ring on.

Daisy's heart skipped as she looked into his eyes. This was all pretend, but somehow, it felt all too real. She forced her gaze away from his and stared down at her hand. The stones glittered in the light.

"What do you think?" Asa's thumb grazed her knuckles.

She swallowed, daring to look at him again. "It's pretty."

"Is it the one you want?"

"Maybe."

"Here's a similar one," the jeweler said.

Daisy tore her eyes away from Asa. She pulled her hand from his and took off the ring. Asa took the one the man offered and slid it onto her hand. This time, Daisy was ready for the flutters that filled her belly.

At least, that's what she told herself. It was a lie, and she knew it, but she refused to acknowledge that fact.

She tried on a couple more rings before she couldn't take it anymore. Besides, she liked the first one. It reminded her of herself. Of growing roots to form something beautiful. Like a life she could be proud of.

"I think I'd like this one." She nudged the ring laying on the velvet mat.

"You're sure?" Asa asked.

She nodded.

"Okay." He looked at the jeweler. "We'll take that one."

"Wonderful. This one has a matching wedding band." He opened the display case and removed a ring, placing it on the mat next to the engagement ring. "Why don't you try them on together?"

Daisy looked at Asa. Wedding rings were not part of their plan. His eyes widened slightly, but he nodded.

"We might as well while we're here. It'll save us a trip later."

"I have some for you to look at as well. Once she chooses a band material."

She hadn't even thought about a ring for Asa. It wasn't necessary since they weren't actually getting married, but the jeweler didn't know that.

"Of course." Asa took the rings from the man and put them together before sliding them onto Daisy's finger. His hands shook, and she looked up, noting the clench to his jaw.

Before she could think much about it, he offered her a tight smile. "They look great." He looked past her to Johnathan. "We'll take them both."

"Excellent." He took a notebook from under the counter between the display cases and set it atop the glass. Daisy handed him the rings, and he wrote down the inventory numbers. "Now, what do you want the bands made of? We carry everything from sterling silver to twenty-four-karat gold and platinum. Though, I wouldn't recommend twenty-four-karat gold for a wedding set. It's too soft."

Daisy glanced at Asa.

He shrugged. "Whatever you want, sweetness."

"I like gold." She looked between the two men. "Especially with the vintage style. Platinum or white gold both seem too modern."

"Okay, then I would recommend eighteen-karat gold," Johnathan said. He walked over to another case and pulled out a tray of men's wedding bands, carrying them over. "Any of these would go well with her set."

Asa, eyes still slightly wider than usual, looked down at the trays. Instantly, Daisy knew which one she would pick for him. She pointed to it. "That one. It has some vining like my engagement ring."

He picked it up to look at it. "Hmm. It's different, but I like it." He gave a quick nod. "Okay. We'll take that too."

"All right. Let's get your sizes." He picked up a set of sizers from the counter and held one up to Daisy. "Try that."

She slid it over her finger, but it was a little loose, so she tried the next size down, which fit perfectly. The jeweler wrote down her size, then repeated the process with Asa. In minutes, he had their order entered into the computer.

Daisy swallowed hard as he read off the total, and Asa

handed over his credit card. That was considerably more than what she expected him to spend on their fake engagement. It was more than she expected a man to spend on her for a real engagement.

Asa's hand on her face startled her out of her shock. He leaned closer, turning his back on the jeweler. "Smile," he whispered. "And act like you like me, or he's going to think you're here under duress."

The lightness to his voice pulled a small smile from her. She laid a hand on his jaw and stood on her toes to place a kiss on his cheek. "Should I exclaim in a loud voice how beautiful it is and how much I love you?" she whispered back.

He laughed and kissed the top of her head. "Later."

"Okay, you two are all set." Johnathan held out Asa's card, smiling at them. "The rings should be ready in about a week."

Asa took the receipt. "Great. Could you have them couriered to us? You can bill the same account for the service."

"Of course. I'll include a receipt for it in the package." He picked up a business card from beside the register. "If you have any questions or concerns, please call."

"We will, thank you." He took the card and pocketed it, then turned to Daisy. "You ready to go?"

She nodded.

He took her hand. After bidding the jeweler goodbye, they left the shop. The photographer who followed them from Pine Ridge stood on the corner behind a signpost, camera raised. Asa changed direction, heading for him.

"What are you doing?" Daisy hissed. She glanced behind her at the truck. Why was he walking toward the paparazzo?

"Marla isn't the only one who can give an interview."

"Interview? Oh, geez. When you said make a statement to the press, I thought you meant through Marty."

The man realized Asa was heading for him and straightened, letting the camera drop. He backed up a few steps.

"I'm not doing anything wrong, man. Just taking pictures in a public place."

Asa stopped several feet away and scoffed. "Not legally, but morally? Everything you guys do is wrong."

The guy shrugged. "People want to know."

"They don't have any right to my private life. But, since you and your friends refuse to leave me alone, I'm throwing you a bone in hopes you'll realize I'm done with the life and just want to be left in peace." He tucked Daisy close. "This is my fiancée, Daisy O'Malley."

The man's eyes widened. "Fiancée?"

"Yes. The story you were fed by Marla Wilkins was nothing more than an old flame, angry I've moved on."

"Why are you telling me this? You denied it when we reported you two were dating."

"Daisy's not part of Hollywood. She just wanted some privacy, so we denied everything. Marla forced our hand. I couldn't in good conscience let the record show that she and I were together when I was about to ask Daisy to marry me."

"Oh."

"Look, I know you're just doing your job, but we would appreciate some privacy. I've retired. Daisy and I want to settle down and raise a family. All you're going to get are pictures of us working the ranch and buying supplies."

The guy stared at them for a moment. "Wait. You retired?"

"Yes." Asa's eyes narrowed. "That was supposed to be part of the statement my manager gave."

"Well, it wasn't." The man shrugged. "From what my boss told me, you're just on an extended break."

"No. I'm retired. Full stop."

"Okay, then. I'll make sure to set the record straight."

"Thank you."

He raised his camera. "How about a picture of the two of you? You give me that and I'll leave you alone. I'll pack up and go home." He held up a hand. "I can't promise others will, but I personally will leave."

Daisy resisted the urge to roll her eyes. She was sure he would. That photo alone would set him up nicely for at least a year. Add the story Asa just spoon fed him, and he'd become the top photojournalist for all the rags. He'd get all the primo jobs now. But if it meant one less person taking pictures of them, she was all for it.

Asa apparently felt similar. He tucked her into his side. "One picture."

The man smiled and raised his camera. "Say cheese."

EIGHTEEN

"Don't answer that!" Daisy flew through the doorway to Asa's office, skidding to a halt. "Dammit!"

Asa glanced up, phone to his ear. He frowned at her, then turned back to the phone. "I'm sorry, say your name again. I didn't catch it."

"Ian O'Malley."

He froze, shock and some dread filling him, then glanced at Daisy. Her eyes were wide and pleading. He had a feeling she wanted him to hang up, but he wasn't about to hang up on her brother. That would just anger the man further. He sighed. He shouldn't have answered the phone. But when it rang, he'd been elbow deep in the ranch books and answered it without looking at the screen. No one had his number except the people he wanted to have it.

"Hello, Mr. O'Malley. How did you get this number?"

"I have resources."

Daisy motioned at him to put the phone on speaker. He pulled it away from his ear and touched the icon, then laid the phone on the desk.

"Look," Ian continued, "I'm not sure what game you're

playing, but my sister is not a toy. She's a naïve young woman who has stars in her eyes."

Asa glanced at Daisy, whose face was so red he feared she would stroke out right there. She shaped her hands into claws and raised them slowly toward the sky while her mouth opened on a silent scream.

He fought to keep a straight face. She was angry, and he didn't blame her. "Mr. O'Malley, Daisy is far from naïve."

"No offense, Mr. Mitchell, but you've only known her a few months. Until she moved out there, I took care of her. She's probably looking for someone to fill that role, and you've taken advantage of that."

The first stirrings of anger hit Asa low in the gut. This man was a total ass. He didn't know how Daisy stood being under his thumb as long as she did. "I'm sorry, but I think you're the one who doesn't know Daisy well. She's done fine out here on her own. I'm not taking advantage of anyone." Sourness filled his mouth at the lie, but it helped to know Daisy was fully aware of the plan. He wasn't deceiving her into doing anything. "She is in this relationship of her own free will."

Ian snorted. "Oh, I'm sure. A man like you pays attention to a woman like her, I'm sure she jumped at the chance. What I don't understand is why you'd want her. You could have anyone. Why my sister? Is it just convenience? Or a lack of other women? Though I don't think that's the problem. I saw the interview from that other woman. Marla. The one claiming to be your girlfriend. Why aren't you with her? You two seem to have a history."

"That's exactly why I'm not. And what do you mean, a woman like her? There's nothing wrong with Daisy. Have you actually looked at her lately? Your sister is a beautiful woman. Inside and out. I'm not marrying her because she's convenient. I'm marrying her because of her." He glanced up at Daisy again. She now stood like a statue in front of the desk, staring at him with a strange look on her face.

"We'll see about that."

"Mr. O'Malley, unless you plan to come here and kidnap Daisy and take her home, there's nothing you can do to stop her. She's a grown woman, fully capable of making her own decisions. My dad and I won't let you bully her into going back to Chicago."

"There will be no bullying. We'll just make her see that marrying you is a foolish decision. I mean, really, what kind of long-term future could she have with a playboy musician?"

Asa resisted the urge to growl. "You're doing little to endear yourself to me. I think we should end this conversation now before either of us says something we'll regret. Have a good day." He stabbed the disconnect icon with his index finger, then sat back in his chair with a huff. His eyes found Daisy's. "Good God, Dais. That's what you had to put up with before you left Chicago? I think I have a new respect for your bullshit tolerance."

Silence greeted him. She stared at him, a small frown between her eyes.

"What?"

"You think I'm beautiful?"

He picked up the pen he put down when Ian called and twirled it between his fingers. "Well, yeah. You are."

Her face colored again. She cleared her throat. "Well, thank you. For the compliment and for telling Ian to shove it. I knew when the story broke, he and the others would go apoplectic, but I never imagined he'd track down your number and call you. When Nori got a text telling her to tell me he was taking things up with you, then I heard your phone ring, I ran in here trying to head him off. I'm sorry."

He waved a hand. "It's not your fault. I'd like to know

how he got my number, though. It's unlisted, and I don't give it out."

She groaned and sank into the chair across from him. Her hair hung in a heavy curtain as she propped her elbows on her knees and covered her face with her hands. "This is a nightmare." She thrust her hands into her thick auburn locks and looked up.

"We knew there would be backlash from your brothers. His anger isn't unexpected."

"No, but it sounds like he's coming here. Like all of them are coming here." She stood. "I need to go talk to Aunt Nori. Maybe she can help me persuade them to stay home."

"Daisy."

She turned, halfway out of the room.

"Even if they do come, I won't let them make you go home. Or convince you that you should. You belong here. Or anywhere that you can make your own decisions and live your own life."

She rolled her lips in and nodded, moisture shimmering in her eyes. Asa hoped she wouldn't start crying. He already had the urge to pull her into his arms and hold her close. Tears would make it worse. If he touched her, he was likely to kiss her too. It got harder every day to resist those full lips.

"Thank you, Asa." She offered him a tremulous smile, then left.

Asa blew out a breath and tossed his pen down. He hoped they hadn't opened a can of worms they couldn't handle. He wasn't sure what he'd do if all of her brothers showed up. Probably punch the oldest one for starters.

Hands full, Daisy danced down the hallway to the music flowing through her earbuds as she put laundry away. She was trying to put the conversation she had with Ian last night out of her mind. After she left Asa's office, she tracked down Nori and told her what happened. She convinced Daisy to call Ian.

She frowned as she set the laundry basket down and yanked open the drawer on Silas's dresser. It hadn't gone well. Not at first. For five solid minutes, he ranted about her naivete in getting involved with such a "worldly" man. About jumping into a relationship with a playboy. Finally, Daisy had enough and hung up. He called right back, of course. When he started ranting again, she hung up again. They repeated that process twice more before he got the hint and let her talk.

Once he calmed down, she told him nothing he could say would change her mind. That she was an adult and could marry whomever she damn well pleased. It wasn't his problem if she ruined her life, because it was *hers*.

That shut him up. It was like he'd never considered it that way before. After he recovered, he told her he still wasn't happy with her decision, but she was right. It was hers to make, and if she wanted to make a dumb one, not to come running to him when everything went to shit.

Daisy assured him she wouldn't. She still wasn't a hundred percent certain he and her other brothers wouldn't show up in the next few days, but she was at least hopeful now they would stay in Chicago.

She finished putting Silas's clothes away and stepped out into the hall to head to Asa's room. Twisting the knob, she threw open the door.

"Daisy! Jesus, don't you knock?"

She shrieked and jumped back, startled, then could do nothing but stare. Asa stood in the middle of the room, naked and dripping wet.

Hands covering himself, he sidestepped to the head of the bed and snatched a pillow to cover up. "What are you doing in here?"

Daisy blinked and swallowed, getting some of her faculties back now that a certain part of him was no longer visible. Did all men look like that? She'd only ever seen a few pictures when one of her high school friends snuck her dad's laptop into her room while Daisy was at her house for a sleepover and they googled naked male models. They only looked at a few before they realized they were flirting with disaster if one of her parents came in to check on them. Sierra deleted their browser history, double-checked it several times, then snuck the computer back down to her dad's office. Asa's package was the first she'd ever seen up close. The pictures didn't hold a candle to what he had between his legs.

She cleared her throat. "I was putting laundry away. Why are you here? Better yet, when did you get here? I said goodbye to you when you left with your dad earlier."

"I came back to shower. I tripped and fell into a pile of cow manure. There was too much for the hose."

"Oh." She didn't move, transfixed by the expanse of his chest and abs. Good lord, he put all the underwear models to shame. There wasn't an ounce of fat on his six-foot-six frame.

"Daisy?"

"Hmm?" Her eyes jerked to his.

A slow grin spread over his face. Pillow still clutched to his hips, he strode closer.

Her breath hitched. What was he doing?

He stopped a couple of feet away, his abdomen bumping her hand that held the laundry basket to her waist. "If you wanted to see me naked, all you had to do was ask."

Her eyebrows slammed down, his words clearing the lust fog from her brain. "Ass." She shoved the basket at him. "Here." He scrambled to take it so all the clothes wouldn't dump onto the floor. "Put your own damn laundry away." She whirled on her heel, her hair fanning out in a smooth sweep behind her as she did so. She made it two steps before she heard a bang as the basket hit the floor, and he grabbed her hand. With a yank, he spun her around, sending her crashing into his chest. His hard, still damp, naked chest.

She grabbed his shoulders to steady herself and looked up.

Bad idea.

His mouth was inches from hers.

The teasing smile on his face died. His pupils dilated, and his gaze locked on her mouth. Daisy's heartbeat ratcheted up. Was he going to kiss her? Did she want him to? Her body screamed yes, but her mind was pumping the brakes and telling her she needed to back away. They were friends. Barely. And friends didn't kiss. Especially when one was naked.

But her body overruled her brain, and she stayed right where she was. No matter how loud she shouted the command for her feet to move, they stayed planted to the bedroom floor.

He let go of her hand to curve it around her waist as he continued to stare down at her. His head inched lower. The fine hairs on Daisy's scalp rose, along with all the ones on her arms and neck. Her fingers dug into the muscles atop his shoulders, anticipating the need to have a good hold once his mouth touched hers. She was already feeling a little jelly-like.

Asa closed the distance, settling his mouth on hers in a soft kiss. It was an exploratory touch. One meant to test the waters. It was heavenly.

Daisy let out a soft gasp as the heat hit her, electrifying her body. That little sound sent Asa past exploratory. He captured her mouth in a more forceful kiss, opening his mouth against hers and encouraging her to let him in. Something soft hit her feet a moment before he speared a hand through her hair. When he thrust his tongue into her mouth, his hips mimicking the action, she realized he'd dropped the pillow. The hard length of his shaft pressed into her belly.

Startled by the feeling, she broke the kiss to look up at him. "What—what are we doing?"

Don't look down, don't look down.

She repeated the mantra in her head several times. If she looked down, she'd want to touch. And if she touched, who knew what would happen? She wasn't ready for that. Nor was it wise. This was a fake engagement. Nothing about their relationship was real except the friendship.

He arched a brow. "Just how inexperienced are you? Because if I have to explain it, then—"

She waved a hand to cut him off, then bent down to pick up the pillow so he could cover himself. Except that put her face-to-face with the part of his anatomy she was so determined not to look at. It bobbed as she stared, moisture glistening on the tip.

Asa growled and hooked a hand under her arm, pulling her up. "Are you trying to kill me?"

"No, I—"

He pulled her close again, pressing a searing kiss to her mouth. His tongue dove past her lips to plunder inside. Daisy's head spun. Feelings she'd never felt before, ones she didn't even know she could feel, flowed through her limbs to pool in her center. Her breasts ached, wanting his touch. She rubbed against him with a moan.

With a groan, he broke away and took the pillow from her to hold it in front of himself. "You should probably go unless you want to find out if all the stories about my prowess in bed are true."

Daisy took a step back toward the door, giving him a shaky nod. "Right. That wouldn't be wise. Because we aren't really engaged. Or dating. This is all pretend." She clamped her lips together to stop the flow of words spewing from her mouth. Her eyes flicked down to the pillow once more, remembering how he felt pressed against her. Fire erupted in her core and traveled up to her cheeks as she looked up at his face again. He stood there, staring at her, his jaw like granite. The same muscles she admired moments ago looked harder, more defined. *Damn*.

"Daisy."

"Hmm?"

He tipped his head toward the door.

"Oh, right. Yes, I'm leaving." She took another step backward, then turned, hurrying from the room, pulling the door closed behind her. Once in the hall, she stopped a few feet from his door and leaned against the wall.

Her head spun, and her heart still triple-timed in her chest. She'd kissed Asa. And liked it. And she wanted more. Oh, hell. This was a problem.

Daisy sank into a booth at Sarafina's. She needed a chocolate shake. And some french fries. Comfort food was a necessity after what happened in Asa's bedroom. Her mind was still in a tailspin.

"Hey, girl. What are you doing here at this hour?" Sara said, walking up to the table. "Not that I'm complaining. I enjoy seeing you, but you're not usually in town for lunch."

"Oh, God, Sara," Daisy said on a groan. She covered her face. "I think I really screwed things up."

"What?" The booth creaked as Sara sat down across from her. "What are you talking about? What happened?"

She dropped her hands to look at her friend. "I kissed Asa."

Sara's eyes went wide. Then she smiled. "It's about damn time."

"Huh?" Daisy frowned. Her expression smoothed out as she realized Sara thought she and Asa should be more than friends. "No." She shook a finger in the air. "No. He and I are not a good idea."

"Why not? I think you're good for him. You don't put up with his shit. And I've seen the way he looks at you. Like he's trying to figure you out. It's cute."

"He probably is, because I won't fall at his feet like everyone else he's met in the last fifteen years."

Sara giggled. "Exactly. You ground him. He needs someone like you in his life." She shrugged. "You're already pretending to be engaged to him. Why not take advantage of some of the benefits that go with being his fiancée?" She waggled her eyebrows.

Daisy's face flamed as an image of Asa's naked body flashed through her mind.

Sara's smile broadened. "I take it the kiss was good?"

Daisy covered her face again and nodded. "And he was naked."

A burst of laughter flew from Sara's mouth before she cut it off. Her eyes sparkled as she looked at Daisy. "I'm almost afraid to ask what happened."

"Nothing crazy. I was putting laundry away, and I went into his room. What I didn't know was that he came home to take a shower after falling into some manure. He was just coming out of the bathroom when I walked in."

"Oh my. Please tell me you looked."

"Of course I looked. Then he opened his damn mouth and said something snarky, so I shoved the clothes basket at him and tried to storm away, but he wouldn't let me. The next thing I knew, we were kissing and I was wishing I was naked too."

Sara giggled again, stifling it when Daisy narrowed her eyes. "Sorry. I don't mean to laugh, but it is kind of funny. I figured something like this would happen eventually. You two were fire and ice from the beginning. There was something there just waiting for you to explore it."

"Yes, well, it can go back to waiting." She glanced around to make sure no one could hear them. "I don't want a relationship with Asa. I don't want a relationship with any man right now. I just got out from under six. I want to be on my own."

"Oh, sweetie." Sara covered one of her hands. "Being in a relationship—a good one—won't feel like you're being smothered or controlled. It'll be a partnership, and it'll make your life feel more full and richer." She frowned. "If your brothers ever show up here, they're going to get a piece of my mind. Assholes."

Daisy giggled despite herself. "They can be that, yes. But I think things are changing. I talked to Ian the other day. He's not happy about the engagement, but he's finally realizing it's my life to screw up."

"Good." She patted Daisy's hand. "So far, though, I think you're doing just fine."

"So long as I didn't ruin everything by kissing Asa. I don't want to create tension in the house because of this. We never agreed to anything physical past handholding in public. I can't live in a place where I'm tiptoeing around again, trying not to make waves. I finally get to be me. I don't want any awkwardness between him and me to put a damper on that. To walk around waiting for the other shoe to drop and for him to get sick of the inexperienced housekeeper who wants to jump his bones. It could be enough to convince Silas to send me packing."

"That's never going to happen. Silas sees you like a daughter. Unless you betray Asa in some way, he'll never send you away. And honestly, I don't think Asa will let things fester between you. He's never been one to not speak his mind. He'll let you know how he feels about the whole thing, I promise."

"What if he wants more?"

"So? There are worse men you could date. And you're already dealing with the media scrutiny, not to mention the flak from your brothers. Why are you so scared of taking things to the next level with him?"

That was a good question. Every reason she could have for wanting to avoid a relationship with Asa was already in play. Except her heart. She had a feeling he could fillet it wide open if she didn't watch herself. There was also one other reason. One that made her shake at the thought.

She sighed and hung her head, running her hands through her hair. "I don't want to leave, Sara. If things go south, I'm the one who has to move. I love it here."

"You don't have to go anywhere, Dais, if you don't want to. Sure, you'll have to leave the ranch, but that doesn't mean you can't stay in town. I'll give you a job in a heartbeat. Hell, if you want to start a baking line, I'll do that now. I'd double my income from your cupcakes alone." She took Daisy's hands. "How about you stop worrying about things that might never happen and just live?"

Daisy huffed. Sara was right. She needed to quit borrowing trouble. Things would work out just as they were supposed to. "Fine. But can I have a chocolate shake and some fries to help?"

Sara laughed. "Sure. I'll even add extra whipped cream. And two cherries."

Daisy grinned. "Awesome." She squeezed Sara's hands, then let go. "Thank you. I needed a voice of reason."

"I'm not sure I'm that, but I am your friend. And I'm always happy to lend an ear." She gave Daisy's hands another quick squeeze then let go and stood. "I'll be back in a few minutes with your food. On the house." She winked and walked away.

Heaving another sigh, Daisy let her head fall back against the booth. Her mind was still a little jumbled—mostly from that mind-blowing kiss—but she felt better after hearing Sara's take on things. She was going to take things a day at a time and see where they went. If that was the last thing that happened between them, so be it. If not, well, she'd deal with it as it came.

Sara brought her shake and fries, and Daisy quickly ate. She wanted to run by the grocery before she went home. They were nearly out of flour, and she wanted to make bread to go with dinner tonight.

After she slurped down the last of her shake, she left Sara a nice tip, then waved to her friend and left the diner. The grocery store was only a couple blocks away, so she decided to walk. The weather today was nice. It wasn't as hot as it had been, but the sun still shone brightly. She wished it would rain, though. They could use some.

The doors to the store swooshed open as she stepped up to them, blasting Daisy with the cooler air inside. She grabbed a basket from the stack and started wandering the aisles, getting the bag of flour she wanted, as well as some wine— because today called for wine—and a box of toaster pastries for Silas. It was one of the few things she hadn't been able to change in his diet. The man loved them. If she didn't buy them on her grocery runs, he would buy himself a box when- ever he went to town and he was out. He even started writing it on her list, so she gave in. There were worse things he could eat.

As she entered the produce section, the whispers regis- tered. Looking up from the display of grapes, Daisy glanced around, noting the people trying not to stare at her. Her cheeks reddened as she realized she'd been recognized. She looked down, doing her best to ignore them. Like the media, this, too, would eventually fade.

Grapes in hand, she moved to the bananas. They had some at home, but they were ripe and she wanted to use them to make bananas foster for dessert. Asa liked to eat them for breakfast, so they would need more.

"So, is it true what they say?"

Daisy jumped. She turned to look at the woman who'd come up next to her. "Is what true?"

"That Asa's good in bed." She sighed. "You're such a lucky woman. I'd give my eyeteeth for an hour with that man."

Color flooded Daisy's cheeks again, but for a different reason. "What it is, is none of your business. Tell me, if he wasn't famous, would you say that to me?"

The woman frowned up at her. "Well, you don't have to get all huffy. I was just saying. He's hot."

"Yes, he is. And he's mine, so I'd kindly ask you to refrain from talking about him like that." Glowering at the woman, Daisy plucked a bunch of bananas off the stand and walked away. It was absurd, the way people thought they could treat Asa like a piece of meat just because he was a celebrity. He was still a man with feelings.

Angry, she didn't see Marla come from another aisle toward the checkout stands until it was too late. Daisy crashed into her cart, sending it into a display of paper towels. With soft thuds, they rained down to bounce and roll across the floor.

Eyes rolling and shoulders slumping, she shook her head. Could this day get worse? She looked at Marla, who stared at the mess in shock for a moment before she turned her eyes to Daisy. A slow smile bloomed on her face. And not a nice one.

Daisy held out a hand to stave off anything she could say. "I'm sorry. I didn't see you." She set her basket down and started chasing down paper towel rolls.

Marla laughed. "You're such an awkward creature. What he sees in you, I'll never know. You must give good head. I remember he likes that."

Her fingers dug into the paper towels she clutched. Every

ounce of control she had went into not heaving it at Marla's head. Instead, she ignored the other woman and looked at the worker who'd come to help her clean up. "I'm sorry about the mess. I didn't see Marla and ran right into her. Her cart hit the display."

The young man smiled. "That's okay. You're actually not the first one to knock it over. Though this one is the worst."

Daisy smiled. "Maybe you should stack them elsewhere."

He shrugged. "I would, but the boss wants them here. I just keep restacking them when they fall."

Marla huffed and steered her cart around them. "Some of us have better things to do today. I need to get back to my store." She tossed Daisy a cutting smile. "It might be worth closing for the day, though, to go find Asa and remind him who's better at satisfying his needs."

Daisy rolled her eyes. "Go for it. I'm sure he'd love to call the cops on you and have you arrested for assault. After that interview you gave, he's just itching for a reason to press charges against you."

Marla's smile died.

"Oh, and don't forget about our court date next week. I think you should probably keep your store open every opportunity you can. Paint jobs on cars aren't cheap." She gave her a sweet smile. "Have a nice day."

Marla's mouth twisted, but she kept her mouth shut and stomped off.

The young man helping Daisy chuckled. "Thank you."

She looked at him with a curious smile. "For what?"

"Telling her off. She's always complaining about things we don't have. Stuff we've never carried. Saying she thinks we need to. She's the only one who would buy it, and she can get it online. I wish I could tell her where to shove it, but I just smile and tell her I'll let the manager know." He took the rolls she offered him and stacked them up. "I'm glad you moved to town. You make people smile."

Daisy blushed. "Well, thank you." She handed him several more rolls.

"You're welcome."

She finished helping him pick up the display, then headed for the checkout to pay for her items. In minutes, she had two bags of groceries and was heading out to walk back to her car. She only made it to the corner before she noticed the man with the camera across the street, snapping pictures of her from a vehicle. She squinted at him, trying to determine if it was the guy from outside the jewelers, but it didn't look like the same man. At least he seemed to have honored his word and left them alone. Now they just had all the others to worry about.

Quickening her pace, she made a beeline for where she parked. She should have just driven to the store, nice weather be damned. Until things calmed down, she wouldn't make that mistake again.

At her car, she pushed the button on her key fob to unlock her doors and got in, throwing her bags onto the passenger seat. Reaching for the button to start the car, she paused as she looked out the windshield. An envelope was tucked under her wiper.

"What now?" Huffing, she got out and snatched it, then tore it open as she sat down. Inside, was a photo, torn to pieces. "What the hell?" She took a few pieces out and laid them on the center console, trying to figure out what they were. It didn't take her long to realize it was a picture of her and Asa as they exited the jewelers. But it wasn't one the paparazzo took. The angle was wrong. Someone else had followed them that day.

Alarmed, she stuffed it all back in the envelope and started her car, then headed for the police station. Once there, she parked in the most obscure spot she could find and prayed the photographers following her wouldn't see her car. The last thing she needed was for one of them to write a story accusing Asa of abuse.

Head on a swivel, she hurried into the building. At the front desk, she asked to speak to Detective Mike Swanson. When she turned the first letter she received over to the police, they referred her to him. He hadn't found any leads yet, but maybe this would help. She didn't particularly care if they arrested anyone. She just wanted the harassment to stop.

"Ms. O'Malley?"

She looked to her left to see the detective leaning around a doorway. He motioned her toward him with a tip of his graying head.

"You asked to see me?" He led her through the door to a larger room full of desks. Several were occupied with plain-clothes cops, each of them hiding behind stacks of paperwork and coffee mugs. They stopped at a desk midway through the room, and he gestured for her to sit down.

Daisy perched on the edge of the chair and took the envelope from her purse. "This was on my car after I went to the grocery."

He took the envelope by the edges and lifted the flap, peering inside. "A torn picture?"

She nodded. "It's from when Asa and I went to pick out rings last week. We knew we were followed, but we thought it was just one reporter. We talked to the guy. I don't think he took that picture. The angle's wrong. He was on the corner. That looks like it was from the other direction and across the street."

He tipped the pieces out on his desk and put on some gloves, arranging them. "And you didn't see anyone else watching you?"

"No. But I didn't really look. The reporter we talked to

was the most persistent and obvious of all the ones following us around, so we were focused on him."

"Okay." He pushed a notepad toward her. "Write down the name of the jewelers and the address, if you know it. I'll check the area for security cameras. Where were you parked when you found this? The grocery?"

Daisy picked up a pen and wrote down the name of the jeweler. She didn't know the address, so she wrote the city name. "No. I went to Sarafina's first for lunch. I left my car parked near there and walked. I only needed a few things."

"Okay. I'll check that area out too. Have you received any other letters since the one you brought me?"

She shook her head. "No."

"Any weird hang up calls?"

"No."

"Good." He picked up a sheet of paper and handed it to her. "Fill that out and I'll add it to your report."

She nodded and wrote her name on the witness statement. "Do you think you'll be able to find who this is? I'm not scared so much as I'm annoyed. I just want to be left alone."

He nodded. "I understand. I'll do my best to find who it is. But keep an eye out. People like this don't always stay in the shadows, so you should be careful. I also need to talk to Asa and that reporter. See if they saw anything."

Daisy sighed. Great. Just great. She'd been hoping not to involve Asa in any of this. He was going to flip.

Nineteen

Asa pulled into the driveway after running to a neighboring ranch to get a piece of equipment Chet loaned to them and stopped at the mailbox out of habit. He called after Asa watched Daisy stumble out of his room and asked if he could go to the neighbors and get it since he was already up at the house.

He used his key to open the hatch on the back—a security feature they put in years ago after a fan rifled through their mail. He was sure Daisy already grabbed the mail, but figured he should check anyway. When he peered inside, he was glad he did. It was still full.

Taking it all out, he went through it quick, looking for anything important. The only thing intriguing was a plain envelope addressed to Daisy. He frowned as he considered what it could be. He didn't know much about her life before she showed up here. Just that she had a lot of overprotective brothers and worked as a baker. Maybe she had an old boyfriend she kept in contact with. Though why he would send letters instead of emails or calling, he didn't know. He tossed it onto the passenger seat atop the other mail and frowned, bothered by the thought some other man might be conversing with Daisy. He shouldn't be. It wasn't like they were together.

The memory of their kiss a few hours ago surged to the forefront. His dick twitched as he remembered the sight of her on her knees in front of him. He adjusted himself in his pants, squirming in his seat. It had taken all he had not to wrap a hand in her hair and urge her forward.

Angry with himself and his continued reaction to her, he put the truck in gear only to throw it back into park when a delivery van pulled up behind him. Asa got out of his truck and walked toward the van.

The driver rolled down his window. "I have a delivery for Asa Mitchell."

"That's me."

"ID, please."

He dug into his pocket and took out his wallet, flashing the driver his license.

The man held up a clipboard. "Sign here."

Asa scrawled his name on the sheet and handed it back.

"Here you go." The driver handed him a box.

"Thanks." Asa stepped back, looking at the label as he went back to his truck. It was from the jewelers.

A heaviness settled in his gut. What they were doing would help them both in the long run, but it still bothered him, lying like this. His dad didn't raise him to deceive people or to pull others into a lie. He'd done both. There was also the idea that the more time he spent with Daisy, the more real this felt. He didn't want a relationship. She didn't either. But he'd be damned if he hadn't looked forward to coming in from a hard day to her smiling face and home cooking the last several days.

He just hoped all that wasn't ruined because of what happened between them this morning. His plan was to ignore it for now and act like nothing happened. He'd just do his best not to end up naked around her again and they should be able to keep their hands to themselves.

Sure. No problem.

Asa snorted as his conscience mocked him. It was probably right, but he would still do his damnedest to continue like nothing changed.

He parked near the house and gathered the mail, climbing out of the truck.

"Mail call." Asa walked inside and tossed the envelope with no return address at Daisy as he entered the kitchen. She let out a yelp as the letter came flying at her, where she stood at the counter, kneading a ball of bread dough. Her hands bobbled it, but she managed to catch it before it hit the floor.

"Thanks." She glared at him.

He grinned and laid the rest of the stack on the counter for her to look through. "You're welcome. That one looked interesting. Thought you might want to read it first. Old boyfriend sending you mail? I hope not, because our rings just arrived." He waved the box at her.

She turned the envelope over in her hands, ignoring what he said. Her face paled, and the smile on Asa's face died.

"What? What's in the letter?" Scenarios flooded his mind. Was she sick and it was from a doctor? Was it about one of her brothers or nieces and nephews? An old friend?

She sighed and motioned him to the table. "You should probably sit down. I need to talk to you, anyway."

"Why? What's going on?"

She pulled out a chair and pointed to it. "Sit."

"Fine." He took the chair and slid into it. "I'm sitting. Now explain, please."

She sat next to him, holding the letter by the edges. "So, I've been getting letters from someone angry about our relationship."

His eyebrows slammed down. "What? For how long? Why are you just now telling me about this?"

Daisy held up a hand. "Relax. They're not that bad. This is only the third one. The first one told me just to back off. The second was a ripped-up picture of us the day we bought those." She pointed to the box.

"Where are they? I want to see them."

"I gave them both to the police. Actually, the picture showed up today. Someone put it in an envelope under the wipers on my car when I went to town." She looked at the envelope. "I'm surprised they sent a letter too."

"Or maybe it's another person."

Her head bobbed in agreement. "Could be. I saw Marla at the grocery. Maybe she tailed us to Billings and we didn't see her because we were focused on the reporter."

He frowned. "Open that. I want to see what's in it."

She got up and found the letter opener in the junk drawer and slid it under the flap, then removed the single sheet of paper inside. He stood up to stand next to her while she unfolded it.

"Actions have consequences. Back off or pay." His frown deepened as he read the letter aloud. Jaw working, he looked at her. "I don't like this. You shouldn't be in danger because of me. Maybe you should leave."

Daisy's spine straightened. "And go where? I'm not running back to my brothers. And unless I completely leave town, whoever this is won't stop. We'll still be near each other. I don't want to go anywhere else, Asa. Pine Ridge is my home. I've made friends here, and I like this place."

"I know, but—"

She turned away, setting the letter on the counter to go back to her bread. "I'm not running away. I'm not giving up the life I've built the last few months because some crazy person thinks they're entitled to you."

He growled, shoving a hand through his hair as he watched her. Her shoulders and face were set. They said he wouldn't be able to persuade her to go anywhere. And he knew his dad would agree with her. He would want her to stay where they could protect her. If they sent her away, she could still be a target, but she'd be on her own.

"Okay. Stay. But you don't leave the ranch alone. If you go into town, someone needs to go with you. I don't care who, but take someone, even if it's just Nori."

She paused her kneading to lift an eyebrow at him. "Is that really necessary? Other than the letters, no one has tried to contact me."

"Yes, it's necessary. I've dealt with my fans for years. Some of them get zealous in their dedication. If one of them sees you as a threat to me or to the fantasy they've created in their minds, there's no telling what they'll do."

She blew a tendril of hair out of her face and went back to kneading the dough. "Fine. I won't leave the ranch alone. Happy?"

"Enough, yes." He went back to the table and picked up the box and tore it open, taking out the two ring boxes. Flicking open the lid on her rings, he stared at them, an idea taking root. "Maybe we should go ahead and get married."

The dough slid across the counter as her hand slipped. She turned to look at him. "Are you nuts? What would that accomplish?"

He shrugged, glancing at her, then back to her rings. "Safety for you in the form of better legal protection from the crazies out there."

"Asa, I don't need any of that. Detective Swanson will find the person responsible."

"And do what? They haven't really done anything to you, Daisy. The most we can hope for is a protection order. Without fingerprints on the letters or any other identifiable information, we can't link anything to anyone, so they could continue to send you stuff without fear of consequence. And a piece of paper won't stop them from shooting you while you're loading groceries into the car, or ramming you off the road, or—"

Daisy laid a finger on his lips. "A marriage certificate won't stop any of that, either."

He sighed and plucked the engagement ring from its box. "No, but it might give them and others the hint that I'm unattainable, and they'll leave you alone." He grinned. "Plus, my lawyer's a shark. Any charge he can convince a D.A. to press, he will." He took her hand and held the ring over the tip of her finger. "I just don't want to see anything happen to you. You might be a pain in my backside on a good day, but I care about you. About what happens to you."

"Which is not a valid reason to get married."

"It's about as valid as any other." He pushed the ring onto her hand, but didn't let go, toying with it with his thumb.

She scoffed. "What about love?"

He rolled his eyes. "A myth."

"You think love is a myth?"

He nodded. "I've never experienced it. And I've looked." He'd been in many relationships through the years, always thinking maybe this was the one. It never turned out that way.

"Well, you've been looking in the wrong places. Or at the wrong women. You said yourself most of the women you date want you for your money and fame. You need someone who wants you for you."

"Like you?"

She yanked her hand away. "No. I don't want you. Not like that." She turned back to her bread, balling it up to put it in a bowl.

"Really? Because you sure looked like you did this morning."

Her cheeks reddened. "I responded the way any straight, hot-blooded woman would when presented with your naked body. I mean, I know you've looked in a mirror, so..." She took the plastic wrap from the drawer and drew out a piece, refusing to look at him.

He walked up behind her, getting in her space to speak directly into her ear. "So, you're saying I'm just a body to you? That you just want to use me like all the other women I know?"

She spun around. "That's not what I said at all. Don't put words in my mouth, Asa Mitchell."

"How about something else?" He kissed her, pushing into her mouth to taste her. He knew it was a bad idea, but he couldn't resist. Putting that ring on her finger shifted something inside him. Logically, he knew they weren't an item, but his body didn't care. It wanted this woman and screamed at him that she was his.

She moaned and circled his neck with her arms. He leaned into her, trapping her against the counter. His free hand traveled up her side. He wanted to touch her generous curves. To fill his hands with them and watch as she responded to his caress.

The ring box landed on the counter beside the bread bowl as he let go to grab the curve of her butt. His fingers kneaded the soft flesh there, holding her hips tight to his. She rocked into him and moaned again. He tunneled his hand under her t-shirt, needing to feel her skin. His fingers closed over the mound of her breast. The peak pushed against his palm through the satin of her bra. He tugged the cup down and rolled it between his fingers.

She broke their kiss with a gasp. "Asa."

He leaned in to rain kisses on her neck, nipping her earlobe as he continued to play with her breast. Her nails raked his scalp as she tunneled her hands into his hair. Any rational thoughts he might have had fled as she gripped the strands and held him close.

Moving back to her mouth, he fused their lips together again, then thrust his other hand under her shirt to grip her other breast. Her hands tugged his shirt from his pants, finding their way beneath it to skim his abs. He moaned as her soft hands flirted with the hills and valleys of his torso. He was a few more caresses away from stripping her shorts off and taking her on the counter.

Knowing his control was slipping, he moved her bra back into place and slid his hands from beneath her shirt, gentling the kiss. Breathing hard, he looked down at her. Her cheeks were flushed and her lips were swollen from his kisses. He pulsed behind his fly and resisted the urge to kiss her again, picking up where they left off.

"So this morning wasn't a fluke."

Awareness crept back into her eyes, lifting the lust-filled glaze they'd taken on. She drew in a shaky breath. "It doesn't matter what it is. It can't happen." She turned back to her bread dough. "I need to get back to this. You should go put the rings in your safe, then go help Chet. I'm sure he and the others are missing you."

His mouth flattened. He hated that she dismissed him so easily, but he wasn't going to press the issue. Especially since his own feelings were all jumbled up. "I'll leave it be for now, Daisy. But what's between us isn't going away. Call Detective Swanson and tell him about the latest letter." He tucked his shirt back into his jeans and headed for the door. "I'll see you later."

She nodded, not looking at him. He stifled a sigh and left. His simple plan to get his life back was turning out to not be so simple.

Dammit.

TWENTY

Sweat poured off Asa's brow as he chucked hay bales from the wagon onto the conveyor belt that led to the barn loft. Chet stood at the top, pulling them inside for Jasper and a couple other hands to stack. Today, they were stocking up for the winter months with a double load of hay. Half would be used over the next month or so. The rest was for colder weather. They'd do this each month now through early fall, so they didn't have to worry about clearing a path through the snow to get hay into the barn. He was thankful he had the funds to do this ahead of time. He'd done restocking in the winter. It sucked, and he had the frost bite scars on his hands to prove it.

His phone rang from his pocket, and he straightened, motioning Chet to take a break.

"You're worse than a woman," he yelled down.

Asa waved him off, smiling, and answered his phone. It was Marty. "Yeah, Marty?"

"You sound winded. Did I interrupt something?"

Asa rolled his eyes at the smile in his manager's voice. "Get your mind out of the gutter. I'm stocking the hay loft. What do you want?"

"So, I know you said you were done performing, but something's come up."

"Marty—"

"It's for Make-A-Wish, Asa." Marty's voice was quiet, but it cut off his protest.

"When and where?" He didn't even have to think about whether to accept the offer. He'd say yes to charities almost any day if they helped kids. Especially sick ones.

"As soon as we can arrange it. And the girl is in Chicago. She's fourteen and doesn't have much time left. Ewing's Sarcoma. It's a bone cancer."

"Where are we doing this? And what all does she want?"

"She wants the full concert experience, so I was thinking you could do a charity event for the foundation. She can invite whoever she wants, and we could sell tickets for the rest of the seats. It could be a small venue."

Asa pursed his lips. "I'd rather not go that route. Then it's only open to people who can afford the tickets outside of those she invites. What if we open it to hospital staff and their families? And I'll make a donation that would match the ticket sales we're surrendering."

"That's thousands of dollars, Ace."

"So? It's not like I don't have it to spare."

"I guess. It's your money, so whatever. I'll call the foundation back, and we'll work on setting things up. There's one other thing, though. This girl, she saw the article about you and Daisy in the paper. She wants to meet her."

Asa pinched the bridge of his nose. "In Chicago? I can ask, but no guarantees."

"Why wouldn't she? If she's the woman I think she is, she'll jump at the chance to bring some sunshine to a dying girl's last days."

Yep, Marty had her pegged. She'd go, even at the expense of herself. And he couldn't hide this from her. Someone would tell her where he was and what he was doing.

"I'll ask and text you later with her response. Let me know when this is happening as soon as you can, so we can plan here for my absence."

"You got it. Talk to you soon." He hung up.

Asa turned off his phone screen and stuffed it back in his pocket, groaning. He didn't mind charity events, but with everything going on, the timing couldn't be worse.

"Everything okay?" Chet asked from the hayloft.

"Yeah, it's fine." He picked up a bottle of water and took a long swallow. "Let's get back to work." He capped the bottle and set it on the ground, then picked up another bale and tossed it on the belt.

Daisy rinsed the last plate from dinner and put it in the dishwasher. She was going to crack open that bottle of wine and settle into her bathtub with a book as soon as she pressed start.

"Hey, you up for a walk?" Asa came up behind her and touched her shoulder.

"I was going to go relax in the tub. Can it wait until tomorrow?"

His eyes darkened, and he cleared his throat. "Actually, no. We won't stay out long. There's just something I need to talk to you about."

She blew her hair out of her face and nodded, reaching for a dishtowel to dry her hands. "Okay, fine. But it better be quick. There's a bottle of wine chilling in the fridge and a brand-new book on my nightstand with my name on them."

A smile quirked his mouth. "I'll do my best. You ready now?"

"Yeah." She pushed start on the dishwasher. "Should we tell your dad or Nori where we're going?"

"I already told dad we were going to step out for a few minutes."

"Sure of yourself, were you?"

His smile grew as he walked with her into the mudroom. "I've been known to be persuasive."

"Hmm, yes, I suppose you have." She giggled and shoved her feet into her tennis shoes.

He put on his boots, then held the door for her. They walked for a minute or so before she broke the silence.

"So, why did we have to come out here to talk? Why couldn't we discuss this inside?"

"I wasn't sure you wanted to chance Nori overhearing our conversation."

Daisy stopped, frowning up at him. "Why wouldn't I want her to hear what we were talking about?"

"Because I figured you'd want to tell her about it in your own way."

"My own way? Asa, what's going on?"

"I got a call from Marty today. Make-A-Wish called him to ask if I would give a charity concert for a girl dying of cancer."

She gasped and covered her mouth. "Oh, that's terrible. I hope you said yes."

"Of course I did."

"I still don't understand why this is something you wouldn't want Nori to just overhear."

"The girl lives in Chicago, so I need to go there."

"Oh."

"And she saw the article about us. She wants to meet you."

"Oh." Her eyes widened. "Okay, I get it now."

"I wouldn't ask if it weren't for the circumstances. I know you don't want to go back there right now."

"No. You're right to ask. And of course I'll go. We just won't tell my brothers I'm in town."

He frowned. "Are you sure that's the right course to take? Won't they be angrier that you were there and didn't tell them? It'll be in the tabloids. They'll know you're there."

Her shoulders sagged. "Damn. I didn't think about that." Her mouth pulled as she thought of something else. "Ian might find out anyway. He's a pediatric oncologist. Though, there are several children's hospitals in the area. Do you know which one she's being treated at?"

"No. And even if it's his hospital, you don't have to see them. I'll make sure of it. But maybe you should leave it up to them if they want to meet you and talk amicably."

"What if I don't want to talk to them? Even amicably." She crossed her arms and looked past him at the horses milling in the corral attached to the barn.

He touched her elbow. "At some point, you need to work things out with them, Daisy. You've been here four months. I think you've all had time to cool off. Don't let things fester."

She arched a brow at him. "What makes you an expert?"

"Nothing. I just know you're hurting by not having that connection. I saw how happy you were when Nori arrived. You love having her here."

"Well, yeah, but she's always been supportive."

"And your brothers haven't? They were there for you when your mom and dad died. Made sure you were safe and cared for even after you moved out on your own. So they took things a little overboard. You let them, and by the time you realized what they were doing, you didn't know how to get out without completely cutting them out of your life. Look, I'm not defending their actions, but I think you've all learned a lot about each other and your relationship in the last few months. I know they love you, and you know it too. The dynamic just needs to change. And it already has, but if you want that to continue, you need to mend fences with them."

Daisy bit her lip. "Dammit. Why do you have to be so logical? Aren't you supposed to be an impulsive jackass?"

His mouth quirked. "They're not mutually exclusive."

She laughed. "True enough."

He took her hand and tugged her close. "Just think about what I said?"

She sighed. "Yeah, okay."

"Good. Come on. Let's walk off some of that excellent dinner and dessert you made and make room for a snack later."

Daisy giggled. "Or in my case, the wine and chocolate waiting on me."

"Oh, there's chocolate too?" He waggled his eyebrows. "How about you let me join you, and I'll bring whipped cream and cherries? We can make some sundaes." His eyes heated.

She felt her face flame. "You're wicked."

He flashed a grin. "Yes, but I guarantee you'll enjoy every second."

Daisy was sure she would, but that was a rabbit hole she wasn't ready to go down. She doubted she ever would be. Not with a man like Asa Mitchell. He'd been with some of the most beautiful and experienced women in the world. She was just a plain Jane whose only experience with men was some heavy petting and awkward kissing. She wouldn't even know where to start when it came to pleasing a man like Asa.

She hummed. "Well, I doubt we'll find out, because we're just friends."

He sighed. "Right. I forgot you're determined that's all we'll be."

"Well, do you blame me?" She glanced at him. "Nothing about our relationship is normal." She shook her hand from his, ready to escape his presence before she gave in to the desire humming through her veins. "Can we go back to the house now?"

"Yeah." He turned around.

"You'll let me know when this trip is, right?"

He nodded. "Once I get the details from Marty, you'll be the first one I tell. It'll be a couple of weeks until we go, at least. Probably around the Fourth of July."

"Okay. That sounds good. That gives me time to make some extra meals for Silas and treats for the hands. Wait. Is Silas coming with us?"

Asa shrugged. "Not sure. I'll leave it up to him. Things have calmed down a bit now that calving season is winding down. We'll have to talk to Chet and see what he thinks."

She nodded. They reached the house and walked inside, but didn't make it much past the threshold. Daisy stopped and stared through the mudroom door at the sight in the kitchen. Asa ran into her back as she slapped her hands over her mouth to contain a squeak of surprise.

"Why did you—" He broke off as he saw what stopped her. "Oh my God!" he whispered.

"Right?" She dropped her hands and just stared as she watched Silas kiss her aunt in much the same way Asa had kissed her earlier. He had her backed up against the counter, one hand tangled in her hair and the other around her waist.

Daisy reached back and put a hand on Asa's chest, pushing against it. "Go back outside."

"What? Why?"

"Because we want to give them a chance to right themselves before we come bursting in. Go out, and we'll come back in making more noise." She backed up, herding him toward the door with her hips. He put a hand on one, but went outside.

Once back on the lawn, Daisy couldn't hold in the laugh

at what they just witnessed. "I knew they liked each other, but I didn't think they'd take things that far."

Asa tried to hold in his smile, giving her a stern look, but failed. "That's my dad you're talking about. Getting hot and heavy with your aunt. I should be angry with you for bringing her here and tempting him."

She smothered a giggle. "Why? It's not like she's Mata Hari."

He rolled his eyes, but smiled.

"I think they're cute together. And it looks like they make each other happy."

"Oh, yeah. They were real happy."

She smacked his chest. "Stop. They deserve to have a loving relationship just as much as anyone else."

"I know. It's just weird. I've never seen him date. Ever."

Daisy lifted a shoulder. "I guess it just took the right woman." She grinned. "So, should we go break up their party?"

He glanced at the door. "Nah. How about we go for a ride instead? Give them some time alone. Your wine and bath will wait on you."

Yes, but was it wise? Being alone with Asa was dangerous to her equilibrium. But she wanted to give Nori time alone with Silas. They were good for each other, and Nori would only be here a few more days.

"Okay, fine. But pick a gentle horse for me, please."

"No rockets for Daisy, got it."

She laughed. "Or broncos. I end up on my butt in the dirt and I can promise you I'll make sure you get nothing but tuna and lunch meat for the next week."

He held up a hand. "Gentle horse, I swear."

They walked to the barn, teasing each other as they went. Asa sent her into the tack room for saddles while he called Storm and another horse, Petal, in from the corral. It didn't take him long to gear up both horses. Once they were ready, he helped Daisy into her saddle, then let them out of the pasture into the yard.

"Where are we going?" she asked.

"Not too far. It'll be getting dark soon. But there's a place nearby I thought you might like to see."

Intrigued, she urged her horse into a trot like he showed her and followed him, trying not to bounce out of her saddle.

He laughed. "Roll your hips."

"How? I just keep getting bumped out of the rhythm with every stride." She tried again, but quickly gave up when the saddle bumped her butt again, this time hitting her tailbone. She was going to need that bath for more than just relaxation later.

Taking pity on her, he slowed them to a walk, which kept her butt in the saddle.

Able to take her focus off her ride a little, Daisy looked around. The sun was dropping in the sky to their west. In an hour, it would start to sneak behind the mountains. The tall grass they waded through waved in the warm breeze of the summer evening, a beautiful background to the songbirds' evening melodies. An eagle screeched, and she looked up, seeing the majestic bird riding a thermal overhead. God, she loved it here. In Chicago, the background music would be cars honking and people cursing as someone cut them off. The peace of this place was hypnotic, and she felt herself relaxing.

They rode for ten more minutes before they rose over a small hill. At the bottom, the river shimmered in the waning sunlight.

"Is this what you wanted to show me?"

Asa nodded. "It's shallow here, so we can wade in it if you want."

"I want." She nudged Petal into a trot, putting up with the punishment to her ass to reach the water quicker.

At the riverbank, Daisy dismounted her horse, doing her best not to fall in the river as she did so. Asa climbed down with much more grace, then took her reins and let them trail the ground. She toed off her shoes, then waited for Asa to take off his boots and socks and roll up his jeans.

"God, you're slow. And they say women take forever to get ready." She grinned.

He rolled his eyes as he straightened from hiking up his pants. "You're wearing a lot less clothing."

"Duh. It's summer." She spun around and picked her way over the rocks on the gently sloping bank to dip her toes into the crystal-clear water. "It's chillier than I thought it would be."

He nodded and waded in beside her. "It's mountain-fed, so it stays pretty cold all year. It's nice when you're really hot, but you don't want to stay in long."

Daisy dug her toes into the sand and rock beneath them and laughed in delight. "I'm so glad I came here. Places like this are ones I only read about or saw in movies. Now I get to live here every day. This is amazing!" She waded out a few feet until the water swirled around her knees, then looked back at him. "I understand why you left, but how could you stay away so long? And how does anyone say the boonies are boring? This is food for the soul."

He smiled. "After a few years, I didn't want to stay away, but obligations kept me elsewhere. And for some people—like Marla—they don't see serenity when they see places like this. They just see emptiness."

"And that's sad." She put her hands in the water, waving them through it.

"I agree. It's why I left that world and don't want to go back. I've had my fill of it."

Her smile died as she remembered they would venture back into it soon for the charity concert. But her thoughts weren't on the city and the stress of being in the limelight. They were on the girl who asked Asa to come. She wished she could give that girl the same peace she felt here in this river and vowed to do everything she could to make the event all that kid wanted and more.

"What are you thinking about?" Asa asked. "Your expression changed."

She sucked in a breath. "I was just thinking about that girl. I want her to have this feeling. Of peace and happiness. Of knowing in that moment, everything is perfect." She shook her head and looked away. "I can't imagine what's going through her head. How she feels right now, knowing she only has weeks to months left. Of what she's already been through. I know there are times Ian comes home just beaten down, and I know those are the days he lost someone. But he gets up the next day and goes back because he saves many more than he loses. He makes a difference." She looked at Asa again. "I want to do that. I may not be able to save her life, but I want to make what's left of it wonderful. Even if it means facing my problems when I'm not ready. They feel insignificant compared to hers."

Asa took a breath and stared at her with an intensity that left her a little breathless.

"We will. We'll make her last days the happiest they can be. I promise you that."

They held each other's gaze for several moments. Something cracked open in Daisy's chest, sending a warm glow through her despite the chilly water moving around her legs. Feelings she didn't want to put a name to seeped out to tickle the deepest recesses of her mind. Asa held out a hand. With only a moment's hesitation, she took it. He waded closer, letting go to brush the backs of his fingers against her cheek and into her hair.

Without a word, he bent his head and pressed a light kiss

to her lips. That crack in Daisy's chest got a little wider. She rested a hand against his jaw, teasing his mouth with hers, keeping her touch gentle. Neither of them pressed for more, and they pulled apart.

He rested his forehead against hers, silently watching her for several moments before straightening to take her hand. "Come on. We better go. It'll be getting dark soon."

She nodded and let him lead her toward the bank. As he walked, little droplets kicked up to splash her. One of his legs dragged in the water, leaving a wake that rose to soak the bottom of her shorts. She gasped as the water hit her inner thigh.

He glanced back and grinned. "Sorry."

She glared at him, amusement shining in her eyes. "No you're not." With her free hand, she trailed her fingers in the water to splash him. Droplets hit his chest and face.

He narrowed his eyes at her. "Watch it. I don't play nice."

Daisy arched a brow and let go of his hand to walk forward like she was going to get out of the water. "But do you play dirty?" As she came even with him, she turned and put both hands on his chest and shoved. On the loose rock and sand, he lost his footing and toppled backward into the water, sending it spraying in every direction as he sank beneath.

He came up sputtering, blowing away the rivulets of water running down his face and off his nose. "Daisy. Sweetness, you better run." He flipped his hair back out of his eyes and lunged.

She squealed and took off for the bank, but only made it two steps before he had her around the waist and sent them both crashing into the water. He let her go as soon as they submerged, and she found her footing to push through the surface.

"Fuck, that's cold!" She pulled her t-shirt away from her torso, trying to create some space between the cold fabric and her body. A shiver ran through her. She was regretting her actions.

He laughed. "You started it."

A giggle slid past her lips. "But the look on your face was worth it."

"Sure. Keep laughing. I might dunk you again."

"I'll take you with me."

"Really? You won't catch me off guard twice."

She eyed him, ready to feign a move to dunk him again, but decided he was right. And she didn't want to end up underwater a second time. The water really was quite chilly. Instead, she high-stepped toward the bank.

Strong arms grabbed her to lift her in the air.

"Asa, don't you dare!" She grabbed his shoulders as he laughed.

He lowered her to his shoulder and walked out of the river. "I'm just teasing, sweetness. Once was enough for both of us. That water's cold. But the next time we're around a pool, you better watch yourself."

She rolled her eyes and pushed against his back to hold herself up. "I'm scared. Really."

He smacked her butt. "You should be."

"Just make sure I'm wearing something that won't pull me down and drown me."

"How about," he set her down, "I promise to rescue you."

Daisy gave him a saccharine smile. "How about you behave and I won't need rescuing?"

"Where's the fun in that?"

The look she leveled on him could peel paint.

He grinned and walked over to grab the reins for their horses, leading Petal over to her. "We should get back. It's already going to be a cold ride. The lower the sun goes, the colder it'll be."

She put her foot in the stirrup and mounted the horse.

He patted her leg. "You get too chilly, you can take that shirt off. Might be warmer."

Another giggle escaped her. "You just want to see what color bra I'm wearing again."

"Oh, baby, I don't need you to take off your shirt to see that. It's quite clear."

With a frown, Daisy glanced down. Her cream-colored shirt showed plain as day that she had on a light pink bra with soft gray leopard spots.

"Mmrow." He made a claw with his hand and raked the air.

Daisy rolled her lips in to hold back the laugh. "Ass."

He climbed on his horse and whipped off his shirt. Daisy's mouth went dry.

"Go ahead. Join the shirtless party."

"Oh!" With a huff, she spun Petal around the way they came, ignoring his laughter as she rode away.

TWENTY-ONE

"Damn, sweetness. You best hope the judge is a man. He'll take one look at you and rule in your favor without question."

Daisy rolled her eyes and picked up her purse from the counter, ignoring his comment about her pantsuit. She wanted to look professional for the hearing, so she and Nori went shopping in Billings with Sara and Marci. They'd found her gray suit and mint green sateen blouse on sale, which thrilled Daisy. She'd added the heels she bought on her last shopping trip and one of the purses to complete the look. She felt confident in her clothes for once. "Not if he's worth his salt. Besides, I think the evidence will speak for itself. If she's smart, she'll plead guilty and I won't have to testify."

He snorted. "Yeah, she's not that smart. But hopefully this time she'll see reason. You sure you don't want me to come?"

"And create a circus? No. I'll be fine. Nori's going with me, so I'm not alone." She gestured to her aunt, who stood near the island with Silas.

"All right. I guess I'll see you both this evening, then?"

She nodded. "Don't forget, it's game night. You better

bring your best guessing skills. We need to crush them in Pictionary."

He grinned. "Oh, we will."

Nori waved a hand. "Oh, please. Your father and I have decades of experience on the two of you. You might not even recognize some of the things on the cards."

"Don't be too sure about that, Nori," Silas said. "Asa's a bit of a trivia junkie."

She looked at him with a frown. "Aren't you supposed to be on my side?"

He held up his hands. "Yes. Sorry." He narrowed his eyes at Asa. "You're going down, son."

Daisy laughed.

"Hmm." Asa lifted a brow, holding in a smile. "We'll see."

"Yes. Yes, we will." Nori wagged a finger at him and grinned, then picked up her purse and turned to Daisy. "You ready to go?"

"Yep." They waved at Asa and Silas, then headed outside to get in the car. Once inside and buckled up, Daisy started the engine and steered them down the drive. "Thanks for coming with me."

"Not a problem. I'm eager to see the woman get what's coming to her for the way she's treated you."

At the end of the drive, Daisy looked both ways before she turned left to head into town. "So long as she pays for the damage to my car, I don't care what they do to her."

"No, I know you don't. You're too kind. Speaking of, are you sure you're ready to go back to Chicago?"

Daisy sighed. "No, but I can't disappoint that girl because I don't want to talk to my brothers. And Asa's right. Sooner or later, I have to anyway. Might as well rip the bandage off now."

"Well, I will be there if you want me to be. Your brothers might be grown men, but they still listen to me. They'll hush if I tell them to."

Daisy giggled. "I know." She sobered. "I'm going to miss you. It's been so nice having you here."

"Oh, don't worry. I'll be back."

"For me, or for Silas?"

Nori blushed. "Yes, well, I suppose I have more than one reason to visit, don't I?"

Daisy smiled. "I think it's great. He's a good man." She glanced Nori's way. "Have you guys talked about the future?"

Nori's mouth twisted, and she looked out her window. "He asked me to move out here."

The car slowed as shock made Daisy lose all muscle tone for a moment. "Wait, what? What did you say?"

"That I'd think about it. I'm just not sure I want to uproot my life like that. I mean, I've only been here a few weeks. I barely know the man."

Daisy scoffed. "You know him about as well as a man you'd been dating for several months."

"How do you figure that?"

"Think about it. When you date someone, you spend what, four to six hours together a week for the first couple of months when you go on dates? You've been living under his roof and you see him at least four hours a day every day. That's like a month's worth of dates every week. And I would argue you know him better than a man you dated for several months because you're seeing him in his element and not all spiffed up to impress you."

"I hadn't thought of it like that." Her look turned thoughtful.

"You don't have to decide now, though, you know that, right?"

Nori nodded. "Yeah. I want to talk to Sofie about it. If I move, it will impact her too."

"How's she doing?" Nori's daughter, Daisy's cousin, was

recently divorced. She and her four-year-old daughter were living with Nori until they got on their feet.

"She's doing okay. Doing her best to find herself and build up some savings so she can buy a nice apartment. I'm just glad she came to her senses and left Lance before he did worse to her. Or before he hurt Olive."

Daisy shook her head. She couldn't believe her cousin was being abused and no one knew until she ended up in the hospital with a concussion, broken arm and cheekbone, and three fractured ribs. Nori suspected, but Sofie would never confide in her. Not until he knocked her unconscious, then left her to bleed on the living room floor while their daughter played in her room. Then she broke down and asked her mother for help.

"And she's been all right while you've been gone?"

Nori nodded. "Lance is still in jail, and I told your brothers to check in on her occasionally."

"Good." If she knew her older brother, he had one of them there every evening to make sure she was okay. Daisy was glad the judge that granted her divorce also saw fit to take all visitation rights from Lance once he got out of jail. She wouldn't put it past him to take Olive and hold her hostage to get Sofie to do what he wanted.

"If you moved out here, do you think she would come too?"

"I'm not sure. It wouldn't be hard for her to work from here. Her jewelry ships easily. But she has friends there. And Olive loves her preschool." Nori sighed. "I just know I won't decide alone. I have to consider my daughter. She needs me."

Daisy reached over and squeezed Nori's hand. "I know. And even if you really want to move out here, I'm sure Silas would wait for you. Besides, with Asa home, he can take more time off to come see you in Chicago."

"That's true." She waved a hand and blew out a breath.

"I'm not going to worry about it right now, though. It will all work out the way it's supposed to. I'd much rather talk about you and Asa."

Daisy groaned. She'd been waiting for the third degree from her aunt, though she'd been hoping Nori had been too distracted by Silas to notice the closeness that had developed between Daisy and Asa lately.

Nori chuckled. "What? It's only fair. So, tell me. What's going on with you two?"

"Honestly, I don't know. He flirts, I flirt, he flirts more. We've kissed a few times—and yes, before you ask, it's fantastic. I just don't know if I want to get involved with him. With anyone, really. Not right now."

"Pfft. You're already involved. Stop denying it. Embrace it, honey. You'll be happier and less stressed."

"Maybe."

"Oh, there's no maybe about it. Multiple orgasms will do wonders to relax you."

"Nori!"

"What? I'm just stating a fact. Asa looks like he'd be good at that."

Daisy felt her face heat. "Oh my God. We are not talking about this."

Nori laughed. "Fine, I'll behave. Just think about what I said."

Daisy hummed and kept her eyes on the road, an image of Asa standing in his bedroom, wet and naked, entering her mind. She tried to think about the upcoming hearing, but the image wouldn't budge from her brain. It was like there was a picture of him burned into her retinas. She squeezed her eyes shut for a quick moment, hoping to make it go away. Crashing the car would not be a good start to her morning.

It didn't help much. Maybe she should just give in to him. Maybe part of her problem was not knowing how it would feel.

She squashed the urge to snort at her thoughts. Sharing a bed—or a wall, or a chair, or a table—with Asa would likely only make things worse. Then she'd just be counting the seconds until they could do it again. She was sure he'd have that effect on her. Why did the man have to be so damn sexy? And nice? He was supposed to stay a grumpy asshole. But the longer he was home, the more relaxed he became, and the harder she found it to resist him.

Her conscience niggled at her. Would it really be so bad to give in to him? To see if they could have an actual relationship?

Daisy put a quick lid on that line of thinking and forced her mind to concentrate on the road. She walled off images of Asa's naked body behind a steel door. She'd just gained her freedom to live her own life. She wasn't ready to tangle it up with someone else.

As she made the turn into town, her engagement ring glittered in the sun as she turned the steering wheel. Her little inner demon noticed and reminded her that ship had already sailed.

"You two just couldn't wait, could you?" Daisy set a bowl of popcorn down on the dining table and raised a brow at Asa and Silas. Both men had a half-eaten brownie in their hands.

"What?" Asa said, swallowing. "We were hungry."

"Yeah," Silas chimed in. "That chicken stuff you made for dinner wasn't very filling."

She rolled her eyes and sat down next to Nori. "I made grilled chicken caesar salad because I knew we were going to gorge ourselves on junk food tonight."

"And because you had that milkshake," Nori said, waving a finger at her. "Don't forget about that."

"I'm not. But I already planned on the salads before we had the shakes to celebrate Marla getting what was coming to her."

Asa scoffed. "She got a slap on the wrist. The judge should have given you a protection order. If you'd let me talk to him—"

"You are not going to use your name and influence to get me a restraining order when I don't need one. It's been a couple of letters. And we don't even know she's the one behind them."

"I'd rather think she is. It's less scary than thinking there's someone else out there who wants to do you harm because of me."

Daisy tipped the popcorn bowl to pour some into a smaller bowl for herself. "Well, Marla's paying for the damages to my car, so I'm happy. And I am not going to think about it —about any of it—for the rest of the night. The only thing I want to concentrate on now is kicking their asses." She gestured to Silas and Nori and grinned.

"Bring it." Nori dragged the Pictionary box toward her and opened the lid.

Silas passed out the pads of paper and pencils he got from the study, while Daisy helped her aunt arrange the pieces on the board. Asa shuffled the cards and stacked them in the middle.

"Who goes first?" Daisy asked.

"You young'uns should go second," Silas said. "So you know what you're facing. Might give you a fighting chance."

Asa laughed. "Sure, Dad. That's why we'll win." He rolled his eyes, sarcasm dripping off his words.

"Fine. You go first." He slid the top card off the deck toward Asa.

Daisy giggled and took it. "I'll draw first. You can do the

guessing." She peeked at the yellow clue and groaned. How the hell did one draw Egypt?

"You ready?" Nori gave her a wicked smile, holding the timer.

"No." She looked at Asa. "I hope your guessing game is as good as your singing game." She glanced at Nori. "Flip it."

Nori flipped the timer, and Daisy started to draw. The only thing she could think of was to try to draw a mummy, so she outlined a quick human figure and drew lines across him and put two black dots on his face for eyes.

"A mummy."

Daisy nodded and made a rolling motion with her hand.

"It's not a mummy?"

She shot a quick glare at him.

"Okay, it's a mummy. Um, a pharaoh?"

She rolled her hand again, then drew several pyramids.

"The pyramids. Egypt!"

"Yes!" She held up a hand, and he gave her a high-five.

Asa looked at Silas. "What was that you were saying about knowing what we're up against?"

Silas just glared at him. Daisy giggled and picked up the dice, rolling it. They landed on blue, so she moved their marker and picked up another card.

They bantered across the table as they battled it out, changing who led several times until finally, Asa and Daisy won.

Silas pushed away from the table. "I need another beer before we take them on again," he said to Nori. "You want one?"

She laughed and stood. "I wouldn't turn down more wine."

Daisy frowned as she spotted the wine bottle on the table. "Aunt Nori, there's still half a—" Asa nudged her, cutting off. She glanced at him, and he waggled his eyebrows, then looked at the older couple, who weren't paying any attention to them.

"Ah. Never mind." She blew out a breath and sat back in her chair as they left the room. "Did Silas tell you he asked Nori to move here?"

"What? No."

She nodded. "She's thinking about it. But she wants to talk to her daughter first. Sofie and her daughter, Olive, are living with Nori right now. She got divorced last year and has been living with her mom to save money for a down payment on an apartment."

He stared at the kitchen door, a thoughtful look on his face. "Do you think she'll do it?"

Daisy shrugged. "Maybe. I know she really likes your dad. And she'll have me here. If she does, I'm kind of hoping she'll convince Sofie to come too. She could use a fresh start. Her ex is a jerk."

"They have a daughter, right? What about her? Won't living here make visitation difficult?"

She shook her head and picked up a frosted brownie. "He doesn't get any. He beat Sofie senseless and is serving a year in jail for it. Even after he gets out, the judge denied visitation until he proves he'll behave." She took a bite of her treat.

"Damn. Yeah, I can see why Nori would want to talk to Sofie first. Well, we have plenty of room for them to stay here until they find a place if they want to move."

"Thank you. I'll let Nori know that."

"Sure." He reached out a hand toward her face.

Daisy froze. "What are you doing?"

"You have frosting right there." He touched the corner of her mouth.

Shivers shot down Daisy's spine. Her tongue darted out to lick away the chocolate, but she connected with his finger instead. His eyes dilated and his lips parted as he stared at her mouth.

"Dammit, Daisy." His voice was a harsh growl. "You're not making it easy to keep my distance."

She wasn't making it easy on herself, either.

Silas's deep laugh and Nori's lilting giggle reached them from the kitchen, but neither of them looked away. Asa leaned forward, replacing his finger with his mouth, licking away the small bit of chocolate.

Heat made her skin prickle as arousal flooded her system. She turned her head and connected her mouth with his. He shifted in his chair, sliding his legs alongside hers and pulling her forward, holding her head to plunder her mouth.

"Well, Noreen, maybe we should have stayed away longer."

Asa and Daisy jumped apart. Daisy's face flamed, and she turned back to the table. Or tried to. Her knees bumped Asa's as she shifted, hampering her efforts. She pushed at his thigh to make him move and lifted her leg at the same time, banging her shin on the underside of the table.

"Ouch, dammit!"

"If you'd wait a second, I'd move."

She glared at him, not really angry. Just embarrassed. Their relationship was supposed to be fake, and they got caught kissing by some of the few people who knew that.

"Don't mind us," Nori said, sitting next to Daisy. "We were doing the same thing."

That startled a laugh from Daisy. She leaned into Nori and wrapped an arm around her shoulder, giving her a squeeze. "I'm going to miss you."

"Same here." She patted Daisy's hand. "But I'll see you in Chicago soon. Are you sure you don't want me to tell the boys you're coming?"

"I'm sure. I promise I'll talk to them, but I don't want them prepping an argument or anything to convince me to stay. I've discovered they're easier to deal with if I catch them unprepared."

"All men are."

"Hey." Silas narrowed his eyes at her.

Nori just smiled and changed the subject. "So, are we ready to do a battle of the sexes now?"

Silas picked up a marker and slammed it down on the start block. "Damn skippy. You're going down, love."

Twenty-Two

"Whoa. This place is huge!" Daisy looked around in awe at the cavernous theater Marty booked for Asa's concert. "How many people are coming to this thing?"

"I told Marty to invite all the hospital staff and their families. He told me he couldn't get a facility large enough on that short of notice, so we pared it down to just pediatric oncology. They sent out a letter to all patients—current and former, who are still under eighteen—and the staff. RSVP total was around a thousand. This theater holds twenty-five hundred."

He pointed toward the balcony where there was camera equipment set up. "We're going to live stream it, too, for the kids who are hospitalized and can't make it. It's supposed to be recorded as well, so Jasmine can watch it whenever she wants."

"Oh, that's wonderful."

"Asa."

They turned at the sound of Marty's voice.

"Hey, Marty. This place is great." He held out a hand to his manager.

Marty took his hand and gave it a quick shake before releasing it. "Yeah, we got lucky it was available. It helped we're doing this on a weeknight."

"For sure. Did the band make it in okay?" Asa had Marty contact his touring band and ask them to play with him. They all jumped at the chance to help out, finding replacements for themselves on their other projects so they could be here.

Marty nodded. "They're all backstage except for Deke. His plane lands in an hour."

"Awesome. They're going to handle soundcheck, right? While Daisy and I make a trip to the suburbs to visit the Richters?"

"Yep. Everything's set up. You just need to be back a couple hours prior, so the sound tech can make sure everything's set up the way you want. Venue doors open an hour before the show starts. The rush shipping from your merchandise warehouse showed up last night, so I've got volunteers bagging and distributing the items to the seats. We assigned seats, so we made sure each family got the correct shirt sizes."

"Wait. You're giving everyone merchandise too?" Daisy asked, looking at Asa.

He nodded. "Among other things." He winked at her. "Wait until you see what I packed for Jasmine and her family."

She beamed. "It's killing me, you know." Though, she had an idea. Every evening this week after dinner, he locked himself in a soundproof booth he had in the barn. And she'd seen him with his guitar more often than not since Marty called to ask him to do this concert. Plus, it was in the back of the SUV. She'd made sure to pack pants with pockets so she could stuff them full of tissues. She had a feeling she'd need them.

He flashed her a rakish grin. "Oh, I know. A few more hours, sweetness." He took her hand and turned back to

Marty. "Thanks for arranging all this. We're going to head out now."

"Of course. It's what I do. I'll see you later."

Asa nodded and led Daisy off the stage and back through the bowels of the theater the way they came in. They'd come straight from the airport to here so he could check on things. Silas went back to the hotel with most of their luggage, then was going to go find Nori.

Once in the parking lot, Asa pulled up the GPS on his phone and typed in the Richter's address, and they were on their way.

"You should call your brothers," Asa said, after they were on the highway.

"They're at work."

"So?"

"So, we're staying an extra day so I can see them."

"Chicken."

"Damn straight."

He laughed and reached for her hand. "I'll be right there. Unless you don't want me to be. Then I'll be there when you come back to the hotel. You can beat on my chest and tell me how dumb they are."

"I hope you brought armor."

He puffed up his chest. "What are you talking about?" He scoffed. "Armor. You see these muscles? They can take whatever you can dish out."

Her lips twitched, but she just raised an eyebrow. He laughed again and she grinned.

"I appreciate the sentiment, Asa. Thank you."

"Always, sweetness."

That feeling of rightness she had that night at the river came back. Things had definitely changed between them over the last couple of weeks. They were more relaxed around each other and bickered less. They'd even shared a few more kisses, but none of the heavy petting sessions. All hands had stayed on top of their clothes. It was bizarre. She thought he wanted her, but he'd been the one to pump the brakes more often than she did when they kissed. She couldn't figure him out. The only thing that made sense was that he was trying to respect her wishes to remain friends. And they hadn't really talked about where their relationship was going lately, or even if they had one.

Maybe it was time to change that.

She took a deep breath and dove in. "Asa, what are we doing?"

He frowned and glanced at her. "What do you mean? You know where we're going."

"Not that. I mean us. You and me. What's going on here? Things have changed. Neither of us can deny that."

He laid his head against the headrest. "Yeah. And honest answer, I don't know. We've both said we don't want a relationship, but I—well, I feel like we're in one. Maybe it's proximity. Maybe it's our agreement to pretend for the masses, but it's feeling less fake all the time." He glanced at her again. "I'm comfortable with you."

Daisy bit her lip. "That's the way I feel too. Like we aren't pretending. But then, at the same time, like we are. You kiss me, but back way off. We spend time together, but not really as a couple. But yet, it feels that way. It's strange and hard to explain."

"I get what you mean. And I back off because we agreed to keep this platonic."

She snorted. "We're failing. Epically."

One side of his mouth lifted. "Maybe we shouldn't anymore." He sent a long look her way before turning back to the road. "When I came home, I wasn't looking to date anyone. Not because I didn't want to have a relationship, but because I didn't think I could find someone I trusted. I was wrong."

"You trust me?"

"Yes. You could have sold pictures of me to the tabloids a million times over by now. Or used my name to get you things, but you don't. All you want is to live your life. If anything, I should be the untrustworthy one. I've mucked everything up by asking you to help me get my own life back."

She held up a finger. "You didn't ask, I offered. And this has been as much for me as for you. I get to be myself. You don't care that I used to be a tall, gangly kid until I sprouted boobs at the age of twelve and suddenly all the boys took notice. Or that I had a hard time balancing a budget because I suck at math and let other people handle my finances until I got sick of always having to ask how much was in my checking account and forced myself to learn it. To you, I'm just Daisy. I don't have to explain myself for being me. And I also get a friend. One who has my back."

"Yes. I second the friend thing. I think you're the first true friend I've made in fifteen years. One who doesn't expect anything from me and there's no subterfuge."

She rolled her lips in. "So where does that leave us?"

"That depends. Are you ready for more? We can go as slow as you want. But I know I want more than just friendship with you, Daisy."

Daisy's world spun on its axis as he put into words what they'd been dancing around. This hunk of a man wanted to date her. Her! He trusted her to be his real-life girlfriend. Not just when others were watching.

Her body hummed as she realized what that meant. She'd get to see and feel more of Asa's beautiful body.

The hum died just as quickly. That meant he'd get to see and feel hers too, and it was nowhere near as perfect as his. Or as the women he'd dated in the past.

"Stop it."

"What?" She looked at him.

"I can see what you're thinking. Stop thinking you aren't good enough. I love the way you look. If you haven't noticed." His eyes went to her boobs.

"Yes, well, there's more of me than my chest."

"Oh, I know. I've watched your ass dance around the house for the last couple of months. Trust me, I'm aware." His eyes heated.

She blushed.

"How about this? Nothing has to change except we admit we're together and not faking it anymore. We'll let things happen as they happen. Deal?"

Daisy bit her lip again. Could she do that? Just let things play out however they did? Let her emotions take control?

It might not be a bad idea. Her conscience niggled at her. The last time she let her emotions rule her life, she moved to Montana. It was the best decision she ever made. Could that happen again? Would she regret it if she didn't try?

Yes. She would, she realized. The not knowing what might have been would haunt her the rest of her life.

She took a deep breath. "Okay. Deal."

The teenage squeal was the first thing Asa heard when the Richters' front door opened. The dark-haired woman who answered his knock rolled her eyes and smiled. "She's slightly excited."

Daisy laughed beside him. "We can tell." She held out a hand to the woman. "Hello, Mrs. Richter. I'm Daisy O'Malley."

"Erin, please." She shook Daisy's hand.

Asa held out his. "It's nice to meet you ma'am."

She took it. "You, too, Mr. Mitchell."

"Mom, move!"

Asa grinned. "Yeah, Mom."

The woman laughed and stepped back, motioning them inside. A girl in a wheelchair rolled forward, an enormous smile on her pale face.

"You're really here!"

He crouched down to her level, smiling at her excitement. "Of course I'm here, Jasmine. I couldn't pass up the opportunity to meet one of my superfans."

She giggled.

"How about we all go into the living room?" Erin suggested.

Asa stood. "Sounds good to me." He moved behind Jasmine and spun her chair around. "Lead the way, Mom."

Erin chuckled and motioned them to follow. He wheeled Jasmine down a short hallway to the back of the house, where it opened up to a living room/kitchen combo. His smile slipped a little as he looked around. A hospital bed was tucked into one corner near the window, an IV pole next to it. A set of plastic drawers sat beside the pole, doubling as a nightstand. Through the clear plastic, he could see the drawers were filled with medical paraphernalia. He fought to maintain his composure. No one's home should look like this. Especially not because their fourteen-year-old daughter was dying of cancer.

"Where am I parking you?" He injected as much cheer into his voice as he could.

Jasmine pointed to an empty spot across from the couch. He rolled her over, then took a seat on the couch. Daisy sat down next to him, and Erin perched on a chair next to her daughter.

"I'm sorry my husband couldn't be here to meet you. He'll be at the concert later, but he had to work today. He's taken so much time off for Jasmine's illness that he works when he can to keep his employer happy."

"That's understandable. Where does he work?" Asa asked.

"He's the finance manager at a local bank."

"My little brother will be at the concert tonight, too," Jasmine said. "He's at school." She smiled. "One good thing about dying, I don't have to go to school."

Asa blinked, shocked at her candor.

"Jazzy," Erin admonished her.

"It's okay," Asa said, finding his voice again. "She's entitled to feel however she wants about her situation. I think I'd probably be glad it got me out of school too."

"Same here," Daisy said. She gave the girl a smile and waved. "Hi. We haven't been introduced yet. I'm Daisy O'Malley, Asa's fiancée."

The girl smiled. "I know. You're prettier than your pictures."

Daisy blushed. "Thank you. So are you."

Jasmine rolled her eyes. "No, I'm not. Not anymore." She touched the fabric cap covering her head.

"Nonsense. I could get a bad haircut and feel the same way, but it doesn't change my face, or what's on the inside. You have a pretty smile, and your eyes are just stunning. I'm betting your mom would tell me you have a wonderful personality, too."

Erin smiled, nodding.

"Daisy's right. Your illness changed your appearance, but it didn't take away your beauty. I thought that the first time I saw the pictures my manager, Marty, texted me. And it inspired something." Asa stood and held up a finger. "Can you hang on for just a minute? I left something in the car."

Jasmine gave him a curious frown. "Okay."

He flashed her a smile and ran outside to get his guitar and the small backpack he brought along, then hurried back in.

"Are you going to play for me?" Jasmine's eyes widened when she saw the guitar.

"Yes." He sat on the couch again and opened the case. "But this song is just for you." Taking out the instrument, he looped the strap over his shoulder and strummed the strings, testing them. After a few quick adjustments, he started to play.

As quietly and inconspicuously as she could, Daisy dug into the pocket of her jeans for a tissue while she listened to Asa sing. His song was beautiful. He sang about a girl with beautiful eyes and a smile that lit up the room. Of a life well-lived and well-loved. How her memory lived on by those who remembered her. It was a promise of better days—for everyone. A life without pain or fear. And of finding solace in God's grace. It was a song for Jasmine's parents as much as for Jasmine herself.

Daisy sniffed and wiped her eyes as he finished. He nudged her shoulder and gave her a soft smile, then offered a bigger one to Jasmine and her mom.

"So, what do you think?"

Erin struggled to hold herself together, but Jasmine beamed through her tears.

"It was awesome. And I think it's perfect for my family. Can you play it at the concert so my dad and brother can hear it too?"

He nodded. "I hadn't planned to—I wrote it only for you —but I will if you want me to. Also," he held up a finger, then bent down to unzip the backpack and reach inside, "I recorded it, so you and your family can listen to it whenever you want." He pulled out a CD. "Marty has your mother's email, so he's going to send her a digital file as well that you can download to whatever device you wish." He passed her the disc.

She took it with a squeal. "This is so cool! Thank you!"

"That was very kind, Mr. Mitchell," Erin said, regaining her composure. "Thank you."

"It was my pleasure, truly. I'm just glad I'm in a position to make her happy."

"So are we. She was devastated when you announced your retirement."

"I still am." Jasmine pouted, resting her head on her fist as she propped her elbow on the arm of her chair. "Why are you retiring, anyway? None of the articles said."

He glanced at Daisy. She gave him an encouraging smile.

"It was time. I only got into the business to save my family's ranch. Things snowballed when my first album hit it big, and I found myself saying yes to things I didn't fully look into before I signed the contracts. I never wanted to be a superstar. I just didn't want my dad to be homeless. I'm not built for the limelight long-term, and I was burned out. You can ask Daisy. When she met me, I was a total bear. And that's not me." He glanced back at her. "I don't know how she fell for me, but I'm thankful she did."

"I'm glad she did too. I didn't like that blonde woman who claimed to be your girlfriend. Marla. She seemed shallow. And mean."

"Well, regardless, all of those rumors were false, and she's been dealt with. Daisy and I are planning our wedding and running the ranch."

Jasmine wrinkled her nose. "I probably won't be around to see it." Her features smoothed out, and she looked at Daisy. "But you'll be a beautiful bride."

"Thank you. And I'm sure you'll be watching wherever you are."

That brought a smile to Jasmine's face. "Oh, for sure. I'll

have God make me a bench so I have a front-row seat." She giggled.

Asa smiled. Daisy could see he was fighting to hold onto it. This kid and her situation were really getting to him. It was to her too.

"Good," Asa said. "So, how about another song?"

She clapped her hands. "Yes!"

"What's your favorite?"

She named it, and he started playing again. Daisy recognized the song. Since she'd been living at the ranch, she'd listened to some of his music. This was one of her favorites, too, and she found herself humming along at the chorus. He noticed and nodded at her to sing. She waved him off, but he bumped her shoulder and nodded again.

"Sing," he said, pausing briefly between lyrics.

She blinked at him. He grinned and kept singing. With a rueful smile, she jumped in at the chorus, harmonizing with him. By the end of the song, Daisy found she was enjoying herself. Singing with him was fun. She'd only ever sang in school choirs and for herself.

"You're really good," Erin said when they finished the song.

Daisy blushed. "Thanks. I'm okay, I guess."

"You're more than okay," Jasmine said. "You should sing on stage with him all the time."

"Oh, no. I think I'm good just doing this. An audience is his thing, not mine." She waved a hand and offered a smile, hoping to placate the girl. Singing in a small gathering like this was one thing, but in front of thousands? She didn't know how Asa did it.

He bumped her shoulder again. "Ah, come on, Dais. It'd be fun."

She blinked at him again, and he chuckled.

"How about another song?" He looked at Jasmine.

The girl named another one, and Asa started playing again. They spent the next half hour going through a list of her favorites. When Asa's throat got dry, they took a break.

"Do you want to see my room?" Jasmine asked while they waited on her mother to get Asa and Daisy some water.

"Sure."

"You know you can't get up the stairs anymore," Erin said, walking into the room. "And your dad isn't here to carry you up there." She handed Asa and Daisy the water bottles she carried, and they thanked her.

The girl pouted. "I wanted them to see my collection."

"I can carry you." Asa glanced from daughter to mother. "If you don't mind, Erin?"

The woman shrugged. "If you're willing. Just be careful of her pain pump. It runs through a catheter into her back."

"Like an epidural?" Daisy asked.

Erin nodded. "The cancer's surrounding her spinal cord, so she was in tremendous pain through the lower half of her body. They placed that for pain control, so she wasn't drugged up all the time. Unfortunately, it means she can no longer walk."

Jasmine snorted. "It wasn't like I could before they put it in. The pain was too bad. At least now, I can enjoy the time I have left."

Asa cleared his throat. "Well, I'm glad. And I hope Daisy and I have made that time even better."

She grinned up at him as he stood. "Definitely. And I get to be carried by you?" She feigned a swoon, falling back against her chair, a hand over her forehead. "What more could a girl ask for?"

He laughed and stepped forward to slide an arm around her knees and another around her back and under her arms. "I'm honored." He straightened with her in his arms, then turned to Erin. "Where am I going?"

She stood and pointed. "This way."

Daisy got up to follow them, taking a shaky breath as she watched Asa carry the frail girl through the house. That crack he opened up earlier ripped open into a full-fledged canyon. Emotions poured out so fast she could hardly make heads or tails of them. Admiration, joy, appreciation for this man and for the fact he was part of her life filled her. But drowning them all out was one emotion. The one making her hands shake. Love.

She loved Asa Mitchell. Was, in fact, in love with him.

As Erin led them all upstairs to Jasmine's bedroom, Daisy did her best to shove her thoughts and revelations aside. Now was not the time for her to ponder such things. This time was about the girl in Asa's arms. Not her. She refused to let anything put any sort of damper on the girl's special day. She didn't want Jasmine wondering why Daisy suddenly had trouble looking at Asa, or why her smile wasn't quite as bright. So she buried the emotions. There would be time later to pull them out and dissect them.

Erin pushed Jasmine's bedroom door open for Asa to carry her daughter through.

"Do you want me to set you on the bed?"

"Sure." Jasmine nodded.

He walked forward and perched her on the edge. Erin took the pillows and piled them behind her back, then picked up a large stuffed bear from the window seat and put it under her feet to keep them from dangling and pulling her down.

"Comfortable?" Asa asked her.

She nodded.

"Good." He glanced around. "Wow. You weren't kidding about the collection."

Daisy agreed. Jasmine had posters of him plastered all around her room. A decorative pillow on her bed bore his logo, and a tote bag and several hats hung on a hook board.

"I have, like, every t-shirt, too. And that's not all. I don't just collect merchandise."

"I can see that." Besides the music posters, horses were the main theme of Jasmine's room. Pictures of horses, both by themselves and with Jasmine in the saddle, lined the shelves and the top of her dresser. Beside them were trophies and medals. "I take it you ride?"

"I used to."

"Jasmine won several equestrian championships. She even placed nationally in the agility competition for her age group a couple years ago."

"Wow." Asa stepped over to a shelf to look more closely at the pictures. Daisy came up next to him.

"I wanted to compete at the collegiate level and go to school on an equestrian scholarship. I wanted to be a vet."

Daisy glanced at her. "I'm sorry cancer took all that away."

"Me too." She waved a hand. "But I've dealt with it. I'm not afraid to die. Not anymore. I know what's on the other side. I'll get to ride all the horses I want soon enough."

Tears formed in Daisy's eyes. She nodded and turned away before they fell. Asa took her hand and squeezed it.

"I want you to have something. Mom, can you—" Jasmine pointed at a shelf.

Erin walked over to it.

"The medal with the blue strap."

She took it off the trophy it was looped over and handed it to Asa.

"It's from the last competition I did. I had a CT scan of my leg the day before, but I didn't want to miss the competition. If I did, it could have kept me out of nationals this year, so I pushed through the pain and came in second. The next day, the doctor's office called and told us they were referring me to a pediatric orthopedic oncologist." She looked at Daisy. "Your brother, in fact."

Daisy's mouth dropped open. "My brother is your doctor?"

She nodded.

Daisy bit back a groan. Fate had a terrible sense of humor.

Jasmine giggled. "He's mad at you, you know."

"I know. I'm mad at him too."

"But he's worried too."

Daisy frowned. "What makes you say that?"

"I was inpatient a few months ago, and my brother, Blake, was getting on my nerves, and when Dr. O'Malley asked me how I was doing, I pretty much unloaded on him about how I wished my brother would leave me alone. He said maybe he was just doing it because he was worried about me. That sometimes siblings go a little overboard when they're worried. I asked him if he'd ever done that, and he said yes. With you. That he'd been trying to protect you and make sure you had a good life, but that in the process he might have forgotten it was your life to live."

A hard lump lodged in Daisy's throat. She swallowed and forced her voice to work. "He did?"

Jasmine nodded. "When the story broke about you and Asa—the first one, not the engagement—I asked him if the woman was his sister. You have the same name and you look like him. He said yes. He still seemed worried, but he was angry too. I didn't really understand why, though."

"He didn't know about my relationship with Asa. I didn't want the judgement I was sure to get."

Jasmine nodded. "Makes sense. I hope you work things out. Take it from someone who knows; life is short."

Well, if that wasn't a punch to the gut...

Daisy nodded. "I'll keep that in mind."

"Good." The girl yawned. "Sorry."

"Don't be. You need extra rest," Asa said. "We should let

you get some, so you're ready for tonight." He walked closer. "I'll take you back downstairs, then we'll let you nap."

Jasmine sighed and held up her arms, looping them around Asa's neck as he picked her up. "Fine."

He chuckled. "Glad to know I'll be missed."

TWENTY-THREE

M usic pulsed as Asa and his band played. Daisy watched from the stage wing. She could see Jasmine and her family in the front row. The girl wore an enormous smile. It made Daisy happy to see her enjoying herself. She was a remarkable kid. There weren't many adults who could handle the same situation with such eloquence.

Asa's song ended, and the crowd cheered.

"Okay, for this next song, I need a helper."

Shouts erupted as people volunteered.

"But not just any helper," he continued. "This song is for a very special girl. The reason we're all here tonight. Jasmine Richter." The spotlight swung to light up the girl and her family in the front row.

Asa looked to security on the theater floor. "Bring Jazzy up here. Mom, Dad, little bro, you can come too."

Daisy watched as Jasmine's father picked her up and carried her toward the stairs, where the security guard moved the barrier to let him through. Erin and Jasmine's brother followed. A stage hand ran out from the other side of the stage with a chair and set it down near Asa.

"Now," Asa said, once they were situated. "I wrote Miss Jasmine a song. It was supposed to be just for her, but she loved it so much she wanted to share it with everyone here. I think it needs another voice, though." He looked at Jasmine and grinned, waggling his eyebrows. "Don't you?"

The girl laughed and nodded.

"I think I know who that voice should be. How about you, Jasmine?"

Daisy frowned. He wouldn't.

"Yes!"

Asa spun around and looked at Daisy. She waved her hands, glaring at him. He grinned.

"Daisy, come out here."

"No!" she mouthed, waving her arms again.

"She's being shy. Everyone, let's give her some encouragement."

The crowd erupted. Daisy groaned and swiped her hands over her face. She was going to kill him later. Sighing, she stepped out of the shadows, waving at the crowd as she walked to his side. She gave the Richters hugs, then looked up at him, doing her best to telegraph that he would pay later.

His grin told her he knew she was mad and didn't care.

"I don't know this song," she whispered.

He leaned in. "Sure you do. You listened to it several times on the way back to the hotel. You'll do fine, so quit worrying."

"I hate you."

He straightened, smiling down at her. "Consider it payback for the yogurt."

"The yo—" The memory of chucking a container of Greek yogurt at him the night they met came back to her, and she broke off to laugh.

Asa laughed with her and turned back to the crowd. "Everyone, this is my beautiful fiancée, Daisy O'Malley. She's going to be my backup for this song. Give her a round of applause."

The crowd cheered again as a stagehand ran out and gave Daisy a microphone. Sweat formed at her hairline, and she prayed she wouldn't screw this up. He was right; she did know it. Not as well as she'd like, but well enough. When they got in the car when they left the Richters, she asked him to send her the song. He emailed it to her and she downloaded it, then ran it through the car's speakers, singing along. It had been easier to focus on it than on the revelations she experienced in the Richters' house.

"You ready?"

She glanced at him. "No, but go ahead."

"You'll do fine. Sing with me on the chorus." He leaned over and pecked her cheek, then stepped back to strum his guitar. The first strains of Jasmine's song floated through the theater.

Daisy took a breath to steady her nerves. She was glad he was confident. Maybe it would rub off on her.

The song entered the chorus, and Daisy lifted the microphone, closing her eyes to help her focus. Feeling the song, she found the harmony to Asa's powerful baritone and let it flow. She loved this song and the message it held. Her confidence grew as the music progressed, and she opened her eyes. Asa's gaze found hers, and she got lost in the words. When the last notes faded, the crowd erupted.

She smiled at Asa, feeling an adrenaline rush unlike any other.

"I told you you'd do fine." He smiled back, then turned to the crowd. "A round of applause for Daisy." The crowd responded. "And for our guest of honor, Jasmine Richter!" The crowd noise grew. Asa shook hands with Jasmine's dad and gave her mother and Jasmine a hug, then ruffled Blake's hair before the four of them headed off stage.

Daisy waved to the crowd, intending to go back to her spot in the shadows, but Asa caught her hand.

"Stay."

"What?" Her eyes widened. "No. I agreed to one song."

"Come on. They love you. Sing the last few songs with me." A naughty smile crossed his face. Before she could respond, he lifted his mic. "Who wants to see Daisy sing the rest of the concert with me?"

Cheers filled the theater.

"Oh, you play dirty."

"Always, sweetness." He tugged on her hand. "Come on."

Daisy rolled her eyes and sighed. "Fine."

Riding a high he hadn't felt in years, Asa stepped off the stage, Daisy's hand in his.

"Asa, that was fantastic." Marty stepped into his path.

"It was. I think everyone enjoyed it."

"Of course they did. You and Daisy together are amazing. We should look into making you a duo."

Asa's euphoria died. He held up a hand. "No. End of discussion." He tugged on Daisy's hand. "Come on, sweetness. Let's go find the Richters and say goodnight."

"Asa—"

"Marty, drop it." It was Daisy who spoke this time. "You'll never get me to do that on a regular basis. I like my quiet life in the mountains. So does Asa. This was a special case for a special girl. Don't ruin it, please?"

The man's mouth snapped shut, and he nodded. "Yeah, okay. Sorry."

She laid a hand on his arm for a brief moment and smiled as Asa led her away.

"Thank you." Asa looked at her as they moved toward the

ready room. Security was supposed to bring the Richters back there before they left. They were going to take a few pictures together.

He rounded a corner and came to a quick halt at the man standing in their way. Around six feet, the stranger looked to be in his mid-forties. Gray laced his dark auburn hair, and he had a distinguished air about him.

"Ian."

"Hello, Daisy."

Asa bit back a groan. Why couldn't the universe just let him ride his high? He let go of Daisy's hand to offer it to her brother. "Dr. O'Malley. It's nice to meet you."

Ian eyed him for a moment before taking his hand. "Same here. I'd say it's long overdue."

"Yes, well, things are complicated."

"Very." He looked at Daisy.

She rolled her eyes. "Now is not the time for us to have this discussion. We're on our way to the ready room to say goodbye to Jasmine and her family."

Ian pursed his lips, considering her for a moment before nodding. "Will you meet with me and the others tomorrow?"

Daisy nodded. "Yes. I was going to call you in the morning and see when would be a good time to stop by."

"How about we all meet for lunch? Marino's okay?" He named a diner near the hospital where he worked.

"That's fine. You'll let the others know?"

He nodded.

"Great. I'll see you around noon, then." She started to walk around him.

"Daisy."

She paused and looked over.

"It's good to see you. And you were great out there."

Daisy offered him a small smile. "It's good to see you too, Ian. And thank you."

He nodded. "Have a good night."

"You too."

With another nod, he walked away.

"You okay?" Asa asked, as she blew out a breath. They resumed their walk to the ready room.

"Yeah. I just hope tomorrow goes as smoothly."

"I think it'll be okay."

She was inclined to agree after the things Jasmine said and Ian's attitude just now.

"Do you want me to go with you?"

Daisy bit her lip as she thought about it. It would be nice to have him there for support, but his presence would keep her and her brothers from having the open discussion they needed to. "No. I'll be fine on my own. Just be ready for me to beat on your chest when I get back."

He laughed. "You got it, sweetness." He hooked an arm around her waist. "Come on. Let's go say goodnight to the Richters."

Sunlight glinted off the windows of Marino's. Daisy swiped her palms down the sides of her shorts, then pulled on the handle to let herself inside. She let her eyes adjust to the lighting, then scanned the restaurant for her brothers. She spotted them all at a booth near the back. Taking a deep breath, she headed over.

Six heads turned to look at her as she stopped in front of them. "Hello, boys."

"What are you wearing?" Kyle frowned up at her.

She bit back a growl. "I will walk right back out that door."

Ian patted the air. "Let's just—play nice, okay? Daisy, sit down. Please."

James, her youngest brother, pushed out the chair next to him.

She dropped into it. "I'm here, so talk."

"We should talk?" her second oldest brother, Brian, said. "You're the one who ran away."

"And I'd do it again. I've never been happier."

Kyle snorted. "Yeah. Because you're living in sin with that musician. Has he got you hooked on drugs? Or alcohol? We read the papers, you know."

Ian nudged Kyle's arm. "Don't be an ass. I don't think what we know about him is necessarily true."

"What?" Kyle frowned at him. "The other day, you were ready to draw and quarter him. What changed?"

Daisy wanted to know that too. She stared at Ian, confused. Who was this man, and what did he do with her asshole brother?

"You didn't see him with Jasmine. My patient, who used her wish to meet Asa? A man who writes a song for a dying girl can't be all bad."

"He's not," Daisy said quietly. She sighed. "How about we start over?" She offered her brothers a smile. "It's good to see you."

Next to her, James smiled back and leaned over to bump his shoulder to hers. "You too. You look good, Dais."

"Thanks."

"Can you explain to us why you left? And what's going on now?" One of the twins, Sean, asked.

Daisy took a deep breath. "It was a culmination of things, really. Mostly, I was just ready to take control of my life, but you wouldn't let me. You all questioned every move I made, inserted yourselves into every part of my life, and no matter how much I protested, you just steamrolled over me and told me it was for my own good. That you knew best. You didn't. But Kyle, what you did was the last straw. That man you set me up with was, well, odd. And not my type. If you bothered to pay attention to who I've grown up to be, you'd know that."

"And Asa Mitchell is your type?" Kyle said.

"Not at first. When I met him, I thought he was a total asshole. But he's grown on me. And shown me he's not the man I thought he was. Or the one the papers make him out to be. They print so many lies, it's outrageous."

"So, he's not dating you and that other woman?" the other twin, Terry, said.

"No. They dated in high school fifteen years ago. She's bitter because he doesn't want her back now that he's home for good."

"And you're really marrying him?" Ian asked.

Daisy spun her engagement ring around her finger, contemplating what to tell them. She decided on the truth. If she wanted a real, adult relationship with her brothers, they all needed to be honest with each other. "I'm not sure. Our relationship started out as fake. As a way to keep Marla and the other crazies at bay."

Six sets of eyebrows slammed down into identical frowns. She held up her hands. "Let me finish before you rip into me."

When they didn't speak, she continued. "The first story you saw, the one that sent Nori out west, was the beginning of it. The papers speculated on it after we told a woman harassing him in town that I was his girlfriend. Someone told the paparazzi following us and they ran with it. Asa denied it, and that's when Marla gave her little exposé. He knew the press would never believe him if he just denied it, so I told him to confirm we were in a relationship." She held up a finger when Ian opened his mouth to speak. "You didn't see him. I couldn't sit there and watch the stress eat him alive. When Asa came home, he was close to a breakdown. Years of touring and being in the public eye had him at his breaking point. It took weeks before he started to relax. The bad press brought all that right back."

She ran a hand through her hair. "By that point, we'd gotten to know each other better and developed a friendship of sorts. I couldn't sit there and watch it tear him apart. Or watch his dad try to hide the pain of watching his only child wade through his own private hell. Not when I could do something about it. So, we faked an engagement."

"So, you're not engaged?" James asked.

Daisy shrugged. "It's not that simple. Not anymore. Somewhere along the way, I fell in love with him." She blew out a breath, making her bangs flutter. A weight lifted off her shoulders as the admission left her mouth. It felt good to get it out there. Now, if she could just work up the courage to say it to Asa.

"So, you are engaged?" Brian said.

"What we are is together. As far as the public is concerned, yes, we're engaged. Whether we stay that way remains to be seen. I just know I've never met anyone like him. Ian's right. The man you know from the media portrayals isn't the real Asa Mitchell. Yes, there have been women, but not as many as you'd think. He's never done drugs, he doesn't drink to excess, and he's not an overly dramatic prima donna. Well," she tipped her head, "except when it comes to food." She smiled. "Then he can be more particular. He hates tuna. And lunch meat." She sobered. "He's a good man. One I think you all would be proud to call a friend. And maybe one day a brother-in-law."

They all looked at each other, doing that thing they did where they came to some decision without saying anything.

"Are you ever coming home?" Ian asked.

"To visit, yes. I'd love to. But I think my home now is the Stone Creek."

He studied her for a moment. "We only ever wanted

what was best for you." He traced lines in the condensation on his glass. "When Mom and Dad died, I was at a loss about what to do with you. Especially as you got older. I kept wondering what they would think if I let you do certain things. Eventually, it just got easier to shelter you from everything. As your body developed, I think I panicked. I knew no matter what you wore, you'd still attract attention, so I figured if you never showed any skin, I didn't have to worry about whether they would think you were dressed too risqué. Then that led to us trying to find a man who we thought would appreciate you for you and not just for your body."

"So you picked men like Ethan Byrnes?" She laughed.

"Hey," Kyle said. "He's a decent guy. He works hard, comes from a good family, and doesn't have a criminal record."

"Um, yes, but trust me when I say he was very interested in my body. Just because someone checks all the boxes doesn't mean they're the right fit. And FYI, Asa checks all those boxes."

Kyle shifted in his seat. "Okay. I guess I can see where I might have been a little pushy."

"A little?" She crossed her arms and raised an eyebrow.

He rolled his eyes. "Yes. A little. But like I said, he's a good guy. And don't tell me Asa doesn't stare at your boobs."

Her cheeks heated. "Well, with him, I don't mind."

"Ew." Brian waved his hands. "We don't want details."

She grinned.

"I'm sorry, Daisy," Kyle said. "Like Ian said, I just wanted what I thought was best for you. If I didn't think Ethan could be a good husband, I wouldn't have pushed you toward him. But you're right. I should have respected your wishes after that first date. I let my own impressions and opinions of him sway me, and I didn't take your feelings into account."

Daisy's eyes widened. She looked around the table. "Okay, who are you all and what have you done with my brothers?"

The six of them glanced at each other.

"We know," Ian said. "This is all out of character, but we've come to understand some things in the months you've been gone. Plus, Nori reamed us all out when she came home. My wife got in on the action too." He shook his head. "Shelly's never been one to get on me about much, but she let me have it. I think that more than anything helped me to understand I treated you differently. You were right to leave. I'm just sorry you had to."

Emotion clogged Daisy's throat. She blinked a few times. "Me too. Despite all your assholery, I love you guys."

He smiled at her. "Can we start over? I can't promise we'll never question a decision you make, but I can promise we'll stop riding roughshod over you." He looked at the others. "Right, guys?"

Five heads nodded.

Her smile wobbled. "Okay."

Twenty-Four

On light feet, Daisy let herself into the hotel suite after her lunch with her brothers. Asa looked up from the couch, where he sat reading a book on an e-reader.

"Hey." He set the device down. "How'd it go?"

She closed the door and put her purse on the table next to it. "Better than I expected."

"Yeah?"

"Yeah. They admitted they were dumb and assholes and apologized. They even promised to do better." She sat down next to him.

"So, no beating on my chest?"

She giggled. "No. Not this time."

"Damn. I was looking forward to restraining you and soothing your pain." He waggled his eyebrows and his eyes heated.

Daisy felt an answering heat flare to life in her belly. She glanced away. "Where's Silas?"

Asa shrugged. "Somewhere with Nori. I don't really want to think about what they're doing."

She laughed and stood. "Well, I know what I want to do." She grabbed his hands and pulled him up.

"What are we doing?" A wolfish smile crossed his face. He yanked her forward. "Why, Daisy O'Malley. Are you trying to take advantage of me?"

Her cheeks heated. With a nervous laugh, she pushed out of his arms, but hung on to his hand, pulling him toward the door. "No. I want to show you my city."

"Sightseeing?"

She nodded.

"Hmm. Okay. Let me put my shoes on." He let go of her hand and found a pair of tennis shoes, then grabbed his wallet, a hat, and sunglasses.

She led him out of the suite and downstairs. They passed the cab stand and kept walking.

"Where are we going?" He glanced back at the taxis.

"To the L."

"We're taking the train?"

She nodded. "It goes right past our first stop."

"Which is?"

"You'll see."

He sighed. "You're loving this, aren't you?"

"Yep." She giggled and led him toward the train station, stopping long enough to purchase their passes at the kiosk. They boarded the train and found seats in the mostly empty car. It was mid-afternoon, so it wasn't too busy. She knew that would change in a few hours when people went home from work.

As they passed through several stops, Daisy pointed out landmarks and other things of interest to him. He asked questions and commented on places he recognized.

The train slowed again, and she pushed him toward the aisle. "This is our stop." They got up and stood at the doors, waiting for them to open as the train came to a halt. On the platform, he took her hand, and they headed for the stairs to take them to street level.

She guided him down the sidewalk, stopping in front of a shop.

"Sugar and Spice." Asa read the sign over the door.

"Yep." She grabbed the door handle. "This is where I used to work."

"Really? That means there's baked goods like what you make at home inside?"

She nodded and opened the door.

"Oh, yeah." He pulled her inside.

"Daisy!"

Daisy grinned as Sandrine called her name, then ran around from behind the counter to envelop her in a hug.

"Oh, it's good to see you." Sandrine pulled back, but held on to Daisy's biceps. "What are you doing here?" Her eyes strayed to Asa, then widened. "And who's the hunk?"

Daisy laughed. "It's good to see you, too, Sandrine. This is Asa. Asa, this is Sandrine Pembroke."

He held out a hand. "It's nice to meet you, ma'am."

"Ditto." She shook his hand. "So, you're the fiancée, huh?" She eyed him up and down, then smiled at Daisy. "Your brother, Kyle, told me you were engaged when he stopped in a while back, asking if I'd heard from you. You sure sent them all into a tizzy when you left. But, you did good, girl. He's cute."

"Thanks." Daisy giggled. "We're on a tour of the city and stopped in to get some goodies."

Asa rubbed his hands together. "If they're half as good as the stuff Daisy makes at home, I can't wait."

Sandrine smiled and led them to the display case. "She learned most of her recipes here, so I'm sure you won't be disappointed."

"You make better cakes than me," Daisy said.

"Maybe when it comes to decorations. Yours always taste wonderful."

Daisy nodded. "Yes, but yours have that fluffiness I've yet to completely master. I'm better at cookies."

"God, yes. Her chocolate chip cookies are the best," Asa said. He smiled at Daisy, then looked at the display again. "I think I'd like to try your raspberry champagne cupcake, though. It's hot today, and that sounds refreshing."

"How about you, Daisy?" Sandrine asked, walking around the counter to open the case.

"Cheesecake. I want cheesecake. The peanut butter swirl kind."

"With chocolate sauce or without?"

Daisy arched a brow.

Sandrine laughed. "Dumb question." She reached for the one with chocolate sauce, putting it in a plastic box.

"Can we get a dozen chocolate chip cookies to go too?" Daisy asked. She was sure Silas would like them. If she could keep Asa from eating them all before they got back, that was.

"Of course." She handed them their treats, then reached for a box.

Asa bit into his cupcake and moaned.

Daisy giggled and took a fork from the cup on the counter, then reached in her purse for her wallet.

Sandrine waved her off. "On the house."

"What? No. You can't give us these and a dozen cookies."

"I own this bakery. I can do whatever I want."

Daisy squinted at her.

"Don't give me that look. I'm just glad to see you. I miss you around here. Your replacement is great, but she's not you."

Daisy's face relaxed. "I miss you too."

"Hey." Asa snapped his fingers and pointed. "Do you deliver?"

Sandrine nodded, giving him a curious frown. "Yes. But I don't ship."

"It's not for me. She can make whatever I want." He pointed at Daisy. "I was thinking about someone else."

"Oh, yes." Daisy nodded as she caught his meaning. "Did you hear about the benefit concert Asa did last night?" she asked Sandrine.

The woman nodded. "It was a Make-A-Wish thing, right?"

He nodded. "I'd like to send some things to the family."

"Sure. Name it."

"I think I'd like to make them," Daisy said before he could. She looked at him. "If you don't mind staying here for a while?"

He shook his head. "Of course not. I like that idea better. I'd like to help."

She beamed. "Perfect. Is that okay with you, Sandrine?"

"Of course it's okay with me. Get your butt back there, girl." She hooked a thumb toward the kitchen beyond the door behind her.

Daisy smiled and took Asa's hand. "Come on."

Dinner in hand, along with all their goodies left over from baking at Sugar and Spice, Daisy and Asa let themselves into their hotel suite that evening.

"Dad?"

Daisy deposited her bags on the table by the window, while Asa went to check Silas's bedroom. She took off her shoes and sighed as her toes sank into the soft carpet.

"He must still be with Nori," Asa said, coming out of the room.

She nodded and headed for the couch. A note on the

coffee table caught her attention. It was addressed to them both. "Oh, here. Look." She picked it up and unfolded it. "It's from your dad. He's staying at Nori's place tonight."

Asa's nose wrinkled. "Not thinking about it." He rolled his shoulders. "Let's eat. I'm starving."

Daisy agreed. She did not want to think about what Silas and Nori were up to, either. She moved their shopping bags to the floor and opened the pizza box, sitting down at the table. Asa sat down across from her and they both lifted a slice from the box, eating in silence. Daisy didn't know about him, but she was ravenous. Her lunch had been minimal; she'd been too busy mending fences with her brothers. Then she spent the rest of the day on her feet, baking. She would not be ashamed to eat half the box by herself.

But after three slices, she was full. Asa polished off the rest.

"That was good." He wiped his mouth with a napkin and sat back in his chair.

She nodded. "Best pizza in Chicago." She sipped her water. "So, what do you want to do the rest of the evening?"

He shrugged. "We could watch a movie. Or play cards. I can run down and get a deck from the hotel store."

"Oh, cards sounds fun."

"Okay." He stood. "I'll be back in a few minutes. You want anything else?"

She shook her head. "No, I'm good. I think I'm going to hop in the shower while you're gone, though. I feel all sticky from baking. Like I have flour in places I shouldn't." Which she probably did. She narrowed her eyes at him, remembering the puff of flour that flew up when he turned the mixer on too fast.

He gave her a devilish grin and held up his hands. "I don't know what you're talking about."

"Mmm-hmm. Go get the cards."

With a laugh, he exited the suite. Daisy cleaned up their

dinner mess, then found her pajamas and went into the bathroom. In the shower, she discovered she did indeed have flour where she shouldn't. Her generous bustline trapped enough to make another batch of cookies.

Scrubbing herself clean, she shut the water off and got out, drying off with a fluffy bath towel. She got dressed and wrapped a smaller towel around her hair, then went back to the living room. Asa stepped through the door as she entered.

"It took you that long to get a deck of cards?"

"Uh, yeah."

She stopped and frowned at the distracted tone of his voice. "Is everything okay?"

He nodded. "Yeah. Sorry. They were busy. Here." He walked over and gave her the deck. "I'm going to take a quick shower too."

"Okay." She took the cards, still frowning. "Are you sure everything is all right? You're not smiling."

He sighed. "It's fine, Daisy. I'll be right back."

She watched him walk away. He'd just lied to her. She wasn't sure why or what it was about, but something was wrong. Maybe he got recognized downstairs. That had happened when they picked up their pizza. It took him a little while to shrug off the stress it induced. Hopefully, the shower and a game of cards would help him relax again.

While she waited on him, she found a bottle of wine in the fridge behind the bar and a couple of glasses. She poured them each some, then got the box of cookies they brought back and put them on the table. With things setup and ready for them to play, she stepped out on the balcony to enjoy the evening breeze. The sun was low in the sky, but not set yet. Traffic noise reached her ears, even from forty stories up. She didn't miss that sound.

Movement from inside the suite drew her attention. She turned to see Asa in the doorway. Gray and black plaid pajama pants hung low on his hips and a gray t-shirt clung to his muscled frame. He smiled at her, looking much more like himself.

"Ready?"

"Yes." She smiled back and came inside. "What are we playing?"

He drew the blinds over the door, and they sat down at the table. "I don't care. What do you want to play?"

"Rummy?"

"Sure."

She dealt the cards, then picked hers up, arranging them. They played several hands, laughing as they tried to outdo the other. When they were even at two wins apiece, Asa grinned at her.

"I'm going to kick your pretty little butt."

"We'll see." She lifted her cards, holding back her smile. She had a good hand, but didn't want to let on to that.

"I can see it in your eyes, sweetness."

"See what?" She schooled her face. Dammit, she hated that he could read her so well.

He laughed. "Cute. But you're not fooling me." He laid some cards on the table and drew one from the deck before discarding another.

Daisy laid down her matches, then picked up a card, discarding another. "I don't know what you're talking about."

"That's like over half your hand." He groaned and picked up another card. "We're playing poker next. I'm tired of losing."

She laughed. "You won two hands."

"The first two."

"What can I say? I'm on a streak." She drew another card. It was what she needed. With a grin, she laid her cards down. "Rummy."

He tossed his cards down. Daisy laughed again. She

pushed away from the table. "I need some water. You want some?"

Asa got up and followed her. "Sure."

She took two bottles from the fridge under the bar and handed him one, then twisted off the cap on hers and took a long drink. The pizza was salty and made her thirsty. The wine wasn't helping.

A bead of water dribbled down her chin. Asa reached out and caught it. When his skin touched hers, a shiver went through her, and goosebumps erupted on her arms. Slowly, she lowered the bottle, trapped in his gaze.

He opened his hand and cupped her jaw. Her breath quickened as he leaned closer. His eyes held hers, silently asking permission. Daisy stood on her toes and sealed her mouth to his.

In a flash, she was lost in the sensations he provoked. He took over the kiss, tangling his tongue with hers. Waves of pleasure spiked her blood until her head spun.

She broke away to realize it wasn't the kiss making her head spin. He'd picked her up.

"What are we doing?" She laid a hand against his jaw.

"I'm not making out with you standing behind a bar."

"Oh."

He bent his head and captured her mouth again. Daisy moaned. She wanted more. Her body was strung so tight she felt like the slightest touch would make her snap. And maybe it would. She didn't know. All this was new to her.

Asa set her on the couch, then followed her down, pressing her into the cushions. Her head fell back against the arm as he left her mouth to rain kisses down her neck to the expanse of collarbone exposed by her shirt.

"I love this top." He nudged the neckline away with his nose. It fell off her shoulder, sagging lower. "It shows just enough to keep me intrigued." He kissed his way back to her neck, then went south into the valley between her breasts. "I'd be happier if it was gone, though."

"Okay," she breathed.

He stilled and looked up. "Are you sure?"

She nodded. "Yeah. I'm dying, here. I need you to touch me. Kiss me."

He studied her, then nodded. "We'll go slow. If you want to stop, all you have to do is say so."

Daisy highly doubted she would ask him to stop, but she nodded anyway. "Slow is good. But not too slow."

A wicked smile formed on his face. "No, not too slow. We'll both die of torture if that happens." He dipped his head and lightly bit the top of her breast.

Daisy's giggle turned into another moan.

He drew back and lifted her shirt. She raised her arms so he could pull it over her head. He frowned at the sports bra he exposed. "Can you take that off yourself? I'm afraid I'll snap your nose or something if I try."

She laughed and pulled an arm through the strap.

"Seriously. I don't know how women squeeze into these things."

Daisy pulled it over her head and flung it to the floor. "It's stretchy."

"Mmm-hmm." His eyes glazed as he stared at her chest. "It's a travesty to restrict such beauty." He wrapped his large hands around her breasts, raising one as he bent his head to take the tip in his mouth.

Wet heat flooded her core. *Dear God in Heaven. That felt delightful.* His tongue swirled around the hard bud. When he bit down, she let out a yelp as a jolt of pure lust sent her hips bucking upward. He let go to look at her.

"Did I hurt you?"

She shook her head. "God, no."

He grinned. "Good to know."

Daisy didn't get a chance to respond. He dipped his head again and took the other breast in his mouth. His fingers worked the other, driving her into a frenzy. She tunneled her hands into his thick hair and clutched the strands as he toyed with her breasts. She never thought it would feel so good to have a man's hands and mouth on them. They were always just a nuisance to her. She'd never look at them the same way again. Not after the way Asa's mouth and hands on them made her feel.

He let go to kiss her again. She wrapped her arms around him and found the hem of his shirt, her hands diving beneath to feel his warm skin. The urge to feel his naked chest against hers hit, and she pushed at his shoulders.

Immediately, he pulled away. "What? Are you okay? Do you want me to stop?"

She smiled. "No. I want you to take off your shirt."

"Oh." He grabbed it at the back of his neck and pulled it over his head, throwing it in the same direction as her bra. "How's that?"

"That's—that's good." Her ability to form a better sentence went sailing away with his shirt. She laid her hands against his chest, feeling the crisp hair tickle her palms. He was beautiful.

But he didn't give her much of a chance to look before he kissed her again. There was more urgency this time, and Daisy could tell his control was slipping. Hers was too. Especially with his chest pressed to hers. Every move he made rubbed that beautiful hair-roughened chest against her nipples, sending waves of heat through her. She needed more.

Feeling bold, she let her hands travel down his torso to grab his ass through his pajama pants. It flexed beneath her touch, and he groaned into her mouth.

"You're killing me, sweetness," he said, breaking away.

"*I'm* killing *you*?" She groaned. "I'm ready to shoot off like a rocket."

"Really? Let's see if we can help that along." With a wicked smile, he sat up. His hands trailed down her torso, over the tips of her breasts, to the hem of her shorts. "Lift your hips."

They rose before she even registered his words, her body recognizing the benefit of following his instructions.

He pulled her shorts and panties off, baring her to his view. Daisy was too aroused to feel self-conscious. She just wanted him to put her out of her misery.

Sliding back, he lifted her outside leg over his shoulder and kissed the inside of her thigh. "I love your legs. I'm a big man, and they're perfect for wrapping around my waist."

A blush stole over her whole body, and he chuckled. "I also love that I can talk dirty and you blush. Let's see what else I can do to make that happen." He ran a finger through her folds.

Daisy sucked in a sharp breath. "Oh, God."

He did it again, and her hips rose to meet his hand.

"Jesus, Daisy. Slow's about to go out the window."

"Fine by me."

Growling, he slid a finger into her channel. She let out an airy moan, and he added another, then another, stretching her. With a few strokes, the dam on the rising tide of heat broke to flood her body. She let out a wild shout and writhed against his hand; it disappeared all too quickly.

"Where are you going?" she asked as he stood.

"Unless you're on the pill, we need protection."

"Oh. No, I'm not."

He gave her a short nod and walked away. Daisy let her head fall back against the sofa and blew out a breath. The first doubts crept into her mind. Was she crazy? Did she really want to give herself to Asa? To take him as her first lover?

But what if he was also her last?

She shut her eyes as her conscience reminded her of her revelations this week. That she'd fallen head over heels for the man. She honestly couldn't imagine herself ever wanting someone the way she wanted Asa. If things went south on them, she wanted the memories to tide her over. They would be good ones she could pull out when she needed them.

He reappeared, naked now. Her eyes widened as she took in his engorged state. He looked bigger than she remembered. Moisture glistened on the tip of his shaft. Her mouth watered, so she did what she wanted to do the day she walked in on him in his bedroom. She sat forward and licked him.

"Holy hell, woman." He grabbed a handful of her hair. "Do that again."

With a knowing smile, she did, then took him into her mouth. She didn't have any idea what she was doing, but figured it must feel good because he had a fist wrapped in her hair and kept making low growls, deep in his throat.

He gave her hair a quick tug, pulling her back. She looked up at him with a pout.

"Don't look at me like that. If you kept that up, we weren't going to get to use these." He held up a string of condoms.

Her eyes widened. "That's a lot of condoms."

He sat down and pulled her on top of him. "And I'm going to use every single one tonight." He tore one off and opened it, smoothing it on over himself. Hands on her hips, he urged her to straddle him.

"Are you sure this is the way we should do this the first time?"

Asa nodded. "I know you don't have much experience, if any, right?"

She rolled her lips in, but nodded, not shying away from his gaze. She wasn't ashamed she'd never been with a man at her age. It made her happy to save herself for the one that mattered.

He wove a hand into her hair. "You'll have more control this way. It'll probably hurt at first, but with you on top, you get to decide how fast or slow we go."

Nerves replaced some of her arousal. She nodded. "Okay."

"Hey." His thumb caressed her cheekbone. "We can stop. I can take care of myself in the bathroom."

She bit her lip, but shook her head. "No. I want to do this. And I know the first time is the worst. It has to happen sometime."

"Are you sure you're ready for that to be now?"

Daisy nodded. "Yeah. I'm sure."

He studied her for another beat, then stretched up to kiss her softly. "You set the pace. I'm just along for the ride this time."

She kissed him again and shoved her wariness out of her mind. She wanted this. Wanted him. Rising up, she inched closer until her knees pressed into the back of the couch on either side of his hips. She could feel his erection tease her core. Her body wanted to slam itself down on top of him, but she knew that would be a bad idea. Asa was a big man everywhere.

Rubbing against him, she worked them both into a state of heightened pleasure before reaching down to grab him. He hissed against her mouth, and she pulled back. "Sorry."

He shook his head. "It didn't hurt. But you are killing me. Slowly and deliciously."

His words made her bolder. She pressed him to her opening and inched down. He groaned as he slid inside her. His muscles strained as he held himself still. Daisy tensed as he met resistance and realized it was now or never. Taking a deep breath, she let her legs relax and sank onto him. A sharp pain pierced her, and she let out a cry, burying her face in his shoulder while it passed.

"You okay?" He stroked her hair.

The pain faded, and she nodded as a new sensation took its place. One of fulfillment. And the first stirrings of pleasure. "Yes." She lifted her hips a fraction and slid back down. They both moaned.

Asa grabbed her hips. "Keep moving, sweetness."

She did it again, going higher this time. In moments, she found a rhythm that left them both panting for breath. That same heat that coiled in her when he sent her over the edge with his hands and mouth grew again, only hotter this time. She boiled with it until her body couldn't take it anymore and she exploded. Searing, white hot pleasure rocketed through her veins to burst through every cell of her body. Her movements sped up as she rode the waves. Asa tensed beneath her for a brief moment before he let out a loud shout, then growled as he ground against her.

He took her mouth, gentling them both with a long, languid kiss. Daisy's bones turned to rubber, and she sagged against him. Her heart sang with love for Asa, but she kept a lid on it. She didn't want to ruin things by telling him how she felt. Not when she wasn't sure he felt the same. She wanted to savor this moment and not taint it with awkwardness.

"When my bones regenerate, we'll move this party to the bedroom." His voice rumbled beneath her ear.

She chuckled. "Sounds good to me."

TWENTY-FIVE

ips swaying to the music coming through her earbuds, Daisy dusted the study. It was amazing how much dirt piled up in this house in such a short amount of time. They'd only been home a day, and she dusted before they left, but the house had a fine layer of dust on everything already. The only thing she could think of was the cattle and horses stirred up a lot of dirt and it floated in the air like a fine smog. It didn't help that she liked to keep the windows open. In fact, opening up the house was the first thing she did when they got back yesterday afternoon.

Her phone rang, cutting off the music. She paused to take it from her pocket, frowning when she saw the screen. It was Ian. Seeing his name didn't fill her with the same dread it did a few days ago. But she still couldn't help but wonder why he was calling her after they just saw each other. She slid her finger over the screen to answer.

"Hello?"

"Hi, Daisy. Um, so, let me preface this by saying I'm not calling out of any sort of malicious intent. I just thought you should be aware of this."

"Of what?" She frowned and sat on the corner of the desk.

"There's a new story in the papers about Asa."

She rolled her eyes. "There's always a new story. What did they make up this time?"

"I'm not so sure they made this one up. They have a picture of him kissing a woman in Chicago. It's not you."

"What?" She frowned and stood up, moving in front of the computer to wake it up and get online. "What paper is it in?"

He named the tabloid. Daisy pulled up its website and scrolled. There in full color was Asa, standing in the lobby of their hotel, kissing his ex-girlfriend. "What the hell?"

Ian sighed in her ear, and she jerked, having forgotten he was on the phone. "I'm sorry, Daisy."

Her frown intensified. "I'm not sure what this is about. But thank you for telling me. I need to go." She hung up before he could protest. Dumbstruck, she sank into the chair and stared at the screen. The woman had her arms wrapped around his neck. His were around her back, holding on. Her eyes narrowed as she saw the object clutched in his hand. It was a deck of cards.

"Oh, that asshole. That's what he lied about." She knew he'd been hiding something when he came back to the room. Anger surged, and she pushed away from the desk, removing her earbuds as she stormed out of the room into the kitchen.

She went into the mudroom and stuffed her feet in her barn boots, then pushed the screen door open with a bang, stalking toward the horse barn. Her anger carried her inside on swift feet. Jasper, who was leading a horse from its stall, paused to greet her.

"Hi, Daisy."

"Hi. Where is he?"

Jasper frowned. "What? You mean Asa?"

She nodded.

He pointed toward the back of the barn. "In the corral with that horse he brought home from Knox's. They're working on some cutting techniques."

She was moving before he finished. Outside, she spotted him atop the new horse, putting the gelding through his paces.

"Asa!"

He pulled the animal to a stop and turned to smile at her. "Hey." He rode over, the smile dying as he took in her expression. "What's wrong?"

"What's wrong? How could you?"

He dismounted and walked over. "What are you talking about? What did I do?"

"How could you kiss another woman, then make love to me?" She rammed a finger into his chest. "I knew you were lying about something when you came back. Were you trying to prove something to yourself when you screwed my brains out on the couch? To convince yourself you would be okay settling for the housekeeper?"

"Daisy, it wasn't like that."

"Or maybe you wanted to give the poor, sheltered girl a pleasurable experience before you dumped her and went back to your supermodel ex."

"Sweetness—"

"Don't 'sweetness' me, Asa Mitchell. I saw the pictures. You were smiling at her, then she was in your arms."

"Honey, it's not what it looked like. If you'd let me explain—"

"Save it." To her horror, her throat clogged up, and tears welled in her eyes. She battled them back. She would not give him the satisfaction of seeing her cry over him. "I don't know why I thought a woman like me could keep you happy. Not when you could have her."

"Daisy, she means nothing to me. Nothing happened, I swear."

"Then why did you lie?"

He glanced away.

"That's what I thought." She spun away and headed inside.

"Daisy! Baby, wait."

She started jogging as the tears rolled over her eyelids.

"Daisy?" Jasper turned as she ran past. She didn't stop.

The need to get away pushed her to move faster. She broke into a full run for the house. Asa's voice carried over the lawn, but she didn't stop. Inside, she snagged her purse off the counter and dashed into the garage to her car. She needed to leave so she could calm down. Just for a little while. Maybe once she'd had a good cry, she could talk to him and explain that this wasn't going to work. But for now, she just needed to get away.

She started the engine as the garage door opened. As soon as it was high enough for her car to clear, she put it in reverse and backed out. Asa changed direction when he saw her, but she didn't slow. Putting the car in drive, she turned around in the driveway and drove away. Tears clouded her vision, and she swiped at them, refusing to look in the rearview mirror. He wasn't worth it.

Her phone rang, but she ignored it, knowing it was probably Asa. Instead, she shut it off. She didn't want to talk to anyone right now.

Brain on autopilot, she soon found herself in town. On Main Street, her eyes went to the sign for Sarafina's. This called for a milkshake. Maybe two. And a double order of fries.

Wiping her eyes again, she parked her car and got out. Sara took one look at her when she stepped inside and ushered her behind the counter to the back room.

"What happened?" She pushed Daisy into a chair in her office.

Daisy took a shaky breath. "He kissed another woman."

"What?" A frown marred Sara's face. "When? I'll kill him for you."

"In Chicago. His ex. At our hotel. Then he—" Her breath caught. "Then he came upstairs and made love to me." A tear spilled over.

Sara stared at her, mouth agape. "Are you sure?"

Daisy frowned at her friend. "What do you mean, am I sure? Their picture is all over the tabloids."

"It's just, that doesn't sound like the Asa I know."

"Well, he did. Can I have a milkshake? I need one. Bad."

Sara nodded. She poked her head out the door and called to one of her staff to make a chocolate shake and bring it in.

"Did you talk to him about it?"

She nodded. "Sort of."

"What did he say?"

"He tried to tell me it wasn't what I thought. But what else could it be? You should see the picture, Sara. They were wrapped around each other."

"Really? Where are these pictures?" She spun around to open an internet browser on her computer.

Daisy named the tabloid. Sara pulled it up and let out a low whistle as she scrolled. "Okay. I can see why you're upset." She looked at Daisy. "What else did he say?"

"Not much. I was so mad, I wouldn't really let him talk. I couldn't. I was on the verge of tears and didn't want him to see me cry over him, so I just left." She sighed and glanced up at the ceiling. "Was I too hasty?"

There was a knock on the door. Sara opened it and took the shake from the young man who carried it. She thanked him and handed it to Daisy, shutting the door.

Sara sat down again and shrugged. "Maybe. Whatever the case, I think you need to talk to him again. Let him explain. Even if it isn't what you want to hear."

Daisy groaned. She pulled what was left of the paper off

the top of the straw and sucked down some of the rich concoction. "Don't ever fall in love with your employer. Especially if you live with him. Even if I wanted to quit, I still have to go back, because I live there."

Sara giggled. "Well, I'm self-employed, so I think I'm safe."

A small smile lifted Daisy's mouth. She took another drink. "Thank you for talking me off the edge." She shook her head. "I really hope I didn't screw things up because I overreacted."

"Just go home and talk to him. If he really was that big of an asshole, I've got a spare bedroom."

Daisy leaned over and gave Sara a hug. "Thank you."

"Any time. Now, take the rest of that shake with you and go fix your relationship."

"Yes, ma'am." She stood, squaring her shoulders. Feeling like an idiot for flying off the handle, she waved at Sara and left.

Outside, she unlocked her car, but as she reached for her door handle, a woman called her name. She turned and groaned as she saw who walked toward her.

"Go away, Marla." She opened her car door.

"You think you won, but he won't stay with you. I saw the gossip columns this morning. He's already tiring of you. It takes a real woman, one who knows how to please a man, to keep someone like Asa Mitchell."

Daisy shook her head. She wasn't even mad. She just felt sorry for Marla. "It's called gossip for a reason. I need to go. Have a nice day." Finished with the conversation, she got in the car and closed the door, refusing to roll the window down to hear what Marla said in reply. She just waved and backed out of her space. She did give in to the urge to look in the rearview mirror as she drove away, though. Marla stood on the sidewalk, watching her. As she reached the stop sign, the woman stomped her foot, then stormed away.

She shoved the woman from her mind. She had bigger problems than Marla Wilkins. Like groveling at Asa's feet. She should have given him the benefit of the doubt. But the timing of his encounter with his ex threw her for a loop. It bothered her that he could kiss her—whatever the reason—then come upstairs and make love to her without mentioning what happened downstairs. Daisy just prayed he was willing to talk and let her make things right.

So caught up in her thoughts, Daisy didn't see the car that came up behind her until it was on her bumper. She slowed down and turned on her flashers to let the other car know it was safe to go around her. But it didn't. She took a long look in her mirror, trying to see the driver. She didn't recognize the car. All she could tell about the person behind the wheel was that it looked like a woman.

The other car sped up and rammed into her. Daisy let out a shriek and gripped the wheel as her car fishtailed. She almost had it under control when the other car hit her again. The rear end of her car swung into the other lane. Daisy tried to steer into the skid, but momentum carried her across the highway. Her eyes widened, and she let out a scream as her car went over the embankment.

Memories of her life flashed before her eyes, ending with Asa's handsome face as she crashed into a tree and the world went black.

Twenty-Six

Asa parked his truck in front of Chet's house and got out. His foreman and best friend was off today. Marci took her mother to an appointment in Billings, so Chet was home with their baby. Asa needed to talk to someone and couldn't wait until tomorrow when Chet came back to work. Things with Daisy were driving him crazy, and he couldn't make sense of any of it.

He mounted the steps to the porch and knocked on the door. After a moment, Chet answered, Sloan in his arms.

"Asa. Hey. What are you doing here?" Chet held the screen door open and let him in.

"You're married. How do you stay that way?"

Chet barked out a laugh, but quickly sobered when he saw the seriousness on Asa's face. "Let's go sit down." He led him into the living room.

Asa flopped into an oversize chair. Chet laid Sloan in a playpen on a play mat, then sat down on the couch.

"I take it this is about Daisy?"

"Yeah." Asa rubbed his forehead. "She flew off the handle at me this morning. When we were in Chicago, I went down to the hotel store to get a deck of cards. My ex, Kim, was there. Apparently, she was in town for some modeling thing and staying at the same hotel. We ran into each other in the lobby. I stopped and said hello."

He sighed. "I should have just kept walking. She gushed about how great it was to see me, and that she missed me. We should do dinner, yada yada yada. I told her I was leaving in the morning and I had plans, so maybe another time. I just wanted to get away. She did that pout thing she does and walked up to give me a hug. So, I hugged her back. The next thing I knew, she planted a big kiss on me. It only took a second for me to push her away, but, of course, there were paparazzi hanging around, and they got that one second shot. I'm sure they got a shot of me shoving her away, too, but they didn't print that."

"Daisy believed the papers?"

Asa nodded. "She wouldn't even let me explain."

"That doesn't sound like her."

"I agree. But the timing was terrible. I went back to our suite, and I didn't tell her what happened. Then we ended up in bed together for the first time."

"Whoa. So she thinks you're double-dipping?"

"Something like that, yes." He groaned and leaned forward, scrubbing his hands over his face, leaning his elbows on his knees. "How do I fix this? I don't want to lose her."

Chet's eyes widened. "You fell in love with her."

Asa frowned. Is that why he felt this way? He groaned again. "I don't know, man. I just know I need to fix this."

"I don't think there's much to fix. It sounds like you two just need to talk. And next time, don't lie. She'll always know. Trust me. So, how about you get out of here and go talk to her?"

"Yeah. I'll have to wait until she gets back. She reamed me out, then ran off. I think she went into town. Maybe to talk to

Sara. But I will once she gets back. Even if I have to lock her in my bedroom to do it. Or hers." He stood. "I think I'll ride out and check on the herd while she's gone. Give her plenty of time to cool off."

Chet got up. "Just don't stay gone too long. You don't want her to think you're ignoring her."

Asa sighed. "It's a delicate balance, isn't it?"

"Yes. But it gets easier the longer you're together. At least it has for Marci and me."

"Good to know. Thanks for listening. I know I haven't been the greatest friend the last few years. I appreciate you sticking with me."

Chet laid a hand on Asa's shoulder. "You've been my best friend since we were in diapers. I knew you'd come around, eventually."

"Still, thank you."

"You're welcome. Let me know how things go. We can always get Marci's opinion if you need it."

"Hopefully, it doesn't come to that." Asa headed for the door. "See you later." He opened the door and stepped through, waving.

Back in the truck, he thought about saddling Storm and riding out, but decided he'd rather have the air-conditioning. The truck could handle the terrain. They hadn't had much rain lately, so it wouldn't bog down. He followed the road from Chet's toward the pasture and let himself through the gate. Asa kept the pace slow, so he didn't spook the cattle and checked on the herd. He'd head deeper onto the ranch and check on some of the animals that were further out, then head back. That would take him a good hour. Surely Daisy would be back by then. And hopefully calmer.

Ninety minutes later, he drove into the yard and parked by the back door. Daisy's SUV was still missing. Frowning, he took out his phone and tried to call her. She didn't answer, but he wasn't really surprised. He called Sara instead, hoping maybe she was at the diner.

"Sarafina's. Sara speaking."

"Hey, Sara. It's Asa. Is Daisy there?"

"No. She was. But she left over an hour ago. She's not home yet?"

"No. Did she say if she was going anywhere else?"

"She planned to go home and find you. To apologize. She should be there."

Unease skated up Asa's spine. "Okay. I'm going to drive the road into town. Maybe she broke down or hit a deer. If she shows up or you hear from her, will you call me?"

"Of course. Same goes for you. Let me know she's safe."

"I will." He hung up and put the truck in drive, turning around to head into town. As he made the turn onto the highway, he prayed he would find her safe and sound, but pissed beside her car. He could handle a broken-down car. Better yet, he hoped he passed her. That she decided to stop at the grocery or some other place in town before heading home.

He did his best not to speed and kept his eyes peeled. Some of the drop offs were sharp, so he slowed to look, his heart in his throat every time. He punched the button on his steering wheel to make a call. "Call Daisy." The phone rang through the speakers, then rolled to voicemail again. "Dammit!" He hung up and kept driving.

Just shy of halfway to town, skid marks on the road made him slow. He looked off the side of the road on either side. A flash of blue in the trees down the embankment on his side of the road caught his attention. He pulled to the berm and put his flashers on, throwing the truck in park.

"Daisy!" He was out of the truck as it rocked to a halt and standing at the top of the embankment. Through the trees, he could make out the rear of her vehicle wedged between two pines. "Dear God." He scrambled down the hill toward her car, his stomach in his throat as his mind went through the possibilities of what he would find.

"Daisy!" He skidded to a halt at her back bumper. He could see her slumped inside, not moving. "Please be alive. Please be alive." He dug his heels into the dirt and walked around the side of her car to the driver's side. The window was busted out.

"Baby, it's me." God, she was so still. He reached in to check for a pulse. To his relief, one beat against his fingers. It was weak, but it was there. "Honey. Sweetness, can you hear me?" He tapped her cheek. She didn't make a sound.

Asa dug his phone out and called 911. Once he reported the accident, he called his dad.

"Hello?"

"Dad, Daisy's been in an accident. I'm down the embankment about halfway to town. I called for help."

"What? Jesus. Okay. I'm on my way." Silas hung up.

Asa pocketed his phone. He knew better than to move her, but he couldn't just stand here and wait for help to arrive. He could at least try to get better access inside the car, so the firefighters wouldn't have to waste precious time trying to get to her.

Her door was crumpled, with a sizeable gap between the top of it and the car frame. He found a sturdy log and wedged it into the crack. Using the leverage his height provided, he pushed on the branch. It took a few tries, but the door finally popped free of the latch mechanism. He yanked on it, forcing the hinge to bend backward.

"Daisy, sweetness." He crouched next to her seat, tapping her cheek again. "Wake up, baby." He lifted one of her eyelids. The pupil didn't react. Fear made his heart skip a beat. He pushed it back and forced himself to focus. It wouldn't serve him or her if he freaked out.

The basic medical training his dad made him learn when

he was younger came back to him. He leaned into the car and started assessing her, looking for obvious injuries. Blood trickled from her head beneath her hair. Gently, he worked his hands into the strands, feeling her skull. Near the cut, he felt a dent.

Hands shaking, he moved to her limbs to check for breaks. Her arms felt fine, but her lower legs moved in ways they shouldn't when he touched them. He left her torso alone, not wanting to jostle her if she had a back or neck injury.

He bit back a growl of frustration. None of her wounds, except the cut on her head, were ones he could treat with the first aid kit he carried in his truck. It wasn't bleeding enough for him to want to mess with it and chance moving her neck.

With nothing left to do, he took her hand and alternated between praying and talking to her for the next fifteen minutes until he heard sirens. When the first one split the air, he scrambled back up the embankment, reaching the top just as the firetruck came into view. He waved his arms, and it slowed, parking in front of his truck.

"She's down there," he said as the firefighters climbed out. He recognized his old friend, Wade Kaczmarek. "I can't get her to wake up."

Wade walked up to him. "She?"

He nodded. "It's my fiancée, Daisy. We had an argument, and she left the ranch to go into town to cool down. When she didn't come back after a couple of hours, I got worried and called around. Sara at the diner told me she was there, but left over an hour before, so I retraced her route home and found her car down there." He pointed down the hill again.

Wade nodded. "You said she's unconscious?"

Asa nodded.

"Has she stirred at all?"

"No. I did a quick assessment without moving her. Both

her legs are broken below the knee, and there's a dent in her skull."

"Okay, that's good to know. We'll get her out of there. Hang tight." He turned to run back to the truck, yelling for the others to grab the limb splints and neck collar as he went. An ambulance and a patrol car screamed onto the scene, adding to the chaos. Asa was so focused on the responder activity, he didn't hear his dad's truck pull up until Silas called his name.

He spun around. "Dad."

Silas jogged up. "How bad is it?"

Tears welled in Asa's eyes. He fought to keep them at bay. "It's bad." His voice wobbled. "Her legs are broken and I think she's got a skull fracture. That's all I could tell without moving her. The firefighters just arrived. They're gathering their gear to go down and get her."

Shock left Silas speechless for a moment. He blinked several times, looking between Asa and what was visible of Daisy's car from where they stood. Finally, he nodded. "Come on. Let's see if we can be useful. They might need some extra hands to pull her up."

They ran up to the firetruck to offer their help. Wade told them to stay at the top of the embankment for now. Frustration ate at Asa's gut, and he paced the edge of the road, watching the firefighters and ambulance crew work the scene below. He heard Wade radio for a chopper.

Asa's anxiety grew as they extracted her from the car. She still wasn't moving, and to him, the rescue wasn't happening fast enough. He wanted to run down there and scoop her out of the car and drive as fast as possible to the hospital. Thankfully, part of his mind stayed rational and he was able to keep his feet rooted to the pavement.

After what felt like an hour, but was only about ten

minutes, Wade motioned them down to help carry her up the hillside.

"Dear God," Silas muttered as he got his first look at Daisy. Blood coated the side of her pale face.

Asa swallowed the lump in his throat. She looked dead.

The beat of a helicopter's blades cut through the sound of them moving up the embankment, growing louder as it neared. They halted at the edge of the road as the chopper descended onto the roadway just past the firetruck.

Two people exited the chopper and ran toward them.

"What do we have?" One of the flight paramedics lifted the visor on her helmet.

"Daisy O'Malley. Twenty-eight-year-old female. Car accident with entrapment. Visible deformities to both lower extremities and skull. Unconscious, but responds to painful stimuli. Pulse is one-thirty and thready. BP is one-oh-two over sixty-six. Respirations are sixteen." Wade rattled off all they knew.

"Okay. Let's get her on the chopper." She glanced at Asa and did a double take. "You the one who found her?"

He nodded. "She's my fiancée."

She tipped her head toward the chopper. "You can come with us. Let's go."

Asa glanced at his dad.

"Go." Silas gave Asa a push toward the helicopter. "I'll make sure your truck gets home."

"The keys are in it."

"Keep us updated."

"I will." Asa took off after the paramedics. The woman was busy loading Daisy into the back and starting an IV. The man with her pointed at the front. Asa glanced through the glass, and the pilot gestured toward the handle, making a turning motion with his hand.

Asa grasped the handle and opened the door to climb

inside. He folded himself into the seat, his knees practically in his chest. The pilot handed him a headset.

"Strap in." The pilot's voice came through the earphones.

Asa slid the straps over his shoulders, adjusting the length and buckling them into the buckle on the front of the seat. It barely clicked into place when the whir of the rotors increased. They were airborne in seconds. He turned, trying to see into the back. All he could see was a glimpse of Daisy's hair hanging off the edge of the stretcher and her shoulder.

"She's in good hands."

He turned back to look at the pilot. "I know."

"And I'm going as fast as I can."

"I know that too. Thank you."

The pilot nodded.

Asa kept one eye on what he could see of the back and the other eye out the cockpit window as they flew toward Billings. It was a quick flight that dragged. He just wanted them to be on the ground with Daisy in the hands of the doctors, who could do what had to be done to save her. He prayed they could save her.

"When I set us down, you stay with me. I'll escort you to the waiting area. They'll take her straight down to the E.R. and work her up," the pilot said, his attention on the ground. The flashing strobes from the helipad lit their way.

The chopper bumped as they landed. As soon as both skids were firmly on the ground, a group of people ran forward with a stretcher, and the rear door opened. Asa watched as the paramedics transferred Daisy to the gurney and the group ran inside. The rotors slowed, and the pilot flipped some switches and removed his headset.

"Let's go."

Asa took off his headset and opened his door. Unfolding from the seat, he exited the helicopter and followed the pilot inside. They rode the elevator down to the first floor, then walked down a winding hallway to the family waiting room near the E.R.

"I hope things turn out okay." The pilot patted him on the shoulder, then pointed to a volunteer sitting behind the desk a few feet away. "Give her your name and the patient's name. She'll make sure the E.R. staff know you're waiting."

"Okay. Thank you."

The pilot nodded and left.

Asa walked over to the desk. "My fiancée, Daisy O'Malley, was just brought in by helicopter."

The woman wrote Daisy's name on a notepad. "Your name?"

"Asa Mitchell."

"And you said she's your fiancée?"

He nodded.

"Are you her next-of-kin on record?"

"Um, not yet, no. I think it's probably her aunt. Or her oldest brother. But they both live in Chicago."

"Okay. Do you have contact information for them?"

Asa took out his phone. "I do for her aunt. Let me call her and break the news, then you can speak to her." He found Nori's name in his contacts and clicked on it. It rang several times before it rolled to voicemail. He hung up, not wanting to leave that kind of information in a message. "Damn. She didn't answer. I think I might be able to get a hold of her brother, though." He looked up the phone number for the hospital where Ian worked and dialed their directory assistance.

"Can you put me through to Dr. Ian O'Malley, please? It's an emergency."

"I can connect you to his office," the young man said. "One moment." The line clicked and hold music played before he could respond. After a couple of seconds, it started to ring again.

"Hem-Onc, this is Carlie."

"Hello. I'm trying to reach Dr. O'Malley about his sister. It's an emergency."

"I'm sorry, Dr. O'Malley's in a meeting—"

"Then interrupt him." Asa's voice echoed off the walls. He blew out a breath and lowered his voice. "Sorry. Please go get him. Tell him it's Asa calling about Daisy. There's been an accident."

The woman paused a beat, weighing his words. "Okay, give me a minute." The hold music came back on.

Asa paced to the window and looked out, tapping his foot while he waited. His thoughts swirled and his fingers itched to do—something. He couldn't get the image of Daisy's lifeless body out of his head. If he hadn't felt her heartbeat for himself, he wasn't sure he would believe she was still alive.

"Asa? What's going on?" Ian's voice came over the line, pulling Asa out of his thoughts.

"Daisy was in a bad car accident. I don't know what happened. She was on her way back from town and ended up down an embankment. I went looking for her when I realized how long she'd been gone and found her car. They life-flighted her to Billings. We just landed a few minutes ago."

"Dear God. What do you know about her injuries?"

"Both her legs are broken. And she's got a skull fracture. She was unconscious when I found her and still hasn't woken up."

Ian cursed.

"I tried to call Nori, but she didn't answer. Can you tell her? It might be better for her to get the news in person."

"Of course. I hope you're prepared for an invasion. We'll all be on the next plane out there."

"That's fine. Tell me what flight you want on and I'll buy the tickets."

There was a beat of silence. "We can buy our own tickets."

"I know. But I can buy the entire plane and not bat an eye. Just send me the info."

Ian blew out a breath. "Fine."

"The staff need to talk to you. You're Daisy's next-of-kin, right?"

"Yes."

"Okay, hang on." He walked over to the desk and held out his phone to the volunteer. "It's her brother."

The woman took the phone. "Hello. I just need some quick information from you." She asked Ian several questions, then handed Asa back the device.

He put it back to his ear. "Hey. Did my number come up on your phone?"

"Yes."

"Text me your cell. I'll keep you updated."

"You better. I'll get you the flight info you want too." He hung up.

"Mr. Mitchell?"

Asa turned to look at the volunteer.

"Dr. O'Malley said you're to make the decisions for his sister's care if we're unable to reach him."

His eyes widened. "He did?"

She nodded.

"Oh." He cleared his throat, shaking off the disbelief. He figured Ian would demand the hospital call the airline and connect to the plane he was on if they needed something while he was in the air before he'd give Asa that kind of authority. "Okay. Thank you."

Her head bobbed. "There's coffee in the corner over there if you'd like some and vending machines down the hall."

"Thank you." He paced to the window again, but was too restless to stand still. He bounced between a chair, the coffee station, and the window, sure he was probably annoying the woman at the desk and the couple sitting quietly along the wall. They were all probably relieved when his phone rang and he stood still.

He glanced at the screen, seeing his dad's face, then answered it. "Yeah, Dad. There's no news yet."

"Good to know, but that's not why I'm calling. The police have looked over the accident scene. They think Daisy was run off the road."

Shock froze his muscles for a moment. "What?"

"There's paint transfer on her rear bumper. Someone hit her from behind, then fled the scene."

"Who would do that? Do they have any leads?"

"The crime scene unit took samples of the paint. The police said they're going to visit local body shops for cars with damaged front ends. But until Daisy wakes up and can tell them more—if she can tell them more—that's all they've got to go on."

Asa ran a hand through his hair. "This is a nightmare. Okay. Thanks for the update."

"Yep. Did you get a hold of Daisy's family to let them know what's going on?"

"Yeah. I talked to Ian. They'll be in the air in a few hours."

"And how are you holding up?"

He paced to the window again. "Um, honestly? It's still a little surreal. My mind knows she's in bad shape, but I can't fathom losing her." That lump in his throat came back. "I don't know what I'll do if she dies."

"Don't think that way, son. Stay positive. She needs you. I'm on my way to Billings and should be there in about forty-five minutes."

"Okay. I'm in the family waiting room near the E.R. Thanks, Dad."

"Of course. See you soon."

As Asa hung up, he sank into a chair, holding on to his emotions by a thread. He couldn't lose Daisy. He loved her.

Why it took this for him to see it, he didn't know. He wished he'd realized it sooner. Maybe she wouldn't be in there fighting for her life right now if he had.

The urge to move hit him again, but he refused to pace. Instead, he let his knee bounce and tried not to watch the clock or the door. Ian texted him a flight number and the number of tickets they needed, for which Asa was grateful. It kept him busy while he waited. The door opened several times while he booked the flights, but it was never to admit the doctor treating Daisy.

Finally, it opened to let in his dad. Asa sprang from his chair.

"Son." Silas met him in the middle of the room and gave him a hug. "Any news?"

"No." Asa shook his head. "Not yet. Soon, I hope. I mean, it has to be, right?"

The door opened again, and a man walked in wearing blue scrubs. "Family of Daisy O'Malley?"

Asa hurried forward. "I'm her fiancé. How is she?"

"Let's talk in there." He pointed to a door on the wall to his right, then led them over.

The three of them filed into the room, and the doctor shut the door. Asa took in the couch and chair that filled the room. The doctor motioned for them to sit on the couch before sinking into the chair. Asa squeezed onto the small sofa beside his dad.

"I'm Dr. Lammers. I treated Daisy when she came in."

"Asa Mitchell. This is my dad, Silas. How is she? Did she wake up?"

"Mr. Mitchell, I won't sugarcoat it. Your fiancée is in very bad shape. She's in a coma. She has a depressed skull fracture and a sizeable hematoma beneath it. Our chief of neuro-surgery is on his way here now to perform an operation to relieve the pressure on her brain. If she survives, she has a long road ahead of her to make a full recovery."

Asa's hands shook. He swallowed, trying to make sense of the doctor's words. "Um," he cleared his throat, "is that her only injury? Other than her legs, of course."

"Her pelvis is cracked, and she has a couple of broken ribs, which are likely from the seatbelt. It was a good thing she was wearing it. It probably saved her life." He paused a beat. "I know this is a lot to take in, but we're doing everything we can for her."

Asa nodded. Thoughts swirled through his brain, but only one was clear. "Can we see her?"

"Just for a few minutes. The O.R. staff will be ready for her soon." He stood. "Do you have any questions for me?"

Asa shook his head. "Not at the moment."

"Okay. Follow me."

Dr. Lammers led them out of the waiting room and down a short hallway to the E.R. They turned down a corridor lined with exam cubicles until they came to an area with larger trauma bays. He pulled back the curtain on one. "If you think of any questions for me, let one of the nurses know, and they'll contact me."

Asa barely heard him or his dad thank him. All his attention was on Daisy. She laid on the gurney, tubes and wires hanging off her body. A heart monitor beeped a steady pace above her head, connected to the leads coming out from beneath the sheet covering her body. Bruises marred the side of her face and what he could see of her arm that hung outside the sheet.

"Oh, dear God." Silas's voice followed Asa into the room.

He didn't remember giving his feet permission to move, but suddenly, he was at her side, taking her limp hand in his. Tears welled, and this time he couldn't stop them from spilling over. "Daisy." His harsh whisper was drowned out by the beeping monitor. He skimmed her forehead with his fingers, lightly tracing the curve of her face and cheekbone. Even now, she was so still.

"She looks like she's sleeping, but then again, she doesn't." Silas's quiet voice broke the silence.

"Yeah." Asa agreed. The stillness was unnatural. Her entire body was in a state of suspension as her brain reeled from the trauma.

He stroked her hair again. "God, sweetness. You have to fight this. Wake up and come back to me. I need you. I wish I'd told you that." He bent down and placed a soft kiss on her forehead. "I love you, Daisy. So much."

Heart aching, he straightened and wiped at his face. The curtain rattled again, and he looked over to see a nurse walk in.

"I'm sorry. We're ready for her."

"Come on, son." Silas put a hand on Asa's shoulder.

Asa nodded. He lifted Daisy's hand and kissed the back of it before tucking it beneath the sheet. "Okay. Take good care of her."

"We will, sir. There's a separate waiting room for surgical cases. If you go out to the lobby, someone at the front desk can show you where it is."

"Thank you, miss." Silas guided Asa toward the corridor. "Come on. Let's get some air."

In a fog, Asa let Silas lead him out of the emergency room. They checked into the surgical waiting room, then Silas led him toward the door.

"Where are we going?" Asa glanced around.

"We're going to get some coffee and sit outside for a bit."

Asa nodded, only part of his brain engaged in the conversation. Most of his focus was on the image of Daisy's still face. It was set to the music of the heart monitor's steady beat and ran on repeat in his head.

On autopilot, he followed his dad through the hospital,

taking the cup of coffee Silas shoved into his hand, then following him again as they went out into a small courtyard off the cafeteria to sit on a stone bench.

"Asa. Asa, look at me."

A little awareness crept back in, and he looked at his dad. "Why did it have to be her?" More tears spilled over. "Why couldn't it be me? She doesn't deserve any of this."

"No, she doesn't, but that's not the way life works, and you know it." Silas blew out a breath. "Look, I know this is hard." His voice broke, and he cleared his throat. "But she needs us—you—to stay strong. When she wakes up, she's going to need us to be there to help her."

"I know. I just—right now, I'm just trying to process it all, Dad." He shook his head and took a sip of his coffee, trying to put into words what was in his head. "When I came home in May and saw her that first time, I hated her. Home is my sanctuary—I need the peace and solitude it provides. I count on it to help set my mind to rights when life gets overwhelming. And then I come home and here's this beautiful woman parading through my kitchen, disrupting all of that. I just wanted her gone. I don't anymore." He glanced down at his cup. "Somewhere along the way, I stopped hating her and fell in love with her."

"Daisy's easy to love."

"Yeah." A corner of his mouth quirked up. "Yeah, she is. I just hope I get the chance to tell her that. To ask her to marry me for real."

Silas put a hand on Asa's back. "Have some faith, son. She's got a lot to live for."

Asa knew that. But he also knew that wasn't always enough.

TWENTY-SEVEN

Commotion in the hallway outside Daisy's room pulled Asa from the book he was reading. It sounded like a herd of cattle coming down the hall.

He set his book down on the table beside the bed and glanced at his dad, who sat on the couch by the window playing a game on his phone.

Silas frowned. "What is that?"

"I don't know." Asa stood and walked to the door to open it. He stepped into the hall, his eyes widening as he took in the wall of men coming at him. They all wore identical expressions and had the same dark auburn hair except for one, whose hair was pitch black. Asa recognized the one in the middle.

"How is she?" Ian demanded.

"I take it this is the rest of the gang?"

"Yes. How's our sister?"

"Quit bullying the man." Nori pushed her way through from behind the men. "Hi, Asa." She stepped forward and enveloped him in a hug.

He returned her embrace, then pulled back to look at her and her nephews. "She's holding her own." He tipped his head to the door. "Come in." Asa led Nori into the room, and the others followed.

Several of Daisy's brothers cursed as they crowded around her bed. Ian stared at her for several moments, taking in the bandage covering the incision on her shaved head, before looking at Asa.

"What's the latest?"

Asa shrugged. "There really isn't anything new since the text I sent you. They're monitoring her intracranial pressure. It's dropped, so now it's just a waiting game."

Ian gave a curt nod. "Good. I'll talk to her doctor about setting up a medical transfer flight and get her back to Chicago."

"What?" Asa straightened to his full height. "No. You're not moving her."

"The hell I'm not. I'm her next-of-kin, so medical decisions fall to me. One of the best neurosurgeons in the world is in Chicago. I'm sure this hospital is adequate, but I want her to have the best."

"She can get the best here. He or she can consult via teleconference if that's what you want. Daisy wouldn't want to be moved. She'd want to stay here, close to home. Did you learn nothing from the past few months? I thought you all talked about letting her live her own life."

"We did, but she can't make any decisions for herself right now."

"No, but if she could, she wouldn't want you to move her."

"Really? You think you know her so well? You only met her a few months ago. I raised her."

"But you never bothered to get to know her. If you did, you would understand that home and family mean *everything* to her. Her home is here now. The only way she would ever want to be moved is if going to that hospital and to that doctor was her only chance at survival. The doctors here have already operated on her. By all accounts, the procedure was a success. We're just waiting for the swelling to go down and her brain to heal. There's no reason to move her except for you to keep your thumb on her care. I promise you, if you push this, push me, I will bring in my lawyers and tie this up in court until she wakes up and can decide for herself. She's not leaving this hospital."

"He's right, Ian." Nori moved to Asa's side. "Daisy wouldn't want to go back to Chicago. Not when she's being well taken care of here. Montana's her home."

Ian cursed and pinched the bridge of his nose. He pulled in a deep breath. "Fine. But if I get any sense that they're not doing everything possible, or I feel like she needs more advanced care, I will have her on a plane back to Chicago in a heartbeat."

"I'll book the flight myself if that happens," Asa said. "But right now, she's fine where she is." He narrowed his eyes at the older man. "I want your word you will talk to me before you make any decisions."

Ian's spine stiffened.

"I'm her fiancé, Ian," he said, softening his tone. "I love her, and I just want what's best for her."

Some of the anger left Ian's face. "She told us the truth about the two of you. That your relationship started out fake, but grew into something else. I'm glad she isn't the only one in love. I promise I will run everything by you." He held out a hand. "We'll decide together."

Asa's heart thumped in his chest. Daisy loved him? He swallowed hard and took Ian's hand. "I'd like that."

"Go home."

Asa's booted foot slid off his knee and hit the floor with a thud at the nudge to his shoulder. He jerked awake and looked at his dad. "What?" He rubbed the sleep from his eyes. "No. I'm good. Just taking a nap."

"You need a good night's rest. And a shower. You've had neither in three days. You heard the doctor earlier. Even with the increased brain activity she's showing, it's still going to be at least a day before she wakes. Go home. Take a shower, eat something not out of a vending machine, and get some sleep." He took his keys from his pocket and held them out. "I'll stay the night with her. If anything changes, I'll call you."

Silas's mouth was set, his eyes telling Asa not to argue. Asa had seen that look before. He never won.

"Fine." He took the keys and stood. "I'll be back first thing."

"So long as you sleep."

"I will." He held his father's gaze. "Thanks, Dad."

Silas smiled. "Of course. Now go home. My truck is in lot three."

Asa spun the keys over his finger and nodded. "Goodnight."

"Goodnight." Silas settled into Asa's chair.

The door closed softly behind him as he walked into the quiet hallway. He waved at the nurse sitting at the nurses' station and headed for the elevator, riding it down to the main lobby. Outside, he glanced at the sky, noting the heavy clouds overhead. Lightning flashed in the distance. It was going to rain.

Using the key fob to make the horn beep, Asa found his dad's truck. Before he drove out of town, he went through a fast-food drive-thru for a cup of coffee to help keep him awake for the hour drive back to the ranch. He contemplated getting food, but Silas's words echoed in his mind about eating something decent. Daisy kept single servings of some of their favorite meals in the freezer for them to reheat for lunch or on nights when she wasn't home. He'd find a slice of meatloaf and eat that. He just wished there were cookies.

Rain pelted the windshield just before he reached the ranch drive. Lightning flashed and thunder boomed. He hoped the storm subsided to a steady rain. It would help him sleep. Turning into the drive, he drove up the lane to the house and pushed the button on the visor to raise the garage door and pulled in. He shut off the engine and closed the door, getting out to go inside.

More thunder boomed through the house as he set his keys on the counter and opened the freezer door. Daisy's cat, Tallulah, jumped up on the counter and meowed at him.

"Hey, girl." He took out a container of meatloaf and closed the door, then scratched her head. She purred and rubbed against him. "I miss her too." He picked her up, and she cuddled against his neck. "Let's find you some food, huh? You can share my meatloaf, but shh. Don't tell your mama. She'll have my head."

The cat chirped and butted his chin. He put the container in the microwave and turned it on, then stroked Tallulah's soft fur while he waited on it to warm up. When it dinged, he set the cat on the counter, then removed the meatloaf from the microwave and grabbed a fork. He sat down at the island and speared a chunk.

Tallulah chirped again and trotted over to investigate his meal. He blew on the piece of meat on his fork and broke off a piece, offering it to the cat. With a delicate nibble, she took it from him.

"We are never to speak of this, you hear?"

The cat meowed. He smiled and fed her another bite. Once he was done eating, he put his container in the sink, then dumped a few scoops of food into Tallulah's bowl before he headed upstairs to take a shower. Tallulah followed him. He figured she was lonely or scared of the storm—or both—and didn't discourage her. He wouldn't mind the company when he went to bed.

Stripping off his clothes, he got in the shower, washing off the grime from the last few days. Once he was clean, he sank onto the seat built into the wall and let the water pelt him. His mind—his whole body—was tired.

When his fingers and toes were pruned, he shut off the water and got out. He toweled off, not bothering with clothes and went into the bedroom and climbed into bed. Tallulah jumped up, purring. She sniffed his wet hair, then laid down on the other pillow. He gave her one last pet, then closed his eyes, letting the rain lull him to sleep.

Dreams plagued him between bouts of deep sleep. Some were pleasant. Daisy's laugh. Her dancing while she cleaned. Others were more sinister. Images of the tangled wreckage of her car. A scramble to find her and failing. The last one jolted him awake. He'd found her, but he was too late. She stared sightlessly at the bright blue sky from the driver's seat of her car.

He sat up and ran his hands over his face, then glanced at the clock. It was still early—only four o'clock—but there was no way he could go back to sleep. He threw back the covers and stood, walking to the closet to get some clothes. After stepping into his underwear, he grabbed a pair of clean jeans and put them on. As he reached for a shirt, he heard movement in the bedroom and rolled his eyes. Tallulah was probably playing with his phone charger again. He'd bought one of the braided cords to keep her from chewing through the plastic.

"Tallie, I swear, if you knocked my phone off the stand again—" He stopped and blinked as his mind registered the woman standing in his bedroom. "Kim?"

She waggled her fingers, smiling. "Hi, Asa."

"What the hell are you doing here? How did you get in?"

She sauntered forward. "You left the door unlocked." Biting her lip, she touched his bare chest with one long red nail. "I've been waiting for you to come home. I'd have been in sooner, but you looked tired when you got back, so I let you sleep."

His eyes widened. How long had she been watching him? "What do you mean, you've been waiting for me? I don't understand what you're even doing here. I told you in Chicago we weren't getting back together."

She rolled her eyes and huffed, going to sit on the bed. "I remember." She leaned back on her hands and crossed her legs. "Because of that housekeeper of yours. Daisy." A frown marred her face, and she shook her head. "She's pretty, but how could you choose her over me? Is it the boobs?" Her nose wrinkled. "Are they even real? I bet she had implants."

Asa's mouth dropped open, and he stared at her. "Kim, why are you here?"

She stood in one graceful motion, moving into his space to put her hands on his chest. "To soothe your pain. I mean, her injuries are just horrid. You must be in need of some comfort. I had an assistant once who was in a skiing accident and had similar injuries. It was terrible to see her so banged up. She looked like Frankenstein with all the staples in her head. I made sure her medical bills were covered, then let her go. I couldn't look at her without seeing her ghastly injuries." She shuddered.

He took her shoulders and gave her a shake. "Why. Are. You. Here?"

She huffed. "Because we belong together. I hoped I could convince you of that in Chicago, but you blew me off for that busty bimbo. And she wouldn't scare away. I tried. But I had to do something. I couldn't let her take you from me."

Suspicion narrowed his eyes. "Kim, what did you do?"

She rolled her eyes again and shook free of his hold. She walked over to the chair by the window and picked up her purse. When she turned around, she had a gun pointed at him. "I tried to warn her off. Sent her letters when I was in Denver, and paid a local kid to put that envelope on her car. When that didn't work, I tried to eliminate her in the hopes you'd come running back to me when I offered you my sympathy, but the dumb bitch didn't die in the crash. I tried to get into the hospital to finish her off, but there was always someone in her room. If it wasn't you, it was your dad, or one of those brothers of hers. She was never alone!"

Asa gulped and tried not to stare at the gun barrel. Instead, he kept his eyes on her, hoping for an opening to take it away.

Kim readjusted her grip on the gun. "But I have a new plan. We'll just go away together. I took a bunch of cash from my bank account and transferred more into an off-shore account. There's a private plane waiting for us at the airport. I figure we can find a nice slice of beach somewhere in the South Pacific until you come to your senses."

"You ran Daisy off the road? And now you want me to run away with you?"

She frowned at him. "Have you not been listening?" She growled. "Put your shirt on so we can go."

"I'm not going anywhere with you. Think about what you're doing. What you've done. Put the gun down before you add murder to the charges against you."

She laughed. "I'm not going to kill you. In case you haven't realized, I want us to be together. It's kind of hard to do that if you're dead." Her expression hardened. "But I won't hesitate to injure you so you can't get away." She motioned to the shirt in his hand. "Put your shirt on."

He studied her for a moment, realizing she would indeed shoot him. Shaking his head at how he never knew she was so nuts, he shrugged into the shirt and buttoned it up. "Happy?"

"Yes. Let's go." She backed toward the door, opening it.

"I need shoes," he said, stalling.

"I saw them by the garage door." She motioned to the open door with the gun. "Come on."

Glaring at her, he walked toward the door. As he came even with her, she pulled her arm back a fraction, the tip of the gun pointing up to make room for him to pass by her. He spun, catching her off guard, and knocked her gun hand up and away, spinning her around. She fired a shot, but it went wild, the bullet slamming into the wall.

Behind her now, he locked an arm around hers, the other going around her shoulders. He tucked her close, immobilizing her. "Drop it, Kim."

She struggled in his hold, but was no match for his strength or size. "No! You're mine. The bitch can't have you."

"It's over, Kim." He grabbed her wrist and let go of her shoulders to take the gun away. He flicked the safety on, and put it in his waistband, still holding onto her.

"No!" She struggled again, and he pulled her in tight, holding her arms to her sides. She yelled again, telling him to let her go, when her screams suddenly turned into sobs, and she sagged against his hold. The fight left her and she bawled in his arms.

Asa blew out a breath, forcing his racing heart to slow. He carried her toward his nightstand so he could get his phone. Holding her tight in one arm, he picked it up and dialed 911. After reporting the incident, he took her downstairs and set her on the couch to wait for help to arrive.

She curled up against the arm and refused to look at him. Shoulders slumped and eyes downcast, she looked defeated and much older than her thirty years.

He ran a hand through his hair and sat down in his dad's recliner to wait. *God, what a night.*

TWENTY-EIGHT

The hum of neon lights and the beep of a heart monitor filtered through Daisy's subconscious as she came awake. Her eyelids fluttered open, but she squeezed them shut again against the bright lights. Her head hurt. And her legs. And her chest.

"Daisy? Sweetness, wake up. Open your eyes and look at me."

She didn't want to. The light was too bright. She moaned and tried to turn her face away.

"Turn down the lights," Asa said. "I think they're too bright for her."

Daisy heard footsteps, then the brightness dimmed. She let her eyelids open a slit. Asa's wide chest came into view. She blinked and looked up. He leaned over her with a broad smile on his handsome face.

"Hey. It's good to see your eyes. Welcome back."

Welcome back? What was he talking about?

She shifted and felt the pull of wires and tubes. She looked past him and saw the clinical furniture and IV pole and realized she was in the hospital.

"Where—where am I?" Her voice came out as a scratchy whisper. She tried to clear her throat, but couldn't work up any saliva. "Can I have some water?"

"In just a minute, sweetie." A nurse moved in next to Asa and shined a light in her face.

Daisy recoiled and raised a hand to block the light. "Stop."

"I just want to check your pupils, then I'll leave you alone." She held up one of Daisy's eyelids, then the other, shining the light in her eyes.

Spots danced in Daisy's vision, and she blinked, trying to dispel them.

"They look good. I'll let the doctor know you're awake and talking." She disappeared, and Asa's face came into view again.

He held up a glass of water with a straw in it. "Here."

She tried to take a sip, but couldn't sit up. He found the controls for the bed and raised her head. The room spun, and she closed her eyes.

"Sorry, was that too fast?"

She gripped the bedrail until her head quit spinning, then opened her eyes again. "I'm okay."

"Good." He held out the water again, helping her take a drink.

The cool liquid slid down her throat, making her feel more awake. She let go of the straw and let her head fall back against the pillows. "What happened?"

"You were in a car accident. Apparently, my ex, Kim, wanted me all to herself and thought eliminating you was the best way to accomplish that. She ran you off the road."

"What? Kim McDonough tried to kill me?"

He nodded and set the water on the tray, then lowered the bedrail to sit on the edge of her mattress. He took her hand in his, tracing the veins on the back. "She showed up at the house in the middle of the night yesterday and tried to make me run away with her. Pulled a gun on me and everything."

Daisy's eyes widened.

"We'll have to patch a hole in the wall, but it all ended well. She's in custody now." He reached out to touch her face. "I'm so glad you're awake. You gave us all a good scare."

The sensation of something on her head made her reach up and touch it. Gauze met her fingertips. And a distinct lack of hair. Her eyes shot to his. "What happened?"

"You had a brain injury. You fractured your skull in the accident and it caused a brain bleed. They had to remove the broken portion of your skull to relieve the pressure. The doctors think it's a miracle you're alive."

"That explains the pounding in my head."

"Yeah. That will probably continue. They have to replace the section of skull they removed, which will probably be soon."

A tear leaked out of her eye.

"Hey. None of that. You're alive. With time and some therapy, you'll heal."

She drew in a shaky breath. That wasn't the only reason she was crying. "I'm sorry, Asa. For what I said about the tabloid photos."

"It's all forgotten, sweetness." He stroked her cheek with his thumb. "I love you, Daisy. I don't want anyone else but you."

More tears spilled from her eyes. "I love you too."

He dug in his pocket, then held up her engagement ring. "When you get out of here, I want you to wear this for real. Along with the wedding band that matches. Marry me, Daisy."

Her breath hitched. "So long as we wait until my hair grows back a bit for wedding photos." A heaviness on her legs registered. She tried to wiggle her toes and met something hard. It took her a second to realize her legs were in casts. "And for my legs to heal, so I can walk down the aisle."

He chuckled. "Anything you want, sweetness."

EPILOGUE

Daisy put down her spatula when she heard a car door shut, then voices just outside the back door.

"Asa! Silas! They're here!" She didn't wait for them to come from the living room where they watched the football game. Picking up her cane, she spun toward the mudroom. Stuffing her feet in her barn boots, she hurried outside to greet their guests.

"You made it!" She stopped in front of Nori and pulled her into a hug.

"We did." She hugged Daisy back. "You're getting around well," she said, pulling away.

"I am. Another few weeks, and I'm hoping I can ditch this thing." She held up the cane and shook it. Her physical therapy was going great. She'd recovered most of the balance she lost from her brain injury. She was working on strengthening her legs to regain the rest. Her hair was also growing back in.

"Good."

The screen door banged, and Asa and Silas came out. Silas

ran forward and scooped Nori off her feet, planting a big kiss on her lips.

Sofie, Nori's daughter, rolled her eyes and stepped up to give Daisy a hug. "You'd think they hadn't seen each other in months. He was in town helping us pack just last week. Only Mom putting her foot down and saying she wanted to make the trip out here herself made him go home."

Daisy laughed, returning her hug. "It's young love." She let go to bend down and give Sofie's daughter, Olive, a hug. "Hey, kiddo." She brushed the girl's rich brown hair out of her face and placed a kiss on her cheek. "How are you?"

"Fine." She pointed beyond them, toward the barn. "I want to ride a horse!"

"Soon, pumpkin," Sofie said. "Let's get settled in before you start demanding Silas take you for a ride."

Olive's bottom lip popped out as she stared up at her mother, but she nodded. "Okay. I'm hungry."

Daisy laughed. "Come inside. I just made cookies."

"Ooo! Yay!" The girl took off for the back door.

"Just one!" Sofie yelled after her. She sighed. "She's going to be a holy terror tonight. Too many hours cooped up in the car."

Daisy waved a hand. They started toward the house. "She can play with the puppy Asa brought home from Colorado a couple weeks ago." She turned to look at her fiancé, who grinned.

"Don't look at me like that. You love Seamus."

"I did. Until he ate an entire ham."

"You left it where he could reach it."

"I didn't realize he'd grown that much."

"How big is this puppy?" Sofie asked.

Silas laughed. "A small horse." He held the door open.

Asa helped Daisy up the steps and they walked into the kitchen. Olive sat on the floor, a cookie in one hand, giggling as she tried to keep Seamus, their three-month-old Irish Wolfhound puppy, from eating it.

Asa snapped his fingers, "Seamus, sit."

The dog's butt hit the floor. He looked up at his master with a whine. Tallulah ran into the room, distracting him. He forgot he wasn't supposed to move and took off after the cat.

"I hope you weren't looking for a quiet life by moving here." Daisy looked at Sofie.

Her cousin grinned. "Quiet is relative. Compared to the city, this is a dream."

"Good. We're glad to have you. Silas, especially." Daisy glanced at her soon-to-be father-in-law and winked.

Silas returned her smile and tucked Nori under his arm. "I am." He looked down at Nori. "Should we tell them now?"

"Tell us what?" Asa asked.

Nori rolled her eyes. "You can't ask that question in front of them and then not tell them." She smacked his chest.

His grin grew. He looked at them. "I asked Nori to marry me. She said yes."

"What?" Daisy said, shocked.

"Dad, that's great."

"Mom! Why didn't you say something?"

Nori smiled. "We wanted to tell you all together. And we'd like to get married soon. Before we leave for Ireland in a few weeks." She looked at Daisy. "I hope that's not too close to your wedding for you."

Daisy shook her head. She and Asa were getting married in a couple of months—just before Thanksgiving. "Of course not." She clapped her hands. "This is exciting! What kind of wedding do you want?"

"Just something small. Family." She looked up at Silas with a smile. "We need nothing else."

"No, we don't. Everything we need is in this room." He kissed her softly. "I love you."

She beamed. "I love you too."

Daisy fanned her face as tears threatened. They were too sweet. "Okay, enough of that. How about we get your stuff in here? Dinner will be ready soon." She'd put meatloaf in the oven earlier. It had about a half an hour left until she could take it out.

"Sounds good." Silas unwrapped himself from Nori's arms. He bent over and scooped Olive off the floor. "Come on, pumpkin. You can help Grandpa."

"Okay!"

As he walked out, Asa turned to her to give her a quick kiss, and she saw the tears shimmering in his eyes. She grabbed his face and gave him a longer kiss.

"Thank you," he said when he pulled back.

"For what?"

"For deciding you wanted to live your own life and forever changing mine. And his. I love you, sweetness."

She kissed him again. "I love you too." She turned him around. "Now, go help your dad."

He laughed. "Yes, Miss Bossy-Britches."

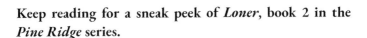

Keep reading for a sneak peek of *Loner*, book 2 in the *Pine Ridge* series.

Thank you for reading Sweetness! I hope you enjoyed it.

Want to read an EXCLUSIVE and FREE book? Sign up for my mailing list. You can find the sign-up form on my website, ashleyaquinn.com. My list also receives sneak peeks of my latest work and access to exclusive giveaways. Also, please consider leaving a rating or review on Amazon and or Goodreads. It would be greatly appreciated!

Thanks again for reading!
   - Ashley

~

Keep reading for a sneak peek at Book 2, Loner in the Pine Ridge Series.

LONER

PINE RIDGE
BOOK 2

ONE

"Olive! Stop chasing the chickens and come help me." Sofie McAllister leaned out the back door of their little two-bedroom bungalow on the Stone Creek Ranch and hollered for her four-year-old daughter. The little girl ran around the yard in her bright purple boots and coat, the pom-pom on her purple stocking cap bobbing as she chased one of the hens. Olive loved the chickens, but right now, Sofie needed her to help carry a few things to the car.

"What do you need, Mommy?" The girl came running up to stop in front of her mother.

Sofie held the door and motioned her inside. "We're supposed to meet Daisy, Sara, Marci, and Grandma to make centerpieces for the wedding." She picked up two sacks of silk flowers from the counter and held them out to her daughter. "I need you to carry these, so I can get the box."

"Okay." Olive took the bags.

Already wearing her coat, Sofie picked up her purse and slung it over her shoulder and across her chest. Gripping her keys in one hand, she lifted the box. "Let's go." She gestured toward the door with her head.

Olive ran to the door and held it open.

"Make sure it's locked."

The girl turned the button on the knob, then jiggled it once the door closed. "It's locked."

"Good." Sofie pushed the button on her key fob to raise the lift gate on her SUV, then set the box inside. Olive deposited her bags next to the box, then ran around to get in the car. Sofie helped her buckle in, then got in the driver's seat.

The trip down the lane to the main house was quick. She pulled into the yard and parked next to her stepdad's truck and got out.

She still couldn't believe after ten years of being single and hardly ever dating, her mother married Silas Mitchell within months of meeting him. Sofie wasn't upset about it, though. He was a good man. And he made her mom smile.

After retrieving the items from the rear of her vehicle, she followed Olive up the steps into the mudroom.

"Take off your boots," she told her daughter before she could scamper into the kitchen for hugs from her grandma and cousin. Not to mention the cookies surely waiting in the cookie jar. Sofie hadn't bothered to bake in the two months they'd been living on the Stone Creek. Daisy always had more than enough to keep their sweet cravings satisfied.

Olive sat down on the floor and tugged off her boots, then stood, tossing her hat and coat onto the pile. She flew inside.

"Grandma!"

"There's my button."

Sofie smiled as her mom, Nori, greeted Olive. She stepped out of her shoes, doing her best not to crash into the wall as she held onto the box.

"Do you want help?" Sara Katsaros asked, as Sofie stepped into the kitchen.

"I've got it." She walked to the island and set the box down. "Olive, you left your bags in the mudroom."

"Oh!" The girl let go of her grandma and ran through the door, reemerging a moment later with the flowers. She held the bags up to Sofie. "Here you go."

"Thank you." She took the sacks and set them next to the box, then shrugged out of her coat.

Sofie's cousin, Daisy O'Malley, pulled a bag toward her and peered inside. "Oh, I like these." She looked up at Sofie. "Thanks for getting them while you were in Billings. I thought we had enough, but Marci said we were short."

"Of course. No sense in you making a trip when I was already there."

"No doubt."

"So, are we ready to get started?" Marci asked.

"I think so." Sofie sat on a barstool and picked up a jar. "So, what exactly are we doing?"

Daisy picked up a jar of her own as well as a ball of jute. "We're wrapping the tops of the jars in this stuff, then filling them with glass beads, lights, and flowers."

"Why did you decide against real ones?" Sara asked. "I'm sure Asa wouldn't have minded spending the extra money."

"No, but some people are sensitive to flowers. I didn't want that on the tables where we were eating. Plus, we can fill the jar with fairy lights since we don't need to add water."

"Kind of like mood lighting," Nori said.

"Exactly."

Sofie picked up a glue gun and plugged it in.

"Mommy, can I have a cookie?"

She looked over to see Olive standing at the counter, pointing at the cookie jar.

"Just one. Once you're done, why don't you go find your coloring books? You can sit at the table while we work."

"Okay." The girl spun around and opened the jar, sticking her hand inside and coming out with a chocolate chip cookie.

Sofie smiled as she took a big bite. It hadn't taken her daughter long to adjust to her new surroundings. Having her grandma and her favorite cousin close by helped, she was sure. It had helped Sofie adjust, that much she knew. She never would have had the courage to leave Chicago if her mom hadn't come with her. Though it was really the other way around. Nori moved, and Sofie tagged along. There was no reason not to. She and Olive needed a fresh start after what happened with her ex-husband. And it meant she could stay close to her family.

"Bring me one of those, too," she told her daughter.

Olive took another cookie from the jar and brought it to Sofie.

"Thank you."

"Welcome!" The girl spun on her heel and ran from the room to get the coloring supplies Nori kept on hand.

"Can you bottle her energy and give me some?" Marci asked.

Sofie grinned. "Trust me, if I could, I would. I need it just to keep up with her."

"I need it to stay awake."

"Sloan keeping you up?" Daisy asked, mentioning Marci's almost one-year-old son.

"Yes. I thought he'd get better as he got older, but he hasn't. Oh, he'll sleep longer stretches at a time now, but he's still up every three to four hours instead of every one to two. And he's always up and ready for the day at five a.m. I've tried pushing his bedtime back to eight or nine, but he's still up before the sun. He'll just take a longer nap in the afternoon." She sighed. "I'm exhausted."

"Is he teething?" Nori asked.

Marci nodded. "So bad. I have to keep a bib on him all the time to sop up all the drool. It's insane. I didn't know such a small creature could produce so much saliva."

Sofie laughed. "Olive was like that. Once all their front teeth come in, it slows down. How many does he have now?"

"Four. The two in the middle, on the top and bottom. He's working on the ones beside those now. I'm glad to know there's light at the end of the tunnel, however dim it may be at the moment."

They all laughed.

"There is," Sofie said. "And if you ever need a break, I'm happy to babysit."

"I might take you up on that. I could do for a few hours of me time. A hot bath and a long nap sound wonderful."

"You just let me know when. I'd love to have him."

Sofie's ringing cellphone cut off any reply Marci might have made.

"Sorry." She stood to get her phone from her purse at the other end of the island. "It's probably a client wanting to place an order." She found the device, answering it. "Hello?" Turning, she picked up the pad of sticky notes and a pen from the basket by the wall and walked out of the kitchen for some privacy.

"Sofie, it's Jim Blackwell."

Her heart stuttered in her chest as her attorney identified himself. She cleared her throat. "Jim, hi. Um, I don't mean to be rude, but why are you calling? I didn't think we had any more business left to discuss."

"We didn't, but I'm afraid I have some bad news, Sofie. Lance has been released from jail."

Sofie's breath left her in a whoosh. Her lungs froze along with her mind as she struggled to process what he said. "What —how?"

"Overcrowding. He's been a model prisoner and served half his sentence, so they let him out two weeks ago. But not without conditions."

"Two weeks? And I'm just now finding out? I thought we were supposed to be notified right away?"

"We were, but his paperwork got stuck in the system somewhere. It just landed on my desk half an hour ago. I verified everything, then called you."

She ran a hand over her face and blew out a breath. "Okay. Um, you said there were conditions to his release?" Sofie walked to the window and looked out. She ran a shaky hand through her hair and drew in a deep breath to steady herself. This wasn't a big deal. She knew he'd get out at some point, and they weren't in Chicago anymore, where he could just show up and threaten her. But it was still a shock. She'd been mentally preparing herself for his release in February, not now, almost four months early. She let her breath out on a slow exhale.

"He can't contact you, even through the guise of checking on Olive. Any inquiries he makes about her have to go through an intermediary. The judge appointed one when he granted Lance's release. You should get a letter soon explaining how it works. I can tell you that if he contacts you at all—and you can prove it—he'll go back to jail. This is for the duration of his parole, not just the remainder of his sentence."

"How long is his parole?"

"He has to meet with a parole officer weekly until his sentence is technically up, then biweekly for six months, then monthly for eighteen months."

Two years. That was good. Hopefully, by the time his parole was up, he would have moved on and their only contact would be about Olive. Though she wouldn't be upset if he decided to just walk away completely. Lance was poison. Sofie wished she'd never met him, but also didn't. She wouldn't have her beautiful daughter if she hadn't. Olive was the best thing in her life, and she couldn't regret her relationship with

Lance because of her. She just wished she'd walked away sooner and spared herself and Olive some heartache.

"I'm sorry, Sofie. If I'd known, I would have lobbied to keep him imprisoned for his full sentence, but he's been a model prisoner, so they let him out."

"It's okay, Jim. I appreciate you trying. Thank you for calling to give me a head's up."

"Of course. If you need anything, please don't hesitate to call."

"I won't. Thank you." She bade him farewell and hung up. Clutching her phone, she rested it against her chin for a moment as her thoughts whirled. She prayed Lance would leave them be and abide by the conditions of his parole. The last thing she needed was to spend all her time looking over her shoulder, waiting for him to find her and make good on the promises he made after she had him arrested. He'd vowed she would regret betraying him.

A shiver ran down her spine. Part of her thought his threats were just a knee-jerk reaction to the situation. But a larger part knew him and what he was capable of, and recognized his threats for the promises they were. When he said he wouldn't let her live without him or take his daughter away, he meant it.

Laughter from the kitchen drew her from her thoughts. She shook off the undercurrent of fear and put her phone away. There was nothing she could do about Lance right now. He didn't know where she was. And even if he found out, she wasn't alone. Plus, the security on the ranch was decent with the upgrades Asa made after the incident with his ex-girlfriend.

"When are the trailers coming for the wedding guests?" Sofie heard Sara ask as she walked back into the room. Her eyes strayed to Olive, who sat at the small table, tongue poking out between her lips as she concentrated on coloring her picture. Sofie's heart lurched as she looked at the girl. She wouldn't let anything happen to her daughter. If Lance came after them, she'd do everything she could to protect her. She wouldn't let Olive end up with her father. She deserved better than the abusive bastard.

"Tomorrow. Along with the first of our guests," Daisy replied. "Asa's friend, Knox, and his sister Alice are supposed to arrive sometime tomorrow afternoon. Knox wanted to help with setup."

"That's cutting it close," Marci said. "Why didn't Asa have the trailers here today?"

Daisy shrugged. "No idea. Asa and Silas both assure me they'll be ready. I guess if they're not, we'll set them up in the guest rooms. And if my family arrives before they're ready, we'll spread air mattresses all over the house until they are."

Nori groaned. "I do not want to listen to your brothers if they have to sleep on air mattresses."

That made Daisy laugh. "No one does. It'll be fine. Asa contracted with a rental company the movie and music industries use. They'll be here."

Sofie forced a smile onto her face and sat down. "Who else is coming besides them? Didn't you say something about another friend of Asa's from Colorado? Brady? Was that his name?"

Nori gave Sofie a quizzical frown. Sofie did her best to hold her smile and turned her face away. She was sure her mom would grill her about it later, but right now, she didn't want to discuss her phone call.

Daisy nodded. "Yes. I think most of the Archers are coming, not just Brady. A few of them couldn't get away from work." She blew out a breath. "But that's still like fifteen to twenty people once you include the kids."

"And how does Asa know them?" Sofie wasn't clear on the connections to all these people.

"Asa met Brady Archer through Knox. The Archers own a large cattle ranch and get most of their horses from him. They've all become good friends over the years. I haven't met any of them yet, but Asa's talked about them."

"And there are twenty of them?" Marci asked.

"Roughly. Lee and Jenny, then their five kids and all their spouses. A few of them have kids of their own. Plus, there are a few foster children in the mix."

Sofie listened with half an ear as she pulled a jar toward herself and picked up the glue gun. Her fingers still shook, so she took a steadying breath, willing them to stop. She didn't want to put a damper on Daisy's wedding in any way.

"How long is everyone staying?" Sara asked.

"The Archers will be here a couple days beforehand and are leaving a couple of days after the wedding. They're driving, so they didn't want to rush out the next morning. My family is coming mid-week. Ian said they're flying back in the evening the next day. They all have to be back at work or school on Monday. My old boss is coming. Sandrine. She'll be here the day before. She's staying in the house, though. She and Alice both."

"I'm glad I live in town," Sara said. "It's going to be crazy out here for a few days."

Sofie agreed. And was glad. All her little cousins running around, not to mention the big ones, would help distract her from the news she just got.

"Mommy, look!" Olive ran up with a picture in her hands of a princess, colored head to toe in purple, Olive's favorite color.

"It's very pretty, sweetie."

The girl beamed and ran back to the table.

"I don't remember ever being as obsessed with a color as she is," Daisy mused.

Sofie smiled. "It makes it easy to buy things for her, though. If it's purple, she loves it."

Nori chuckled. "You were like that, but with pink. Do you remember that? Everything had to be pink, right down to your underwear."

Sofie laughed. "Yes. And my room too. It looked like bubblegum. I suppose her obsession is payback for what I put you through."

"Of course it is." Nori grinned.

"I'm just glad you went with purple as one of your colors, Daisy. It made it easier to convince her to wear the white dress once she saw it had a purple sash, and she saw she got to carry purple flowers." Sofie had steeled herself for an argument with Olive when she showed her the dress Daisy wanted her to wear. Olive was not a fan of dresses, but the purple accents kept the whining to a minimum.

"Good. That wasn't my goal when I picked the colors, but it's a nice bonus."

They all chuckled as they worked, the conversation lulling as they concentrated.

Nori leaned over, laying a hand on Sofie's arm. "Honey, what's wrong? Ever since you took that phone call, your shoulders are stiff and your smile is strained."

Curses flew through Sofie's brain. She should have known she wouldn't be able to hide her feelings from her mom. No one knew her better. "It's nothing."

"Don't give me that load of bull. I know you better than that."

Sofie huffed. "I know, but I don't want to talk about it. Not here."

Nori's eyebrows winged upward before she narrowed her eyes. "Later, then. No secrets, Sofia Grace. Not anymore. You promised."

Sofie nodded. "I know. And I'll tell you. Later." Her eyes

darted around to take in the other women. Thankfully, none of them were paying attention to Sofie and Nori's whispered conversation.

Nori straightened. "Okay. I'll hold you to that."

She was sure she would. After Lance beat the snot out of her the last time, Nori made her promise not to keep secrets again. But in all honesty, she didn't want to. The only reason she kept the abuse a secret before was out of shame. Her mother cautioned her not to marry Lance. She'd never liked him. But Sofie hadn't listened. She'd been in love. Then bullied into being too afraid to leave. The next thing she knew, she was married, then pregnant. Once Olive was in the picture, Sofie had been too afraid of what would happen to her baby if she left. She only had her meager jewelry business to support them. Lance was a successful sales rep for a pharmaceutical company.

If Nori hadn't found her after the last beating, she wasn't sure she would've had the courage to leave. It was only the presence of her DNA in his class ring and the matching wound on her face that convicted him. He'd tried to claim someone broke into their apartment. She thanked God for her mother and the detective who wouldn't give up. It was because of both of them she was free of the monster.

She just hoped she stayed that way.

About the Author

Ashley started writing in her teens and never stopped. Her first novel, Smoky Mountain Murder, came out in 2016, and she has since published two more series and has plans for more. When not writing, you can find her with her nose stuck in a book or watching some terrible disaster movie on SyFy. An avid baseball fan, she also enjoys crafting and cooking. She lives in Ohio with her husband, two kids, three cats, and one very wild shepherd mix.

Website: https://ashleyaquinn.com

goodreads.com/ashleyaquinn

amazon.com/Ashley-A-Quinn/e/B07HCT4QST

Also by Ashley A Quinn

Foggy Mountain Intrigue

Smoky Mountain Murder

Smoky Mountain Baby

Smoky Mountain Stalker

Smoky Mountain Doctor

Smoky Mountain K-9

Smoky Mountain Judge

The Broken Bow

A Beautiful End

Wildfire

In Plain Sight

Close Quarters

Scorched

Light of Dawn

Pine Ridge

Sweetness

Loner

Shark

Katydid

Homespun

Printed in Great Britain
by Amazon

41419096R00179